THE MARINE'S
TEMPTATION

BY
JENNIFER MOREY

MILLS
BOON

Published in Great Britain 2015
by Mills & Boon, an imprint of Harlequin (UK) Limited,
Eton House, 18-24 Paradise Road, Richmond, Surrey, TW9 1SR

© 2015 Harlequin Books S.A.

Special thanks and acknowledgement to Jennifer Morey for her contribution to The Adair Affairs series.

ISBN: 978-0-263-25407-5

18-0315

Harlequin (UK) Limited's policy is to use papers that are natural, renewable and recyclable products and made from wood grown in sustainable forests. The logging and manufacturing processes conform to the legal environmental regulations of the country of origin.

Printed and bound in Spain
by CPI, Barcelona

Two-time RITA® Award nominee and Golden Quill Award winner **Jennifer Morey** writes single-title contemporary romance and page-turning romantic suspense. She has a geology degree and has managed export programmes in compliance with the International Traffic in Arms Regulations (ITAR) for the aerospace industry. She lives at the feet of the Rocky Mountains in Denver, Colorado, and loves to hear from readers through her website, jennifermorey.com, or Facebook.

For my twin sister, Jackie,
my number one supporter.

Chapter 1

Perceptions didn't always reveal the truth about a man. What he appeared to be and what he was could be two different things. Surface and depth. The surface reflected the shell of the man, what he looked like, what he said, what he did. Underneath that, a well of secrets lurked. Painful secrets that death exposed. Ruthless and indifferent in life. Human in death. That about summed up Reginald Adair. Few had liked him, but then, no one had really known him, had they?

Carson Adair marveled over how little he knew his father when he thought he had. He spread his hands over the top of the desk. How would his father have felt sitting here? Powerful. Accomplished.

Detached.

Sad.

Human…

Carson would not have associated that word with his dad prior to his murder. But a gnawing curiosity had nestled inside him. If his father hadn't been who he'd thought, who had he been?

He imagined what it must have been like to be the man at the top of a thriving telecommunications corporation, running the competition into the ground, doing whatever it took to keep shareholders happy and revenue flowing. Not caring about anything or anyone else. Maybe he rarely noticed the spectacular view of downtown San Diego. Maybe he rarely enjoyed a lunch or dinner for anything other than a business meeting.

His wife. His kids. He couldn't have had many fond memories about them. Turns out Reginald had been consumed by the kidnapping of his first-born son. Indifference had hidden his grief. No one had known about Jackson Adair until the reading of the will. Carson had seen the reports from his father's secret investigation.

Lost in what it must have been like to be Reginald Adair, he still couldn't say he knew or even liked his father. He definitely couldn't say he loved him. But he was moved by the discovery that the man had real emotions, that he'd carried such a weighty burden all these years—and kept to himself. It explained so much. That his father was capable of love, that he must have loved his firstborn son and his first wife, two things he'd never mentioned to anyone. Carson wondered if Patsy would have been a different woman had she been able to make Reginald love her the way he must have loved his first family. Had his aloofness led to her killing him? It would appear so, since she had fled the country and was the prime suspect in his murder case.

Although his father was dead, Carson was getting to

know him for the first time. That dredged up so much conflict in him. Until now, he'd strove to be everything his father wasn't. Do and be whatever earned his father's disapproval. Now he felt a connection to the man. He cared about giving him justice and finding the son who had been taken from him. And in the process, knowing him as he'd never had.

People said he was just like Reginald and that had always annoyed him. Maybe it still did. Back then, he'd wanted to get as far away from his father and his empire as he could. His mother, too, but as a boy, it had been his father's approval he'd craved. To get that, he'd have had to devote his life to his father's dream. AdAir Corp. When he'd grown into a young man, he'd done the opposite. He'd rebelled and joined the Marines. His father had been so angry when he'd informed him. And Carson had been nothing but glad that he was mad.

His gaze fell to a photograph facing him on the desk. It was of Landry and Whit with Reginald. They stood in this office, smiling with warmth Carson would have called fake before learning about Jackson. Something in the background caught his eye. It was a blue ceramic bowl on top of a wood-and-glass display case along the wall next to the door. Carson looked there. The cabinet was there but the ceramic bowl was missing. The picture looked fairly recent.

Where was the bowl, and was there anything significant about it?

"Meeting's started, Mr. Adair."

Whit's secretary stood in the doorway of the office.

Carson stood. "Right. Thanks." He'd lost track of time. "You have the envelope?"

"Yes, sir. I'll wait for your call."

"Thanks." He hoped he wouldn't have to call her.

Taking the papers he'd been studying earlier, he left the office and walked down the bright and wide hallway of AdAir Corp with a limp that embittered him when he dwelled on it too much. Nothing like facing the rest of his life with a constant reminder of what he could no longer have. Mobility. A career in the Marines.

Reaching the conference room where the mediation meeting had been scheduled regarding Patsy's dispute over his father's will, Carson entered. Everyone was already there: his brother, Whit, sister, Landry, Georgia Mason and her stepmother, Ruby, and two attorneys— one Patsy had apparently hired on her own to represent her dispute, and the mediation lawyer. Despite the crowd of people, Carson noticed Georgia right away. Long, luxurious, dark red hair cascaded over her shoulders. The pencil skirt trimmed her curvy waist and her long, slender legs were bare from the knees down. Her dark green eyes glared at him from across the room. Everyone else had taken a seat but her. She was still mad at him. Mad at every Adair in the room. But her beauty struck him just as much as the first time he'd seen her. The sight of her really got his testosterone going.

"Glad you could make it," she said.

"Sorry. I got hung up in Reginald's office." He limped over to her. It wasn't a horrible limp, beastly but only a little.

After nodding to Whit and Landry, he put the papers facedown on the table, then went to Georgia and pulled out a chair for her.

Her eyes traveled down and then rose up his body, curious about his limp and then all fire when she met his eyes.

"Have a seat, Ms. Mason," he said cajolingly.

"After you, Mr. Adair." She didn't reciprocate his tone, hers having a decided edge.

He grinned and saw Ruby smiling at the exchange. At sixty, she was a little thin but attractive with light brown hair and hazel eyes. She looked nothing like Georgia, although Georgia would probably age just as gracefully as Ruby had.

"Mrs. Mason," he said.

"Mr. Adair."

After acknowledging the mediation lawyer, he saved his next greeting for last. It was Patsy's attorney. Before she'd left the country, she'd given him explicit instructions regarding her dispute over Ruby Mason's inheritance and the authority to sign on her behalf. Carson planned to squash her intentions today.

The beady-eyed, short, stocky, balding attorney gave a nod in greeting.

"Shall we begin?" the mediation lawyer said. His name was Schmidt. He was skinny and had all of his blond hair. Georgia had chosen him, and the rest of them had agreed to meet to sign an agreement today, to settle this dispute outside of court.

Carson waited for Georgia to sit down.

When she did, he took the seat beside her, seeing how she sat straighter, ramrod stiff. She didn't like him at first sight, and his desire to charm her went beyond what would be required for a casual acquaintance. Luckily, he had enough of his father in him to maintain a business sense and stay professional.

"We're here today because Patsy Adair doesn't think Ruby Mason should have any share of the inheritance," the mediator started things off.

"I believe I speak for my brother and sister when I say Ruby is entitled to whatever our father decided to give her." Carson took over the meeting.

Schmidt looked at him, not approving but not stopping him.

"He obviously wanted her to have something," Carson continued, "so I propose we make this meeting short and simple and agree that it isn't our right to change his will. Are we all in agreement?"

"I am," Whit said. Dressed in a dark suit, impeccably trimmed and looking the part of Adair's new leader, he sat in a confident pose.

"I am," Landry echoed. She seemed loopy, as if she'd taken something before coming here. Ever since their father's murder and especially the announcement that Patsy was his suspected murderer, she had not been herself. Carson was getting worried about her.

"Speaking on behalf of Patsy," Patsy's attorney said. "I—"

"You'll sign this agreement or I'll contest *her* share. I've already spoken with Whit and Landry. They support my decision."

"You can't do that," Patsy's attorney said. "All parties have to be present and sign a mediation agreement. Patsy would never agree to this." He swung his hand toward the document on the table in front of Schmidt.

"Yes, I can contest her share. She *is* suspected of murder, as you are well aware."

"Being suspect and proven guilty are two different things, Mr. Adair. I won't sign any agreement that gives Ms. Mason any portion of Reginald's will."

"You're authorized to sign on her behalf."

"Yes, I am." He wore a smug look. He had the power.

All right. Carson preferred to keep this civil, but Patsy's attorney gave him no choice. "Might I have a word with you in private?"

Carson stood. He extended his hand to the conference room door.

Patsy's attorney's smug look changed to confusion.

"Anything you have to say should be said in front of everyone," Schmidt said.

"I'm sure you won't want me to say what I have to say in public."

Patsy's attorney's eyes twitched in question. And then concern. A guilty person always knew when their crimes had been discovered.

Whit looked at him with a nod of encouragement, and Landry looked as if she didn't care. She probably just wanted to get out of here.

When the attorney didn't move, Carson said, "I'm more than happy to oblige Mr. Schmidt."

Patsy's attorney stood. "Excuse us a moment."

Carson led him across the hall to a smaller conference room he'd had one of the assistants reserve. On the table was an envelope that contained copies of what Whit's assistant had.

"I hired a private investigator to obtain these photographs. If you don't sign on behalf of Patsy, they go to your wife."

Patsy's attorney looked from the envelope to Carson. Then he snatched up the envelope and slid out the first of several photos. He didn't look at any others. The first one was enough, as Carson suspected it would be.

"What kind of businessman are you?" Patsy's attorney asked.

"I'm not." He'd run as far and fast away from business as he could. He didn't even work for AdAir Corp. And he didn't like feeling as though he was acting just like his father, using blackmail to get what he wanted. His only justification was that he had to right a wrong, Patsy's wrong, and to honor his father's wishes. For that, he'd do anything. This was a quick and sure way to see that Patsy no longer poisoned his family.

"You think you can get away with blackmailing me?"

"I prefer to think of it as blackmailing my mother."

Patsy's attorney scoffed. "Your family is despicable."

"I'll be sure to tell Patsy that if she isn't guilty of murdering my father." Otherwise, he'd have to agree that at least his mother was despicable.

"Your mother has a legitimate reason for disputing Reginald's will."

"Jealousy is not a legitimate reason." Carson took a step closer. Taller than him by six inches or more, he loomed over him. "Sign the agreement or your wife finds out about your double life."

"Don't you care at all about your own mother's wishes?"

He shook his head. "Not in the least."

"This is preposterous!" Patsy's attorney slapped the envelope down onto the table. "I won't stand for it."

"Your choice." Carson pressed the speaker on the phone and called Whit's assistant.

"Yes, Mr. Adair," she said.

"Go ahead and deliver the package."

"Right away, sir."

"Wait!" Patsy's attorney jerked forward toward the phone as though the assistant could see him try to stop her. "That won't be necessary."

"You'll sign?" Carson asked.

"Yes."

"Never mind, Carol. Wait for me to stop by your desk."

"Yes, sir."

Carson ended the call. "If you don't go into that conference room and sign the agreement, I will have those photos couriered to your wife this morning."

"You're as ruthless as your father."

Carson had never blackmailed anyone before, and it didn't come easy to him. "Perhaps you should be more particular about the clients you represent." He stepped toward the door.

"What about these?" Patsy's attorney gestured to the photos.

"They're yours. The originals will go into my personal safe."

Anger flared from the attorney's eyes. He picked up the envelope and took it with him.

Back in the conference room, Schmidt looked suspicious. Whit already knew what this was about.

"I signed the agreement, Carson." Landry stood. "I'm going to go now."

"Okay, I'll talk to you soon."

She left the room while Schmidt, Georgia and Ruby watched Patsy's attorney stuff the envelope into his briefcase.

"We're all ready to sign the agreement."

Georgia looked stunned, gaping at him, no doubt wondering how he'd done it. And why.

Patsy's attorney signed the agreement and stood, picking up his briefcase. With a last glare at Carson, he stormed out of the conference room.

"What did you do?" Georgia asked.

"That's between me and him." He handed Ruby a pen. "It's not important anymore. What's important is that he signed."

She took it and signed the mediation agreement.

"I'll let you know when the transaction takes place," Carson said.

She smiled warmly up at him. "Thank you, Mr. Adair. Your father would be so proud."

He grunted derisively. "You have no idea."

You're as ruthless as your father. He'd done whatever was necessary to repair the damage Patsy had left behind when she'd fled. He wasn't happy about having to use a strong arm to make her attorney do the right thing.

Whit came up behind him with a pat on his back. "Thanks for taking care of this, Carson."

"No problem. Hey." He stopped Whit from leaving. He leaned over and picked up the papers. "Did you know about these?" He showed the pages to Whit, who studied them.

"No."

"There's contact and background information on Reginald's housekeeper and the neighbor. He must have gotten this just before he died."

"And planned to go to North Carolina to talk to them?"

"That would be my guess."

Whit put the papers down and looked at Carson. "Are you going to check it out?"

"Police report said they talked to everyone, but maybe Dad had a reason for talking to them again."

"I'd have to agree with that," Whit said. "Where'd you find these?"

"On his desk. Your assistant said she had it among

Elizabeth's things. It must have passed to her before anyone noticed what it was."

"I'll have to thank my assistant for being so good at her job."

When Whit left, Carson turned back to the remaining attendees. He saw Georgia and Ruby stand from their chairs. Unlike her stepmother, Georgia was not all aglow over the outcome of the meeting.

"Mrs. Mason," he said to Ruby.

"Please, call me Ruby."

"Ruby." Carson caught the roll of Georgia's eyes. "As you know, none of us were aware that our father had another son. Your son."

"Yes, that came as a shock to me. I was sure he'd have told you."

"My father wasn't the same man who married you."

"So I've heard." Ruby looked sad over that, as though thinking of what could have been had Jackson not been kidnapped.

"We need to go, Mother."

"It's all right, Georgia."

"Whit and I have decided to take over the investigation our father was conducting to find your son, Jackson. We… I was hoping I could meet with you some time to talk about what happened. His kidnapping."

Ruby's face fell. She was still, even after all this time, distraught and quite possibly full of guilt.

"No. I won't stand for that." Georgia turned to her stepmother. "Mother, it's bad enough you had to take their money. You don't have to put yourself through that again."

"Georgia, hush. If Mr. Adair can find Jackson, I want to do everything I can to help."

Georgia pinned him with a ferocious glare.

"Please, call me Carson." Carson met Georgia's spitfire energy and found himself enchanted all the more. "You, too, Georgia."

"Come by the hotel anytime," Ruby said.

"I have a better idea. Why don't I arrange for some rooms at our ranch. There's plenty of space and we'll have more time to talk."

Georgia's eyes rounded in horror as Ruby readily agreed. Then her mouth dropped open and she beamed accusation at Carson.

"It's all set then. Carol has directions for you, and a car if you need it."

"Why, thank you, Carson." Ruby was all smiles.

Carson gave Georgia a slight bow, having more fun with this than he should. "I've got to run, but I'll see you two lovely ladies tonight." Saying farewell to Schmidt, he left the conference room with a chuckle he didn't understand. Why was he so charmed? He didn't have time for a girlfriend. Besides, Georgia had made it clear how much she despised the Adairs. Wouldn't he be wasting his time trying to convince her she was wrong? She might not be wrong. He had, after all, just blackmailed Patsy's attorney.

Georgia watched Carson leave the conference room and fought a mixture of awe and angst. He'd done what she'd least expected. She and Ruby didn't have to fight for the inheritance. He'd made sure Ruby would have it, uncontested. Carson had become a hero for the day. But she could not allow him to suck her stepmother into a long, hopeless search for Jackson.

Schmidt was talking to Ruby about what to do next

to get her inheritance. Georgia touched Ruby's arm, interrupting them. "Wait here, Mother. I'll be right back." With Ruby's perplexed look, Georgia hurried out of the room and went after Carson.

She armed herself against gushing gratitude and physical awareness—he was too handsome for her impression of him and his family. Inviting them to his family's ranch was more in line with what she thought of them. It was more of a lure with the promise of pampered hospitality. He'd played Ruby, dealt her right into his hands. She wouldn't know what hit her until it was too late. Why had he done it? So she'd cooperate and help him find Jackson? Everything this family did had to have a reward. Invite them to the big ranch. Wow them with generosity and extravagance.

Ruby had suffered a great deal after her son's kidnapping. She'd talked about it enough for Georgia to know how deep her scars were. She'd loved Reginald and he'd turned his back on her. From the sounds of it, he'd turned his back on everyone. And raised his sons to be just like him.

"Mr. Adair!" She caught up to him at the elevator. In jeans and a long-sleeved Henley, he dressed casually for a man in his position at AdAir Corp. Short-cropped, light brown hair gave him a clean-cut, disciplined look, and those blue eyes dazzled, especially when he'd entered the conference room and seen her. He hadn't just seen her, he'd touched her with his gaze, lingering on her breasts that were hidden behind the layers of her shirt and tailored jacket. Only she would know the tingle that had chased through her when he'd done that.

He held the door for her, surprise rendering him silent.

She stepped into the elevator. "You can't involve Ruby in your new investigation of Jackson's disappearance."

He dropped his hand from the elevator door. "Involve her? Jackson is her son. She hasn't seen him since he was an infant. And the investigation isn't new. My father started it. Ruby is happy that we're going to search for him. Why aren't you?"

"She's suffered such loss with the kidnapping. I've seen what it did to her. She'll only be hurt more when you fail to find him."

He cocked his head as the elevator doors slid closed. "You're that certain I'll fail?"

"No one else has succeeded in thirty-seven years. What makes you so special?"

He looked at her without reaction. Some men would be insulted, but not him. "My own mother is the prime suspect in my father's murder."

That gave Georgia pause. She looked up at the numbers as they rode the elevator to the parking garage level. He had justifiable motivation for trying to find the kidnapper. She couldn't argue that.

"I *will* find Jackson. It's only a question of when."

"Do you think your father's death is linked to Jackson's kidnapping?" If Reginald had been investigating and discovered something, the kidnapper would have cause to kill.

"It's possible. But not if my mother killed him."

Ruby was an irrational woman. She could have any number of reasons for killing her husband.

She faced him, imploring with her eyes. "My stepmother is so vulnerable when it comes to losing Jack-

son. She lost a lot more than a son when he was taken."
Her entire life had been torn apart.

Carson's eyes blinked in sympathy and understanding. He turned as she had, and now they faced each other in the elevator.

"It isn't my intent to upset you or Ruby," he said. "I want to help you both, not hurt you. Reginald was my father. Jackson is a half brother I never knew I had. So you see, helping you helps me and my family, too. My intentions are for the good of all of us."

And hadn't he proved that today? He defused her. He removed any argument she had.

When he noticed, his blue eyes took on that playful look again, just as she'd seen them do in the conference room. He'd enjoyed being her champion, taking that lawyer to another room and coming back with a prompt signature.

The elevator doors opened to the parking garage. Neither of them moved. She fell into the long moment, daring to toy with the temptation of believing he was different from his father.

The elevator doors began to slide closed. He reached out and stopped them.

She stepped out ahead of him, not ready to go back up to the conference room and get her stepmother.

"What did you say to that lawyer up there, anyway?"

"I reasoned with him," Carson said.

"Reasoned?" He had to give her more than that.

"I helped him see that Patsy isn't of sound mind right now."

She had run before she could be arrested in connection to the attempted murder of Whit's wife, and suspicion had turned to her over her husband's death.

Who wouldn't agree that she was crazy? He must be some negotiator if he could maneuver a haughty lawyer like that.

"Well…I feel like I should thank you," she said.

"My pleasure." He gave her a slight bow of his head.

She warmed to him and the instinct to resist quickly followed. His chivalry didn't change who he was—an Adair. A wealthy man. He represented everything she didn't respect.

She had to stop herself from fantasizing about tracing her finger along that strong, square jaw with unruly stubble sprouting before noon. Maybe he'd foregone shaving this morning. He had a fun-loving side to him. That went against the rich-man, better-than-everyone-else persona she had assumed he had.

"Why did you do it?" she asked. "Why did you help Ruby?"

"It was the right thing to do," he said.

"That's it?" He'd only wanted to do what was right? "What about your mother?"

He grunted. "First of all, I was never close to my mother. And she severed all ties when she went after my brother's wife. I have no loyalty to her, but regardless of the kind of person she turned out to be, I'd have made sure Ruby got what my dad wanted her to have."

His integrity confused her. "But…Ruby isn't part of your family."

"That doesn't matter. She was married to my dad and they had a child together." He studied her awhile. "What's all of this really about, Georgia? Why are you so against my family?"

"I'm not against you." She searched for the right words. "I…I've just seen what being part of your family did to my stepmother. The kidnapping. Reginald leaving her. The blame. It destroyed her." She regained her purpose in chasing after him. "I'll be damned if I'll let anyone make her suffer like that again."

"Maybe I can understand your concern, but none of us—my brother, my sister or I—would harm Ruby. What happened in the past isn't going to stop me from trying to find Jackson."

"Fine. Look for him, just don't involve Ruby."

"I'll protect her as much as I can." He watched her awhile. "I know what it's like to want to protect your family. I felt estranged from my parents, but I love my brother and sister. I would do anything for Whit and Landry."

She smiled, believing he would. Carson didn't strike her as the type to abandon those close to him. He was a doer.

But what would she do about him searching for Jackson and dragging Ruby through that hell all over again? She'd never find closure. She would have to relive that nightmare.

"What makes you think you'll find Jackson any easier than your father?" she asked.

"I don't know if I can. But I have to try. I'm sorry, but I do."

"What if you don't find him? What then? I'll have to take Ruby back to Florida and pick up the pieces you shattered."

He put his hands on her shoulders. "You care about Ruby a great deal. I can see that. My father suffered, too. No one knew how much until it was too late. Try to see this from my point of view. I need to finish what my father started. He started his own investigation. I'm going to finish it."

He was so sincere. And she did understand. She couldn't fault him for trying to find Jackson. She just hoped Ruby could cope with another disappointment if he didn't succeed.

Realizing he'd put both hands on her shoulders and that she was looking into his earnest eyes, Georgia averted her head and stepped back. He was so handsome, a perfect specimen of hotness in a gentleman package. Not her vision of what had ripped Ruby's heart out. And not a man she'd expected to encounter.

"What's this really about?" he asked again softly.

What did he mean? This was about Ruby suffering. Didn't he see that?

"You tried to convince Ruby not to take the inheritance," he said. "Why? Why would anyone refuse that kind of money?"

"It's the money that destroyed her to begin with," she said. "Jackson's kidnapping only made everything worse."

"Adair money? How?"

"Your family treated her like trash and supported Reginald divorcing her. They never liked her."

"Who? My grandparents? Things have changed, Georgia. I don't see them here. It's just me, Whit and Landry. We had nothing to do with how anyone treated your stepmother."

Well. He certainly had a way of putting her in her place. The worst part was he was right. She was tossing blame around wherever she could. If it had the name Adair attached to it, there was plenty to spread around.

She didn't know what to say. She still didn't trust

him or his family, his money, their money. It was really that simple.

He leaned forward and pressed the elevator call button. "I'll see you tonight."

She watched him walk away, an inner struggle warring inside her.

The elevator doors opened but she didn't get inside. Impulse made her walk after Carson.

"Carson?"

He stopped and faced her.

"I'm sorry. Maybe I am out of line. Ruby married a rich man and all it got her was a broken heart. His family never accepted her. And now the inheritance is pulling her back into that life. I'm afraid of what it will do to her. That's why I can't help wishing Reginald had left Ruby out of his will."

A sexy grin curved up on his face. "I'm glad he didn't."

Georgia stared at him in slow comprehension. He wasn't glad for Ruby, he was glad for himself. Because he'd met her.

The sound of a car approaching penetrated her awareness. They stood in the middle of the parking garage lane. Georgia stepped back to get out of the way when she spotted a man wearing sunglasses and a hat aim a gun out of the driver-side window.

Carson tackled her right as fear consumed her and the gun fired. She landed hard on the concrete behind the protection of a pickup truck. More shots rang out, pinging as the bullets hit the truck. Carson stayed on top of her while tires screeched and the sound of the car grew fainter.

Georgia sat up when Carson stood to peer over the hood of the truck. Georgia could no longer hear the car.

"Who was that?" she asked, breathy with wild adrenaline.

"I don't know." He reached for her hands to help her to her feet. "Are you hurt?"

Stepping back from him, she surveyed her body, wiping her hands down her now-dirty skirt suit. She had a minor scrape on her leg and her hands were a little sore, but other than a little shaken up, she was okay. "No bullet holes, so I couldn't be better."

Her attempt at humor fell flat on him. His brow was dark and low in grave contemplation. He must have some ideas about who had just shot at them. Wait. Why would anyone shoot at her? The inheritance? It didn't seem likely. And as she recalled the way the man had aimed the gun, it hadn't been directed at her. It had been directed at Carson.

"Why would anyone want to shoot you?" she asked.

His eyes met hers but he'd closed up. "Go back inside, Georgia. I'll take care of this."

Take care of it how? He ushered her to the elevator.

"But—"

He gave her a gentle push when the doors opened. She stepped inside and faced him.

"The police may want to question you."

"I can wait for them to get here."

"Go back inside. I want you out of danger. What if the car returns?"

"What about you?" He was in more danger than her.

"I was a marine. I can take care of myself." Instead of sounding conceited, he spoke out of honesty and in a teasing tone. Sexy. Manly. A molten shiver ran through her. Then she checked herself. If she wasn't careful, she could fall head over heels…for an Adair.

Chapter 2

After the detective questioned them and AdAir Security gave him the recording of what had happened in the parking garage, he left to begin an investigation. Now Carson turned to Whit, who stood behind his desk, too charged up to sit down. He leaned against the wall with his feet crossed and arms folded, and Georgia sat on a sofa next to Ruby. The detective had asked them about Reginald's murder and, after cautioning them over carrying on their own investigation, seemed to think the shooting might be related to their meddling.

"Why would Dad's killer shoot at you and not me?" Whit asked. "We're both looking into his murder and Jackson's kidnapping."

"Maybe he hasn't tried to kill you yet," Georgia said.

"I don't think it was Dad's killer who shot at me."

Whit's brow lifted. "Oh? You didn't mention that to the detective."

No, but his thoughts were filled with other possibilities. Disturbing possibilities. "We don't have anything on the murder. No leads. Our best suspect is our mother and she's not in the country. Why go to the extreme of killing us when it appears our mother is the one who murdered Dad?"

"Who do you think it could be?" Georgia asked.

Carson looked at her but didn't say anything. He wasn't sure how much he *should* say.

"What motive would Mom have?" Whit asked. "That's always bothered me. Why would she kill Dad?"

"Who knows?" Carson said. "She tried to kill Elizabeth. Dad was so distant with her, she could have done it as a result of his neglect. Their relationship wasn't good."

"No, it wasn't. Not true love, that's for sure. But is that enough to make her kill him?"

Maybe Patsy had taken all she could and finally snapped, beginning with the murder attempt on Elizabeth. But if the kidnapper had killed Reginald for getting too close, then it seemed unlikely that Patsy could have been that person. He supposed the kidnapper could have killed Reginald and was now going after Carson and Whit, but Carson didn't think that was what happened in the parking garage.

The way the shooter had carried out the shooting, covertly moving in and making a clean getaway, was tactical and planned. Would Jackson's kidnapper be so professional? Possibly, but Carson didn't think so.

"What are you thinking?" Whit asked, moving around his desk. He must see Carson's doubt and concern. He stopped before him.

"What's wrong?" Georgia asked.

He looked over at her, again unsure of how much he should say.

"Do you have any idea who might have shot at you?" Whit asked.

Slowly, Carson nodded.

"Who?" Georgia asked. Beside her, Ruby followed the thread of conversation by looking from one to another.

"My last mission didn't go as planned," Carson said.

"You were shot."

Yes, he'd been shot, but a lot had happened before that. He glanced at Ruby and Georgia again. "It was a classified mission."

"Were you in the military?" Ruby asked, innocent of what Carson might be implying—that someone from the failed mission had come shooting at him.

"Yes. I was part of a four-man team in MARSOC, which stands for the Marine Corps Special Operations Command. Our missions were assigned by US Special Operations Command." He looked pointedly at Whit, who understood the brotherly code. His team had done top-secret reconnaissance missions in some of the most dangerous places in the world. In this case, he'd gone to Myanmar, an arms-embargoed country and a conduit for illicit trade. If Carson had made an enemy there, the shooting in the parking garage could only be the beginning. But it was probably best not to discuss that in front of Ruby and Georgia. He could only trust Whit right now. And for the women's safety, he'd keep them out of it.

He looked over at Georgia, who sat wide-eyed in fascination he doubted she welcomed. She had known he was in the Marines but not that he'd done special forces. Did that put a chink in her anti-Adair armor?

Seeing Ruby notice with a tiny smile, Carson wondered if she shared Georgia's animosity or if her disgruntlement centered only on Reginald. Interesting, that Ruby had been the one who'd been hurt by an Adair and it was Georgia who carried the torch. The two were close, but Georgia was Ruby's champion. Ruby had a frailty about her, whereas Georgia was a rock.

"Georgia is a librarian," Ruby said.

"Mother," Georgia said, a warning for her to stop playing matchmaker.

A lover of books. Carson wasn't sure if the profession fit her fiery disposition.

"How do you propose we handle this?" Whit asked.

"We wait for the detective to study the evidence. See what he comes up with from the video surveillance. Then I'll take it from there." If he had to involve his colonel, he would.

There was a lot to consider here, namely, the safety of his family and Ruby and Georgia.

"What was your rank in the Marines, Carson?"

The way Ruby asked made Carson wonder if she was asking for Georgia, who, although intrigued, would not give in and ask herself.

"Lieutenant." He saw how Georgia tried to hide her awe while her stepmother asked all the questions.

"You didn't want to leave?"

He shook his head. "I'd have retired a marine."

"Why did you have to leave?" Ruby asked. She may have noticed his limp but hadn't made the connection.

"I can't be a marine with this." He gripped his lame leg. Resentment and regret rose up as it always did when he was reminded of all he'd lost. He struggled with that reaction, one he always had when people asked him about it.

"Oh," Ruby breathed her realization. "That's where you were shot?"

He really didn't feel like talking about this anymore. He saw how Georgia hadn't missed a thing, and pushed off the wall.

"There's a limo waiting in front of the building." He went to the office door. There, he looked back at Whit. "We'll see you later."

Ruby left the office, and Georgia's dark green eyes met his as she passed. Out in the hall, she let Ruby go ahead of them.

"What did you mean *we*?" she asked.

"Whit and his wife are having a barn dance tonight. They finished their new house and are having something of a house warming. Since you and Ruby are staying at the ranch, you may as well join me."

As Georgia's mouth parted to reject the invitation—Carson was sure that's what she would have done since she'd rejected the invite to Whit and Elizabeth's party that had ended up being their wedding—Ruby stopped and faced them with a cheery smile. "Oh, how delightful. We'd love to."

Georgia didn't look excited at all about the prospect of going to a party. Maybe it had more to do with a party that an Adair put on. It would do her some good to see for herself that his family wasn't a bunch of mean people with money.

"Dress casually," he said to her, loving how easy it was to rile her.

* * *

Carson found Georgia and Ruby in the living room, sitting on the big off-white leather sectional. They'd both changed into jeans, Ruby much more conservative. Georgia wore a teal-green scarf over a white boat-neck T-shirt and distressed jeans that were nearly worn through in places. She had teal accessories, belt, shoes and jewelry. She was so put together. Completely different than the suited woman he'd seen at AdAir. The librarian had sparks. A librarian who hated money. Or was it only his money? He wondered if he should stifle the urge to test her on that.

"I have a little surprise," he said. "Follow me, ladies."

Ruby stood with an excited smile and came toward him. Georgia was much slower, woe to be her, subjected to an evening with awful Adairs.

Leading them to the front door, he opened it to a waiting horse-drawn carriage, complete with a driver.

He helped Ruby up and then offered Georgia his hand next. She didn't take it. Amused, he sat beside her and not Ruby. Ruby looked on in approval, and Georgia scooted over to put space between them. He almost chuckled.

But business had to come first. The carriage was a tool, part of his strategy to relax Ruby enough to broach the subject of Jackson.

He waited for the carriage to start moving.

Ruby sat prim and proper, rail-thin, salon-finished nails, light brown hair dyed to hide her gray. Even her physical appearance supported his expanding theory that Georgia had taken on too much responsibility where Ruby was concerned. It was sad that Ruby had lost her son so long ago, but Georgia had her own life to live.

"I don't know how you could have ever dreamed of leaving all of this," Ruby commented, in a fairyland all her own as she took in the landscape.

"I could never have stayed." This was actually a good way to lead into asking her about Jackson. "It's what my father wanted."

"Did Reginald expect you to stay?"

"He expected me to go to college for some kind of business degree and, yes, follow him and Whit. My father and I were never close. He had little interest in being a father. He spent most of his time working." He glanced over at Georgia, who listened like a mama bear, ready to attack if Carson said anything harmful to Ruby. He was about to take the risk of being clawed. He turned back to Ruby. "If I'd have known his first son was kidnapped and much of his aloofness came from that, things might have been different. He never talked about his feelings, but he must have been heartbroken over losing Jackson."

"He was. Reginald was a changed man after Jackson went missing. When Jackson was born, I like to think we fell even more madly in love. Our love for Jackson made us close. Until Jackson went missing." She gazed off into the darkness, unaware that Carson had begun the questioning he'd been itching to do since they'd arrived in California. But Georgia was. Her eyes had narrowed in warning.

Carson ignored her. "It wasn't your fault, Ruby. Someone took your baby. You didn't give him away."

Some of the sorrow left her as she looked at him again. "That's very kind of you to say, Carson, but no one back then believed I was a competent mother. I left him outside to go answer the phone."

Reginald and his family had blamed her. "In your own backyard. He should have been safe. You should have been able to leave him out there without worry."

"It was the middle of the day," Ruby said, encouraged. "I was in the backyard with him, doing some gardening. He was in his carrier. The phone rang and I went in to answer it. I was only gone one or two minutes. When I came back outside, he was gone."

"Who knew you had a baby?"

"Everyone. Family. Friends. The police questioned all of them. I've always thought my neighbor at the time was holding something back, but the police didn't find any reason not to believe her. That's something that has always bothered me."

"Why did you think she was holding something back?" Carson asked.

"She had a lot going on in her life at the time. She just seemed… I don't know…distracted. The police didn't talk to her long. I guess I've always felt she might have seen something and didn't tell police because she didn't want to be involved. It was an impression I had, nothing more."

Something she'd noticed in the way her neighbor spoke to her? It may be important.

"Did you ever tell Reginald any of this?"

She turned from her lost gaze out across the dark landscape. "He called me about a week before he was killed and asked me about her. He remembered that I'd mentioned what I'd thought of our neighbor and he wanted to confirm it."

Reginald had called Ruby? She must not have

minded. She must be over him. Of course she would be. Their marriage had been so long ago. And Ruby had been happy and in love with Georgia's father.

"He was going to look into the neighbor," Carson said aloud.

"Yes, but I don't think he had the chance."

"I don't, either, which is why I plan to talk to her." Carson stopped questioning her. He had enough for now.

"Are you going to go to North Carolina?" Ruby asked.

Beside him, he sensed Georgia's tension over the desperate hope coming from Ruby.

"I'll need to in order to talk to some people."

"Georgia and I could go with you."

Ruby seemed to want to help, but it was clear that Georgia had other ideas.

"Why don't we just let Carson handle this?" Georgia said. "You've already been through enough. Leave it up to him."

"It's much easier if we're there. We can help him."

Carson doubted she'd be of much help, but he also wasn't so sure that was her main reason. More likely, she couldn't bear to wait to hear what kind of progress he was making. Waiting here would be harder than being there. But if he made no progress, wouldn't that be worse for her?

"Let's decide that later," Georgia said as the carriage came to a stop in front of the barn.

He watched her take in the grandeur of Whit and Elizabeth's new house with reluctant admiration and decided right then to enjoy proving her wrong about the rich—the Adairs.

* * *

Georgia hopped down from the carriage, still marveling over Whit and Elizabeth's big house. It was on the ranch property and it was as spectacular as the Spanish hacienda from where they'd just come. This afternoon she'd gazed out over rolling hills of alfalfa fields, horse pastures and citrus groves and several outbuildings. The guesthouse was three times the size of hers in Florida. She didn't want to be impressed or like it so much, but she was and she did.

Seeing Carson watching her, she marched toward the barn. She didn't want to be impressed by him, either, but the deft way he'd handled Ruby had softened a part of her heart. He may not be finished talking to her about the kidnapping, but he had enough to go on for now and backed off. She appreciated that. But he didn't have to know it.

Reaching the open barn doors, where light poured out onto a corral, she stopped. People ate at tables and danced in the middle to a live country music band. There were Adairs everywhere. And nice or not, Carson was part of this family, the one who had treated Ruby so horribly and attracted people like them. Reginald had loved Ruby, but it was his family that had destroyed them. It hadn't just been losing Jackson.

Georgia didn't shun all rich people. Not all rich people were snobs or magnets to draw others like them into their circle. People could make a comfortable, secure living without amassing enormous wealth. There was a difference between struggling to get by and making a comfortable living. People didn't need hundreds of millions or even billions to survive. Yes, the rich created jobs and kept the economy going. But without those who kept the wheels turning, the ones struggling to get by or making a comfortable living, they'd have nothing. People like Reginald and his parents were just plain greedy. And even if one or two in a family managed to remain humble, there was bound to be someone or several who weren't. As far as Georgia was concerned, getting involved with a rich man wasn't worth the risk of happiness.

Carson and Ruby stood on each side of her. Everyone looked normal, but Georgia braced herself for the backlash. Ruby was the first to step forward and introduce herself to a young couple. The happy light had returned and she was ready to mingle. Affection and love swelled up in Georgia. She didn't have any trouble melting right into the crowd. It was as though she'd stepped into another world and wasn't an average Lake Mary, Florida, resident anymore. Free for the night. Maybe she was remembering what it had been like to be married to Reginald, to be well off. She had loved Georgia's father, but he hadn't made millions.

Georgia followed Ruby and was disappointed when Carson joined her. The young couple wandered off and a man about the same age as Ruby appeared before the three of them.

"Carson." He stuck out his hand. "I heard you were back. So sorry to hear about your parents."

"Hayden. Good to see you."

"Who are these lovely ladies you have with you?" He spoke to Ruby, who all but gushed over the attention.

"I'm Ruby Mason. How very nice to meet a charming devil like you."

Georgia gaped at her stepmother. She'd never seen her act this way before. Maybe she had when she'd met her dad, but Georgia had been so young, she didn't re-member. A traitorous thought came to her: socializing with the rich made her this way.

Hayden spent extra time greeting Ruby, lifting her hand to give it a kiss before saying, "A pleasure."

Ruby blushed a little, and Georgia was shocked over the transformation in her. Clearly, Ruby loved the atten-tion. Back in Florida, nothing made her shine like that. Most of the time she was sad and lonely.

"Hayden runs a ranch bordering ours," Carson said.

"Oh," Ruby said, sounding awed.

Georgia gaped at her again. What was wrong with her?

"What brings you to the Adairs'?"

"Ruby was married to Reginald. She's Jackson's mother," Carson said.

Hayden sobered. "Oh. Tragic. We were all so shocked to find out that Reginald had another son." He turned to Carson. "Your family certainly has had its share of bad news of late."

"Yes, but we'll overcome. An Adair doesn't give up easily. Whit and I will find Jackson. And we'll find my father's killer."

Hayden turned to Ruby. "Then you'll be in town awhile?"

"I…" She looked at Georgia and Carson. "We may be taking a trip to North Carolina. That's where I lived when my son was taken."

"Too bad. I was going to offer to show you around."

Wasn't that a little sudden? Hayden sounded as though he were quietly trying to get her to change her mind and not go to North Carolina so she could stay here and get to know him.

"Oh," Ruby breathed, clearly delighted he'd made the suggestion. "I would be thrilled to have you show me around. Maybe some other time?"

She'd spend a day with a man she had just met? Georgia was taken aback. Was it his money? Who was this stepmother and what had she done with Ruby? Carson knew the man, so maybe that changed things. That was when an idea struck her.

Distancing Ruby from the search would minimize the amount of pain she suffered along the way. The less involved she was, the easier it would be on her, particularly if they never found Jackson.

"You did say you wanted to see the old lighthouse," Georgia said.

"Yes." Ruby looked disappointed.

"And the museums…?"

Ruby stared at Hayden forlornly. "Yes."

"When are you leaving?" Hayden asked. "Perhaps we can take a day or two."

"Why don't you stay here, Ruby? Carson and I can go to North Carolina." Beside her, Carson turned a sharp look her way. "I'll call you every day with updates." If there were any. "You don't have to be there with us."

"Oh…I…" Ruby's happy light began to shine again. That and the shameless flirt Georgia had never met before.

"There's Beachfront Village I could show you, as well," Hayden said. "There's a fabulous place to have lunch there."

"If you like, you can join up with us later," Georgia said. Or not. Hopefully, this mutual interest Ruby had with Hayden would keep her here and away from Jackson's kidnapping investigation.

"Well…if you're sure." She smiled coyly at Hayden.

"I'm sure." She met Carson's wry look. He knew what she'd just done. At least he didn't fight her on it. Now all they'd have to worry about was being alone together.

Carson brought Georgia a glass of wine and put his beer down before sitting beside her at the picnic table they had all to themselves. They had made their way around the barn, and she had met more people than she could possibly remember.

"What do you think so far?" he asked after sipping his beer.

What did he mean? "About what?"

"All these rich people."

Oh, he was teasing her. "I think they're rich." She sent him a mock smile.

With a grin, he left it at that, making her wonder why. Was he playing games with her? Or was he just pushing her because he was offended by what she thought of him? Carson, offended? No. He was way too confident for that. He seemed amused. Charmed, even. Why would her opinion of him and his family charm him? What was her opinion of him? When she'd first arrived, she was full of animosity. She'd expected Patsy's kids to carry through with what she'd started and keep her stepmother from the inheritance that was rightfully hers. But Carson had surprised her. Some in his family may be coldhearted snobs but he was not. Was just being a part of the family that had so hurt Ruby enough to keep her reticent? She didn't know him, after all. And didn't everyone put on their best face when they first met someone? Maybe the evil side would emerge later. If she gave him that much of a chance.

Dismayed that her thoughts had even gone down that path, she looked toward the dance floor and spotted her stepmother doing a two-step with Hayden. They were really hitting it off, ogling each other, oblivious to anyone else. They hadn't run out of things to talk about, either. It worried her that her stepmother had taken to the rancher so quickly. Would she end up repeating old mistakes? She hadn't taken any money from Reginald when they'd divorced. It had been a matter of principle. And guilt. Poor Ruby. But she didn't look like a woman to feel sorry for right now.

"She fits right in," Carson said.

Realizing he'd followed her gaze and that he was likely challenging her again, she said, "They just met. He could turn out to be no different than Reginald." Just like what she'd been thinking about him.

"Hayden is a good man. He lost his wife five years ago. She was his high school sweetheart and he made his millions the hard way…on his own. Not only is she safe with him, he would take care of her like a gentleman."

Would Carson do the same with a woman? And what did he mean by take care of her? That he *kept* his women?

She wasn't prejudiced against all rich people. He had to know that, so she took the risk of offending him again and said in a light tone, "Well, then it's probably a good thing he isn't an Adair."

He wasn't. He just grinned, enjoying what he perceived as her misconception. Maybe she did have a misconception, but the agony Ruby had suffered when she had been a part of this family was too deeply ingrained in her. She couldn't just turn off years of conditioning. And letting down her guard with him would be a recipe for unhappiness, as far as she could see.

"How much did this cost?" He fingered her scarf.

She looked down at his masculine hand lifting the soft, silky green material and then letting it fall back against her chest. She met the playfulness in his eyes.

"I don't remember." She did. It had been expensive. She saved her money so that she could go on a few hundred-dollar shopping sprees every so often. She could spend an entire day putting outfits together, and then loved organizing them in her closet and wearing them until she saved enough for her next spree.

"The purse?"

She couldn't say she didn't remember that one. It was a famous American brand. "Three hundred or thereabouts."

He whistled. "You like expensive things."

"I like clothes." Lots and lots of clothes. Plus, accessories. The accessories were the best part about putting outfits together. But she'd never tell him that.

"That could cost a good amount of money if you do it often enough," he said, sipping his beer without removing his gaze from her.

She did. Something else she wasn't going to tell him. But then, she didn't have to. He'd figured that out on his own. And, oh, he was having fun. She discovered that tickled her. He had an infectious sense of humor.

She couldn't stop a brief laugh. "Okay, you got me."

His deep chuckle did more than tickle her.

"There you are."

Carson's brother interrupted what would have ended up being a long, hot stare.

"Georgia," Whit said in greeting.

"Mr. Adair." She sat back, realizing she'd leaned toward Carson as though his charm had enticed her to.

"Call me Whit. We are in a barn, after all."

She smiled and then Whit turned to Carson.

"I've finally managed to get away from Elizabeth," he said. "And we don't have mediation lawyers and police around anymore." He looked over the crowd in the barn. "Just a bunch of neighbors and friends."

What was he talking about?

"Why do you need to get away from Elizabeth?" Carson asked.

"I've been meaning to talk to you about something. I want it to be a surprise for her." Something caught his eye to stop him.

Georgia followed his look along with Carson. Landry had arrived. She laughed exuberantly with a group of men who were clearly taken by her. She looked like Scarlet O'Hara in that infamous scene, only—Georgia looked closer—maybe a little tipsy.

"She's later than she usually is," Carson said.

"Yeah. Have you noticed how different she's been?" Whit asked. "She's taken Dad really hard, but I expected her to be moving on by now."

"Mom's behavior shocked her, I think," Carson said.

"Well, maybe it's time to shock her out of her funk. Did you know she had to cancel a charity event last week?"

Carson turned a sharp look to him. "No."

"Yeah. Stayed out late the night before. Come to find

out she hadn't finished making arrangements. I doubt the sponsor will use her again."

Carson stared at his sister awhile. "It's so unlike her. She's usually so punctual and together."

"Yeah. *Bad girl* isn't a term I'd stick her with but…"

Both brothers watched Landry swing an arm around one of the handsome men in her circle. She spilled a little of her drink and tipped her head back to laugh at her clumsiness.

"I'll talk to her," Carson said.

"So will I. Between the two of us, maybe we can talk some sense into her."

"She needs to accept what happened."

"Something I could say to you, too, brother."

Carson turned another sharp look toward his brother. "Me?" Carson wasn't a partier and he'd grabbed his father's death by the horns. He was having no trouble coping. Except…

Georgia understood what Whit meant. Carson hadn't accepted his injury and its impact on his future.

"It's why I need to talk to you. It's about AdAir Corp. I've been hesitant up until now to broach the subject. I'm not sure how you'll feel about it."

Perplexed, Carson's brow rose. "This sounds serious. Feel about what, Whit?"

"I should have pulled you into my office for this discussion, but there never seemed to be a good time for that."

Not with their father's murder, Jackson's kidnapping and someone shooting at Carson mucking things up.

"Okay. You've got my attention. This is about the business."

Whit pulled out a chair and sat, flattening his hands

on the table. He was still hesitant. Whatever he needed to say, he had major reservations.

"Whit? It's me. Carson. Just tell me."

"You might not like it. And it's something I really need from you."

"Okay. What is it? I'm sure we can work it out."

Georgia began to feel like an intruder. "Maybe I should go talk to Ruby."

She started to stand, when both men said, "No," at the same time.

"You can stay," Carson said.

She leaned back against the chair, and Carson turned to Whit again, who hesitated yet again.

"Carson, I know how you felt about Dad. His business. But with Elizabeth pregnant, I don't want to spend so much time at the office. Now that you're back and out of the Marines, maybe you'd consider taking over for me?"

Georgia felt the internal shock wave that rendered Carson still and speechless. He did not react well to that request. He hadn't expected it, either. Whatever he'd thought they could figure out hadn't included this.

"Nothing you need to decide now. I wasn't planning on leaving soon. But give it some thought, okay?"

"What will you do?"

"I'd like to stay close to home. Work the ranch, maybe."

How sweet. He wanted to stay close to his wife and raise a family. Beside her, Carson's profile told a different story, as if he felt squeezed into a corner. Not just cornered. Pressed there. Crushed.

"Maybe you should hire someone," Carson said.

Whit's head angled and his mouth frowned in disappointment. "I didn't expect you to react positively to this, not right away. But I don't want to hire from the outside."

"I'm not qualified."

"Yes, you are. You know the business. Whether you like it or not, you know it. And I'd train you, help you with the transition."

"Whit, I don't think—"

"You need to put the Marines behind you, Carson. What happened."

Whit meant when Carson had been shot. There was so much emotion radiating off him that Georgia became certain whatever conundrum he had over leaving the Marines affected him greatly. He hadn't wanted to leave. He'd been forced because he'd been shot. And now the idea of taking over for Whit, taking his father's place, did not go over well with him. He recoiled against it.

"All I ask is that you consider it," Whit said.

Carson stood. "Yeah. Sure. I'll think about it. What else am I going to do with my life than run Dad's company?" Bitterness dripped from his tone.

He looked down at Georgia. "I'm heading back to the house. You coming or waiting for your mom?"

He sounded curt and annoyed. No, troubled.

"Oh…" Georgia was so stunned by his reaction that she fumbled for a response. "I'll wait."

"Carson, I didn't mean to put you on the spot, but I had to talk to you about it. I don't want the company controlled by an outsider. It's a family business."

"I said I'd think about it, Whit." With that, he stalked off.

Georgia watched him go, more than a little curious

over what had made him so surly. When he disappeared outside the barn, she turned to Whit.

"Well, that went worse than I thought it would," he said.

She looked toward the barn doors. Carson was home, but he didn't want to be here. He was here not by choice. He was a man who needed to be in charge of his own direction. Take that away and what was left? A man going through a life change. Resisting it every step of the way.

"He hates the idea of following our father," Whit said, bringing her gaze back to him. "But he has nowhere else to go."

"He could do worse than running a successful company."

Whit grunted his doubt. "Tell him that."

Maybe she would. Because she was sure something more than being shot had put all that emotion in him. More than rebelling against his father. And more than his father's murder. What dismayed her was that something she couldn't control made her want to find out.

Chapter 3

Today, Georgia wore a long-sleeved, soft orange T-shirt with a flowing black tank top over that. Carson walked beside her on their way to the plane. Her top had subtle floral embroidery and all her accessories matched the soft orange. Flower earrings, bracelet, purse, belt. Black skinny jeans that had him checking out her butt too often.

"How many suitcases did you bring?" he asked.

"Huh?" She stopped at their gate. People glided by on the moving walkway. A woman passed with a pet carrier.

He indicated her purse. "You seem to have a purse for every outfit."

"I have a suitcase for those and shoes. And one more for the rest."

"For someone who doesn't like money, you sure have a knack for fashion."

She cocked her head. "Shopping is a fun stress reliever for me. And I like putting outfits together. It doesn't have anything to do with money."

He gave her a skeptical look and then guided her to the seats in front of their gate. She must spend a wad each time she went out to buy a new outfit. He couldn't wait to see what she wore next—and he disagreed. A woman could shop a lot more with money. She had to have money to put those outfits together. Was she being defiant when she said it had nothing to do with money? Suppressing an inner craving to spend, spend, spend? He could have some fun with that, shower her with luxuries and see if she liked it. Starting with right now, as soon as they boarded.

Georgia slipped her purse off her shoulder and placed it on the seat next to her. He'd checked his carry-on since she'd had two bags. They were traveling light as a result. He sat beside her, trying not to overtly notice her thigh in the snug jeans as she crossed one sexy leg over the other.

"Why do you have to meet with your ex-commander?"

So far she hadn't tried to pry information out of him. He'd told her they'd stop in Camp Lejeune, North Carolina, first, before heading to Raleigh, and that was all. Now he realized she'd strategically waited until she had him alone. Maybe now she could get him to talk.

"He's got some things he wants to discuss in person about my last mission and since the mission was classified, we have to meet in a SCIF. Sergeant Major Mark Copeland of the 2nd Marine Special Operations Battalion was a hands-on kind of man and had been upset over the failed mission."

"What's a skiff?"

"Sensitive Compartmented Information Facility, a secure office or meeting facility where classified information can be processed or discussed."

As she tipped her head to the side and smiled her intrigue, her dark red hair slipped down from her shoulder, shiny and thick. "You have a clearance?"

Was he ruining her disparaging opinion of him? "Top secret."

"Why do you think that man who shot at you is connected to your mission?"

He couldn't discuss most of it. "If you had a clearance, I could bring you to my meeting and tell you."

"Does Whit have a clearance?"

He'd discussed everything with Whit. "Yes." AdAir Corp had a SCIF on-site. Carson could have talked to his commander from there, but his commander wanted him to meet in person because he had some intel to share. That meant they'd continued their surveillance after Carson had come home. He was encouraged by that. He'd had a hard time leaving after the mission in Myanmar failed.

"Why didn't your mission go as planned?" she asked.

"We were discovered," he said. "To this day, we don't know how." That was pretty much all he could say.

"You were attacked?"

"Yes." His mind started wandering where he didn't want it. Seeing Georgia catching the change in him, he faced forward and hoped she'd drop the subject.

"What happened?"

"It's classified."

She eyed him awhile, her smart librarian brain adding things up. "Not all of it's classified."

No, but he still wasn't going to talk about it.

"Did your father know you were shot?"

He wondered why she would ask such a question. "Yes. He was killed after that." He recalled the last conversation he'd had with him. He had still been in the hospital and his father had called, insisting on speaking with him.

You get shot and I have to get a call from your commander? Reginald had roared. *Were you going to tell me?*

I was shot, Carson had replied, thinking to himself, *Why did he even care?*

His father's apparent offense was more about control. He'd been angry that Carson wouldn't have called to let him know that he'd been shot.

I told you joining the Marines was a mistake. When are they sending you home?

I'm not coming home.

I've had enough of your attitude, Carson. You're coming home where you belong.

I don't belong anywhere near you.

At that time he hadn't known he'd be honorably discharged from the Marines. The next day, the doctors had informed him he'd be lucky to walk again. Hearing that had been a tough blow. He'd denied it flat out at first. Not walk? Screw that! He'd walk again, damn it. It had been a long recovery. Once he was released from the hospital, he'd begun a rigorous physical therapy regimen. And he had walked again. But the injury was too severe to pass the physical requirements for the MARSOC. Finally, he'd had to accept his fate. He would never be a part of a Marine Special Forces team again.

It was then that he'd gotten the call from Whit.

"Carson. I'm sorry to tell you this over the phone, but Dad is dead..."

The last words he'd ever spoken to his father were the first that had entered his mind right then. As Whit explained the murder, all he could think was, *I don't belong anywhere near you.*

The guilt had only stung sharper when the reading of the will had revealed Reginald's secret agony that had turned him into a heartless businessman.

"Why don't you want to take over his company?" Georgia asked.

He looked at her and realized she'd been watching him while he reminisced. "I'm not an executive."

With the subtle but dubious lift of her eyebrows, she said, "But you said you can't be a marine anymore."

She was fishing for something. "I'm still not an executive."

"Have you ever worked at your father's company before?"

"Oh, yeah. He forced Whit and I to work there as soon as we turned sixteen. When I was eighteen I didn't have to do what he told me anymore." Looking back, he was frankly amazed his dad hadn't cut him out of his will. And then again, not. Now that he knew about Jackson, he could understand how his father would choose not to turn away from his kids, no matter how distant he'd been. Somewhere inside him had been a father who'd loved all of his children.

"And you've been helping Whit, haven't you?"

"Occasionally." He'd stepped in and helped after Reginald was murdered. He knew the business. He'd grown up around it. But being an executive…just like his father… It just ate at him. Maybe it was residual from when he was younger. Rebelling had become habitual. Or maybe he still hadn't forgiven his father for not being a father. It wasn't his or Whit's or Landry's fault that Jackson had been taken from him. Hadn't he realized that his new children needed love, too?

Carson felt weak for thinking that way. So his dad hadn't shown them love. Was he going to cry about it?

"You seem really upset over it," Georgia said.

She was going to have to stop being so intuitive.

"Do you regret not being close to your father before he died?"

"My father wasn't close with anyone."

"And that's what upsets you."

This was getting too personal. "It upsets me that he didn't tell us about Jackson."

"You wish you knew your father better?"

Yes. And he wished he would have been kinder on the phone the last time he'd spoken with him.

"I didn't know my mother," Georgia said. "I can see how you'd be upset. It seems like your relationship with your father was like not having one at all."

"You had Ruby."

She smiled, a radiant, toothy smile that lightened his mood in an instant. "Yes. I do have Ruby."

Carson heard the attendant announce that it was time for first-class passengers to board.

"That's us," he said, standing.

She looked up at him, smile fading, completely caught unaware. She hadn't guessed they'd fly first-class. She hadn't thought of it until now. She was accustomed to flying coach and not boarding first. He grinned, and she frowned at him as she stood up, more of a smirk.

They were the first to board.

Georgia had never flown first-class and she was pretty sure Carson had done this on purpose. Of course he'd get first-class tickets, but he was enjoying this far too much. It was a nice introduction to the benefits of having money, which she suspected was his intent. Show her that having money wasn't bad.

She sat on the spacious, comfortable seat next to the window, watching him bring down the tables in front of them and begin to spread out the papers he'd gathered on the people they'd question once in Raleigh, North Carolina.

"Have you ever flown coach?" she asked.

"No, but I flew in military planes. Is that common enough for you?"

He hadn't asked in a mean way. His tone was teasing. "Doesn't your family have a private jet?"

He stopped sifting through the papers. "Yes, but I thought you'd be more comfortable flying commercial."

"This is first-class."

"You're not comfortable?" He surveyed her seated form with animated flare.

She had to suppress a smile. How could she be enjoying this? He was taunting her.

"I'm comfortable."

"You look comfortable." He surveyed her again, only this time some heat made its way into the play.

Ever since her last relationship, she hadn't been eager to seek out a new man. Actually, she hadn't even thought about finding anyone. It hadn't ended well and she wasn't anxious to start over. Besides, Ruby needed her right now. She paused. Why was she thinking in terms of a relationship with Carson? She had just met him. Were these sparks she felt leading to something? She wouldn't allow it. He was the son of the man who'd broken her stepmother's heart. Reginald and his rich family hadn't accepted Ruby. So why would they accept her? Why would Carson? He was just having fun teasing her.

"Uh…" She looked down at the table in front of him. "Maybe we should…" She indicated the papers there. She couldn't possibly be interested in Carson. He was putting on a good face now, but who was he, really? Reginald's son.

"Right." He picked up the first report. "Penelope Johnson was Ruby's neighbor. She's moved since then. At the time of Jackson's kidnapping, she was going through a divorce. She took her son with her. Problem is she lost custody of him in the divorce."

"She took him?" She took the page he held from him. "Where did you get these?"

"From Whit's assistant. They were among Dad's things, but we don't think he's checked into them yet."

"Wouldn't the police already have talked to them?"

"I'm sure they did."

She searched the document but didn't see anything significant.

"Penelope had just moved in a week before Jackson was taken. Police caught her and she was arrested. The charges were later dropped. She still lives in Raleigh."

"Why did she lose custody?" She handed the paper back to him.

"Drug addict. She did go to rehab, though. Two years after she lost her son."

Penelope didn't seem like a very reliable witness. If she was wigged out on drugs, what would she remember? And she'd essentially kidnapped her son. Would she have kidnapped Jackson? It didn't seem likely, but probably best not to discount the possibility.

"Who else is there?" she asked.

Carson handed her another report.

She appreciated that he included her, but she needed time to read through these.

"Evita Marrero was the housekeeper," he explained for her. "She quit after the kiddnapping and according to my father's report, not on friendly terms."

Georgia sat back against the seat. "Ruby told me about that. Reginald was hard on her. She hates him. She won't feel like helping us."

"We'll see."

"Why did Reginald want to talk to them? I can see the neighbor, because of the trouble she was in, but the housekeeper? Do you think he had an affair with her that ended badlly?"

"No. He was faithful to Patsy, although I don't know why."

"He wasn't the same person back then, though, was he?" He was nicer as far as Georgia could tell.

"No," Carson reluctantly answered.

She took in his perturbed face. It bothered him that his dad might have been different. "And if he was faithful to his wife, then he must have hung on to some of his principles."

"Yes."

"It is important that your woman stays faithful?" she

asked. Those pesky sparks had compelled her. She was curious about him. Or was she hoping she was wrong about him?

"Well, yeah. Who wants the person they're involved with to cheat on them? Anyone who does has no respect for the one they've betrayed."

She told herself that she'd already started this conversation. She may as well finish it. "You talk like a man who's experienced it firsthand."

A flight attendant stopped by and greeted them, interrupting and offering menus.

Carson put the papers down and took the menus, then asked for a specific bottle of champagne with strawberries.

Georgia eyed him as the flight attendant said, "Of course, sir."

They'd get into Raleigh well after dinner, so they'd have to eat on the plane. That hardly warranted champagne. Georgia saw what he was doing and didn't comment.

"Strawberries?" she asked.

"Delicious with champagne. One of my favorite combinations." He leaned closer. "And something we rich people love to indulge in."

Champagne and strawberries. Where was the caviar?

"I've had it before."

He leaned back. "There you have it, then. You have rich tastes and I bet you never even knew it."

She couldn't help smiling, and even breathed a laugh. "How much is that champagne going to cost you?"

"More than you've ever paid."

Was he being deliberately pretentious? "I could let

you spoil me. Use you for your money just for a good time."

His gaze floated all over her upper body and face. "You aren't that type of woman."

"How would you know? I made a promise to myself never to get trampled by a wealthy man." The way Ruby had. She'd stick to her own class. One never could predict the future. Ruby sure hadn't been able to. "I could be using you."

He actually chuckled.

"You barely know me," she said.

"I have a first impression. And I'm good at reading people. Your only hang-up is you don't really know jack about rich people."

Georgia had no idea why she was enjoying herself so much. He'd be insulting if he wasn't talking in such a witty tone. But then, so would she.

"Oh, and is it your job, now, to teach me about them?"

"I think it's going to be the first thing I've had the privilege to choose to do on my own since I was forced to leave the Marines."

What did he mean by that? Before she could ask, the attendant returned for their dinner order.

"Do you mind if I choose?" he asked Georgia, showing her the menus.

She shrugged. He was playing some sort of game with her, and she discovered she didn't mind. And he liked being able to choose on his own. He could try to prove rich people weren't all snobs and the middle class had it all wrong. She wasn't going to buy it. "As long as it's not slimy or has tentacles, I'm okay with that."

"Right in line with my taste."

With another one of his sexy grins, he read the menu
and then waited for the attendant to return. Then he ordered the filet mignon with grilled asparagus.

Georgia let him have his fun, telling herself it was
harmless as long as she was immune to him. And it
could be worse. She could be on his private jet.

When the attendant left, he said, "To pick up from
earlier, I wasn't speaking from experience. No one's
ever cheated on me, and I've never cheated on anyone.
It's up there with robbery and animal cruelty for me."

It was so nonchalant that she had to stop and think
about what he was saying. Why was it so important to
him that she know he'd never been cheated on? Because
of her perception of him? Maybe he didn't want her to
think that rich people didn't have morals. It wasn't his
fault he was part of a ridiculously wealthy family.

"You feel strongly about it."

"Yes."

This wasn't because of her perception of him. He really didn't like cheaters. "You're a real stand-up kind
of guy, aren't you?" Her surprise came out in her voice.

"Has anyone ever cheated on you?" he asked.

"No." But that brought up thoughts she'd rather didn't
enter her conscience. She turned away from him.

He angled his head as though trying to see her face.
"Something I said?"

"No." She shook her head, shaking off the dark
thoughts along with it.

He watched her a moment and then didn't ask her
any more questions. He gave her space. He'd nudged,
but he knew when to back off, and she appreciated that.
More than he could possibly know, and more than she'd
tell him.

The champagne arrived, strawberries floating on the surface. Georgia took a glass from the attendant. The woman left and she met the play of mischief that had returned to Carson's eyes.

"Is this what you do when you fly on your family jet?" she asked.

"No. Never."

Never? She didn't believe that. "This is just for me, huh? Have you ever treated a woman to champagne in a plane?"

"No. Never."

She laughed softly. "I don't believe you."

"I haven't. I've been in the military. If I'd have been here all this time, maybe I would have. I didn't use the jet in the military."

So, she was his first. She clinked her glass with his. "Here's to trying new things."

"To new things."

She sipped some champagne. It was delicious. Sweet with a touch of dry.

"Is it the best you've ever had?" he asked.

She had to be honest. "Yes."

"Good. I'm going to give you a lot of those." He focused on the pages on the table before him, as though what he'd just said was an everyday thing.

"I don't want you to spend money on me, Carson. I can pay my own way on this trip."

"Hmm." He nodded. "I know. But you aren't going to."

She twisted on the seat to face him more fully, still holding her glass. "No, Carson."

He turned his head. "Relax, Georgia. I want to spend

money on you. You need someone to spend money on you."

Their meals arrived, and Georgia refrained from arguing with him. The dishes were gorgeous. She could forget she was on a commercial plane.

She dug in, savoring the flavor of the meat and loving that Carson had thought of this.

Carson stuck a forkful of meat in his mouth, all very *not* in a posh manner. He was more of a mountain man the way he ate the meat.

She laughed but had to set him straight. "I don't need any of this. I'm happy with my humble existence. In fact, I prefer it."

"You need to eat."

"You know what I mean." She spread her hand over her plate and lifted her champagne glass.

"Nobody *needs* it. But it sure is nice. Don't you agree?" He waited while she debated how to answer.

She couldn't lie. "It is nice." But what was nice about it—first-class or him?

Chapter 4

Stepping up to the old redbrick building with rows of narrow windows and a flag waving out front, Carson entered the lobby of the Marine Corps Base Camp Lejeune and told the receptionist he was here to see Major Sergeant Copeland. He'd left Georgia at their hotel. When he finished here, she was going out with him for ice cream, and not just any ice cream.

Copeland appeared moments later, his green suit decorated with rows of badges, ribbons and medals above the left breast pocket and rank insignia on his arm. Carson walked toward him, ever aware of the limp he couldn't hide.

"Lieutenant Adair." Copeland shook his hand. "Good to see you up and moving. You healed well."

"Better than expected." Better than not walking. He had to keep telling himself that.

"Come with me."

Copeland wasn't a man who wasted words. Carson followed him down a hall, certain that the man would someday rise to lead MARSOC. Through a secure door and down another hall, they entered a windowless office area. A woman worked behind a desk there, her pictured badge marked with her security level in a code the military base had chosen.

Through another secure door, they entered a conference room. There was a table to seat eight, a safe, a shredder and two computers at a desk in the back. A state-of-the-art computer monitor hung from the wall and there was a phone in the middle of the table. There were some papers lying out and some high-resolution satellite images.

"We had the local police in San Diego send us over what they have on the shooting attempt," Copeland said, reaching for the papers and handing them to Carson. "I've had our guys looking into it and passed the information over to our marine in South Korea."

Carson began to skim over the first report. "Is it Morris you've got over there?"

"Yeah."

Morris was one of his teammates. Only three of them had made it out alive on their botched mission.

Copeland saw the grim change in him. "They all miss you. Hell, I miss you. You were one my best soldiers, Carson."

Unwilling to talk about it, Carson moved to the table where the photos lay. There were several of North Korean facilities that must be used for weapons research and development. The photos didn't show much, only changes in vehicles parked there, but the same vehicles showed up, nothing new and no increase in number.

"As you can see, there's been no sign of unusual activity there," Copeland said. "Nothing to indicate they've stepped up engineering efforts. There's been no change in government activity, either."

That suggested the North Koreans had failed in securing the information Carson and his team had been sent to intercept. Their intel had exposed a group of terrorists who were talking to North Korea's leader and would have accepted money in exchange for information on pressure transducer technology. That was all Carson and his team were able to glean. The terrorists in Myanmar were in contact with someone, presumably someone from the United States, who had access to technology that would help North Korea manufacture their own transducer.

Transducers were used in gas centrifuges to produce weapons-grade uranium. That had been enough to send Carson and his team in to stop the transfer. They were never able to confirm success.

They had never learned the identity of the person who was going to bring the technology, only knew through the terrorists that the meeting would take place. Somehow the terrorists discovered their presence and a gunfight had erupted. One of Carson's teammates had gone after the man the terrorists were supposed to meet. But the man got away, and Carson's teammate had been killed. The plan had been to capture the man and interrogate him, along with stopping him from transferring sensitive US technology to an arms-embargoed country.

"They didn't get the technology," Carson said.

"Right. But then why did someone go after you?"

Why would the terrorists or the mystery man try to kill him if they didn't have the technology? "Maybe the mystery man still had it and they're waiting to arrange a new meet."

"So they think killing you would facilitate that?"

Copeland was right. It didn't make sense. Killing Carson and anyone else on the team wouldn't stop the US military from organizing a mission to stop another transfer attempt.

"They'd want me alive if they thought I had it." But why would they think he had it? And if the mystery man had it to begin with, what had happened to cause him to lose it? "Maybe they want revenge."

Carson may not have been the easiest target to find after leaving the military, and it would take planning to attack him in San Diego. AdAir Corp had security, and the ranch had a security system. And if they believed Carson and his team had taken the data, they would presume they had given it to the US government. Carson or his teammates wouldn't hang on to it. The revenge motive made sense in that regard.

But how had the mystery man lost the data? Carson had gone over the mission many times. He could think of no incident during the gunfight when someone could have taken the data. The mystery man had to have gotten away with it, or not had it with him at all.

"I've asked Morris to talk to the North Korean border guard he's coerced to help us."

"He's in contact with a North Korean guard? How'd he manage that?"

"We'll get him out of North Korea in exchange. He's getting scared, though. Just before you called with the news that someone tried to kill you, Morris learned two North Korean engineers were executed and their families sent to prison camps. We believe this occurred after they failed to obtain the technology."

"Isn't it a little rash executing the brains behind his nuclear weapons program?"

"He recruited another engineer. Dual Chinese-Canadian citizen who got a green card and an education."

"Who's the engineer?"

Copeland gave him the name. "He isn't the man we're looking for."

The engineer might be part of another mission. In fact, Carson didn't doubt it. He felt a moment of regret that he couldn't be part of it. But he was part of this mission.

"I'm happy to continue to be bait," he said. "Draw the mystery man out." If he'd shot at him once, he'd try again.

Copeland nodded. "That's the main reason I asked you to meet me here. This all has to be kept secret. You aren't part of the team anymore, but you're my best chance at catching that man."

"Thanks."

"I'm not doing it because I feel sorry for you. Man up if you're having a tough time dealing with that." Copeland pointed to his lame leg.

Carson grinned. The commander had set him straight. "Yes, sir. I'll do my best."

"Good, because I need you. Our problem here is that if the North Koreans didn't get the technology and we didn't bring it home, where is it?"

The best way to find out was to expose the mystery man, whom Carson believed was the same one who shot

at him, the one who would have made the transfer, but
for whatever reason, hadn't.

"What did the San Diego police have?" Carson
asked.

Copeland's face lit with the good question. "Ah. They
traced the car to a rental company. Whoever rented it
used false identification. A background came up with
somebody who's been dead for fifteen years. They're
looking for the car now and I'm looking into who might
have traveled from Myanmar, or anywhere near there,
during the time of the mission."

Carson nodded. That sounded promising. And despite Copeland's lack of sympathy, Carson was thrilled
to be part of the team again.

Georgia's bracelets jingled as she brushed her long
hair back over her shoulder and stepped by a row of
treasure-lined shelves inside a village bookstore. It was
an independent bookstore and the most delightful she'd
ever seen. Converted from an old house, it had nooks
and cozy seating areas and walls of books. Carson had
reserved rooms at an old Victorian inn a short walk
from here. The inn was on a farm with white fences and
cows. Very upscale and also very soothing in a country
way. The village was full of boutique shops and there
was even a spa. She was glad Carson wasn't here to see
her melt in pleasure.

He'd left her here and drove to Camp Lejeune to
meet with his commander. A classified meeting. Carson had been part of an elite military team and his
missions fought terrorism and protected national security. The notion of him in that role clashed might-
ily with what she expected to encounter when she and

Ruby arrived in San Diego. A hero. Carson Adair. An Adair. Hero. The two bounced around in her head, and she kept pushing back the hero version. The bookstore helped. It was like therapy, being among the thing she loved most on earth—books—in a place like this with creaky old floors and the smell of candles, potpourri and ink, made it easy not to think of Carson as a big bad heroic soldier.

Georgia purchased a book amid the soft tinkle of piano music and left with a satisfied smile. Walking up the street toward the white inn, she passed a linen-table restaurant that was only open for dinner and a gift shop. As she drew closer, she saw a limo parked in front of the inn. And then she saw Carson. He stood next to the open back door, waiting for her. Standing tall and lean and handsome in dark jeans and another Henley, he looked as if he'd just stepped out of an ad for a yacht.

She saw him notice her outfit, from the silver flower earrings to the silver boots that went with her gray knitted cardigan over a white T-shirt and dark low-rise jeans.

"Hi," she said, and then feared there was too much enthusiasm in the greeting. Big bad soldier. Hero.

"Hi." He grinned. "Let's go get ice cream." He opened the door wider and stepped out of the way to allow her inside.

She slid onto the leather seat and he got in after her.

"How did your meeting go?" She looked down his muscled torso to his long, thick legs. If not for his injury, he could probably run really far for a long, long time. He probably had when he was in the military. But he still had stamina for other activities...

"Good."

His brief answer diverted her attention. "Just good?" That's all she'd get?

"We're a long way from finding out who shot at me." He looked down at the small shopping bag she'd put beside her with her purse. "Did you buy something?"

"There's a bookstore in the village." She restrained her excitement and stopped herself from going on to say what a fabulous bookstore it was. She could talk about books all day and probably bore him to death. Unfortunately, she couldn't keep the beaming smile off her lips.

"Exactly why I chose this place."

Because she was a librarian, and he knew she'd love it here. He'd known about the bookstore.

"I do love to read. I collect them, too."

"Antique books?"

"Yes. It's a challenge finding first editions at reasonable prices. But when I do…" She raised her eyes heavenward, enough to indicate the joy she felt when she found something special.

"What did you buy?"

Still smiling, she parted the tissue paper the clerk had wrapped her book in before putting it into the bag. It smelled like the store. She handed him the hardcover, a novel about a young girl who ran away from home and overcame countless obstacles. An underdog story. Her favorite.

"Not something I would have chosen but good for you." He handed it back to her.

"What would you have chosen? *Machiavelli*?"

He chuckled. "Something Jack Reacher."

She tucked the book back into its nest of tissue paper as the limo stopped in front of a gourmet ice-cream shop. It was every bit as quaint as the village she'd just left. How much more of this was he going to inflict upon her? And what was he trying to do? Win her over or just prove her wrong?

The driver opened the door. Carson got out and took her hand to help her out. She felt a little ridiculous. Not only was she unaccustomed to this, she was capable of getting out on her own. But he was going out of his way to be a gentleman. He even held the door for her as they entered the ice-cream shop.

"Ah, Mr. Adair," the mid-forties man behind the counter said with a big smile. "You finally came back to North Carolina for a visit?"

The man knew Carson, which made him a regular here, which also pricked her curiosity.

"Yes, for a few days."

"The Marines give you some time off?"

"Yeah. Quite a bit."

Only Georgia knew the cynicism in that reply.

"You here for your aunt's party? She ordered dessert. Is that what brings you here?"

His aunt? Who was his aunt?

"That's one reason, yes." He glanced at Georgia. "She's expecting us."

Her immediate reaction was that she did not want to go hang out with his family. Her next was incensed that Carson had planned to take her without telling her. Part of his ploy to prove she was wrong about his kind.

"That was supposed to be a surprise," he said, doing his best to show contrition, albeit with a hint of humor.

That he was doing this all in fun helped, but she was beginning to think she should put the brakes on his shenanigans. "Haven't you surprised me enough for one trip?"

"No. Not nearly." He faced the man behind the counter. "We'll share a butter pecan sundae."

Georgia read the menu. A butter pecan sundae had four scoops of salted-butter caramel ice cream, pecans and whipped cream. Drizzled over all of that decadence was hot fudge and a caramel sauce. Oh, my...

He put his wallet away, and they moved out of the way to allow an older man in line behind them to order something.

"Ice cream is one thing, but a party?" she said. "What kind of party is it?"

"It's a fund-raiser for missing children."

How appropriate. He couldn't have done it on purpose, though. Had he convinced his aunt to throw the party? She didn't think so.

"Didn't she know about Jackson?" she asked.

"Yes, but it never came up after years went by with no progress in the search. And my dad moved to San Diego, where he lost touch with his family. I kept in touch with Kate, though."

"You're close to your aunt?"

"As close as I can be."

She wasn't sure what he meant by that. Close to him was his brother and sister. So maybe his aunt was sort of close. But not close enough to warrant talks about a kidnapping that happened before he was even born.

"What is her full name?"

He looked taken aback that she didn't know. "Kate Winston."

Winston. "Former vice president of the United States Kate Winston?" She opened her mouth and let out an incredulous grunt. "You're kidding me."

"No. Not kidding. She's Kate O'Hara now. She's been reunited with her first love and their granddaughter."

"I read about her. She was led to believe her own daughter died at birth, but she actually was killed in a car accident at the age of twenty-four. It was such a sad story."

"Yes, very sad, but she's happy now. And she's normal. You'll like her."

Vice president of the United States wasn't normal. Georgia was normal. She had an average job and an average income and an average home. She wasn't known by all. And she didn't have parents who would scheme against her the way some of those in Carson's family did. They seemed to be mounting in number. That had her tensing a little. *Careful*, she warned herself, *don't start liking this man too much. Appearances aren't everything.* He seemed as nice as he claimed his aunt was, but things weren't always what they seemed. Hadn't she learned that from Ruby?

Their sundae was ready. Carson took it from another clerk at the pickup end of the counter and took it to a small round table with a shiny metal post.

She sat on a cushioned chair across from him. "How can anyone be normal if they're in politics?" *Vice president.* She was fooling herself even entertaining the *idea* of enjoying his attention! They were so different there was no way they'd make a good couple. He came from such a different background. He couldn't possibly know what it was like to grow up in middle-class America. He was surrounded by people who ran good people like Ruby out of their lives.

Carson leaned forward. "Stop thinking so much."

He picked up the spoon he'd set in front of her and handed it to her.

"I'm not going," she said, taking the spoon.

"Yes, you are. And you're going to enjoy yourself around all the nice people in my family."

His grandparents were not nice. She watched him guess her train of thought with only the look of her eyes.

"All right," he said. "Some of them have their moments. But just give them a chance. I promised Kate I'd be there. She's doing this fund-raiser because of Jackson."

And a tax credit. Georgia tucked that barb away. The party was for a good cause. It was more than a way to show off how much money the host had. She'd go, but only for Ruby. Only for the cause.

Scooping up a large spoonful of the delicious-looking sundae, she brought it to her lips. The flavor was incredible, and she took her time savoring the bite.

"Mmm."

With the shine of triumph in his eyes, he took a bite of his own. When he finished, he said, "This is one of the top-ranked gourmet ice-cream parlors in the country."

And he'd had to take her here. Show her what money could buy. She pointed her spoon at him. "You know, aside from the limo and first-class, I could afford all of this on my own."

"I'm warming you up for the really expensive extravagances."

He was planning more? "The party?"

Shaking his head, he mumbled, "Uh-uh. Better. You'll have to wait and see."

Now was probably a good time to tell him to stop.

"Carson, don't spend money on me. We aren't even dating. It would be a stretch to even call us friends. Why would you do that anyway?" She scooped a bite of ice cream and put it into her mouth, licking off some caramel from her lips.

Carson noticed and swallowed. She hadn't tried to be sexy, but her tongue rolling over her mouth must have gotten to him, and he hadn't expected to react that way. He lifted his gaze from her mouth to meet hers. She swallowed her bite, unable to look away for a few seconds. Then she got ahold of herself and put her spoon down. What if they did start dating?

"Uh…" he stammered, "your bias compels me. And I happen to think I'll enjoy proving you wrong." His gaze fell to her lips as though recalling how entranced he'd gotten over her lick. "You will, too."

She lifted her brow. "*I'll* enjoy *you* proving me wrong?"

"It's a point I hope to make."

That she'd enjoy the money he was going to spend on her, that she'd enjoy what his money could buy? She grew a little uncomfortable, and then, not. He was making this fun. He wasn't out to shove her nose in it. He would really, truly enjoy showing her how nice money was, how nice it was having it and that it was okay to enjoy the luxuries.

"As long as you don't turn me into a snob, I suppose that's okay." She tried to sound bored in a humorous way. She wasn't sure she'd pulled it off.

It wasn't only watching her enjoy the money that would give him satisfaction or the only motivator for starting this game. He couldn't stand being equated with his father. Carson was a good man. A military man. A man who stood up for good and fought evil. He had a fearlessness about him. That's what made him go after Jackson's kidnapper and the man who shot at him. But Georgia would not set herself up for disaster by putting herself into a family like the Adairs. Ruby had likely thought Reginald was a good man. Tragedy had changed him into the same people his parents were. Would Carson be influenced that way? Even if he wasn't, there were people in his family who were not good people. His own mother had attempted to kill Elizabeth.

Georgia didn't hold his family against him. She wouldn't do that. They could be friends. Maybe they could even sleep together. Beyond that? Georgia had to remain steadfast and firm in her resolve. She refused to end up like Ruby, who had thought she was walking into happily-ever-after and had gotten the opposite.

Even while she worked to convince herself to steer clear of any future with an Adair, a nagging sense kept bubbling up that he was different, that the mean people in his family wouldn't matter because he had such strong conviction about the man he was and the man he would become. He wouldn't resist going into his father's corporation so much otherwise.

"Is it really that important to you to be disassociated from your father?" she asked. "I mean, why commit to this relentless—which some might call hopeless— search for Jackson if you hold so much resentment toward your father?"

He swallowed his latest bite of the sundae and put his spoon down, looking at her as though she'd hit on something he struggled with. "I don't resent him… Well, I used to, but…"

Georgia waited for him to think through what he was trying to say.

"He never told us about Jackson," Carson said at last. "That is so odd. I can't figure out why he did that. He didn't seem to want to spend much time with any of us. Wouldn't having more kids help? Or was he so grief-stricken that shutting everyone out was the only way he could cope? I can't imagine him grief-stricken, but that must be what it was."

Georgia nodded. "Ruby was the same way. Withdrawn. Quiet. She never got over losing Jackson. Never."

"No wonder you're so protective of her." He smiled softly.

"She's had enough sadness in her life. She lost Jackson. Then she lost my father. All she has left is me."

Carson had lost a father, one he hadn't had a chance to know. His father hadn't shared himself with his own children. All he'd seen was the man who made hoards of money, a powerful man. In death, he had a glimpse of another side to that man, a man hardened by terrible loss and a sense of helplessness. Maybe that was what had driven Reginald to accumulate riches. He didn't feel helpless when he was in control of an empire like AdAir Corp.

"Do you ever wish you wouldn't have run away?" she asked. She didn't sugarcoat what it was. He had run. He'd run from a father who had never been a father to him.

"No. Losing Jackson doesn't excuse my father from not being a father to his other children. Do I wish I'd have tried to get to know him? Yeah, maybe a little. But I wouldn't have changed my course. I'm a marine. And I still don't want to be like him. He was a cold man. Unhappy. Lonely. And it was all self-inflicted. He might have convinced himself that building AdAir Corp gave him all the joy he needed, but did he really have to shut everyone out?"

Carson was bitter about many things when it came to his father, and all centered around Jackson's disappearance. It had shaped the man he was now, whether he realized that or not. Even knowing about Jackson all along wouldn't have changed that. Reginald would have still been heartbroken and he'd have still shut everyone out. Carson would have still rebelled and joined the military. The only difference now was that Carson was torn over following his father to run AdAir Corp. A career in the military had been taken from him. Would choosing to run the corporation mean he'd follow his father? And would he be all right with that?

I'm a marine.

No. No way. Carson would not be happy feeling as though he'd followed his father, done as his father had wished. But where was his choice in the matter? His brother wanted to resign from AdAir Corp and Carson's leg would keep him from staying in the Marines. What else would he do?

She saw Carson rubbing his lame leg under the table. He was thinking what she was thinking, only much more in depth—and with a lot more turmoil.

"What will you miss most about the Marines?" she asked. What once had been a way to distance himself from his father had turned into something he loved. It defined him. Now he didn't have an identity. And if he didn't find one, he wouldn't find happiness.

"The camaraderie. The exotic places. The excitement."

He liked the adrenaline. Being good at what he did in a dangerous situation. Fighting terrorism and conquering evil. She pushed back her awe and attraction. "You can still keep in touch with the friends you made." And he could travel whenever and wherever he pleased.

With that, his face grew much more somber and he turned away. "Not all of them."

All the fun was gone from this ice-cream excursion. She'd hit a sore spot.

"Was one of your teammates killed on your last mission?"

His head bowed, and she could feel him go back to that day, relive it in horrible detail. "He was my best friend. Leif Louis."

He said it so quietly that she almost hadn't heard him. His best friend. Oh, that was terrible.

Given his relationship with his father, the few friendships he'd acquired in his life must have meant a lot to him. He didn't get that kind of closeness from his family. He did from his siblings, but his siblings had been neglected as much as he had. A best friend would have given him camaraderie he didn't get from anywhere else. And that best friend had been killed.

"Why do you want to be back in the Marines if your best friend was killed?" she asked.

"I wasn't the one who killed him."

And a man like him would want to avenge his death. Being forced out of the military would prevent him from doing that.

"I'm sorry," she said.

"You didn't kill him, either."

"I mean for your loss. That must be so hard for you."

He nodded a few times, going into thought. "He was

a good man. He had a wife and a three-year-old child. Unlike me, he was going to serve his time and get out. He was only in for the experience. And the schooling. He was trying to make a better life for his family."

"Why did he choose the Marines, then?"

He grunted as though he couldn't believe his friend had. "I asked him that same question. His dad was a marine. He joined to make his dad proud. And to be a hero for his son because he grew up idolizing his dad. But it was with his family where he wanted to be. He used to talk about them all the time. How much he loved them. I knew them even though I had never met them."

Carson had gotten a glimpse of what it was like to have a father who loved his son.

"He was like a brother to me," Carson said.

The emotion in his voice touched her. The relationships Carson had in his life meant everything to him. His brother. His sister. His best friend. He didn't have many, but the ones he had were the most important. She wondered if that would ever extend to loving a woman. A wife.

"Didn't you want to have a family, too?" she asked. "You sound as though you didn't agree with your friend's decision to join the Marines. He did it for his dad."

It took him a while to respond. She'd gotten him thinking about it. "I don't know. It wasn't important. Besides, I have a family."

Did he mean his brother and sister were his family and that was enough?

"When I'm ready to have one of my own, I suppose I will." He wasn't like Whit, who'd decided to stay and work with their dad. Carson had gone to make his own way. Getting married would have tied him down, maybe chained him here, too close to Reginald. Part of the reason he'd joined the Marines was that it took him far away from that. Marriage and family was difficult when you were never home.

"What about you?" he startled her by asking. "Why haven't you started a family?"

Everything in her tensed. This wasn't something she relished sharing. But she had brought it upon herself.

"No reason," she said, hoping that would suffice.

Carson didn't say more, but she caught how he observed her. He'd picked up on something, and if she was lucky, he wouldn't try to pry the truth out of her.

Chapter 5

Evita Marrero worked in a street-corner bar in a dangerous section of Raleigh. Georgia and Carson had gone to her trailer, and her husband told them where they could find her. The place had dim lights, a concrete floor, twenty-year-old wooden tables and red-cushioned chairs with torn upholstery. The bar itself was cluttered and the rear shelf of liquor was crammed. Most of the activity was at the bar. A couple of tables had groups of two and four.

Her hair messily pulled back in a clip, Evita wiped the bar in front of the silent drinkers. These were loners with sad pasts. Georgia felt it just with one glimpse. And Evita was one of them. It seemed to Georgia that many who had a connection to Reginald's life ended up like this or with some other type of scar.

Evita came over to them when they each took a bar stool. "What can I get you?"

"We're not here to drink. We're here to talk to you about Jackson Adair," Carson said.

The woman's head drew back a bit. "Jackson Adair... now, there's a name I haven't heard in decades."

"You were a housekeeper for the Adairs," Carson said.

"An unfortunate fact." She looked back and forth between Carson and Georgia. "Who are you two? What do you want?"

"Reginald Adair is dead," Carson said.

It took a while for that to sink in. And then she smiled. "You don't say. How did he go? Was it painful?"

"I imagine so. He was murdered. We just now discovered he had another son. Jackson Adair?"

"How was he murdered?"

"He was shot. The police are investigating. Did you know he had a son?"

Evita took out three shot glasses and filled them with Scotch. Setting them down in front of Georgia and Carson, she said, "Anybody that comes by with good news like that gets a drink on the house."

"Nothing for me, thanks," Georgia said.

"No, thanks," Carson said. "Did you know Reginald had a son?"

The housekeeper tipped the shot glass and sipped, going against Georgia's initial impression. She'd picture this woman downing the entire drink in one gulp, not savoring it as if she was sitting with Winston Churchill.

"Yes, I knew they had a son."

Having drifted off into memory, she shook her head. "Poor little Jackson. Innocent child. It was having a father like Reginald that got him kidnapped." Then her attention returned to the present. "What are you trying to find out about him after all this time?"

"I'm Reginald's son," Carson said. "He was conducting his own investigation when he was killed. We suspect his death may be related to the kidnapping, that maybe he was getting close to finding the person who took Jackson. I found some of his notes that suggested he was planning to talk to you."

"Reginald's son, huh?" After grunting over that revelation, she studied him. "You resemble him."

Georgia saw Carson blink and quickly recover from what must feel like an insult to him. That wasn't a compliment to him.

"When your father was young, he was a handsome man," the ex-housekeeper said. "Like you are."

Georgia had to agree. Carson was a very good-looking man.

"Had a good head on his shoulders, too," the woman continued. "Didn't fall in line with his parents, not in the early days. He did his own thing. And then..."

And then Jackson had been kidnapped.

"You tried to steal a necklace?" Carson said.

Evita sighed. "If I could go back and do it over, I'd have never done that. I realized I made a big mistake, stealing from him and Ruby. Even though it wasn't an expensive necklace, just a few hundred dollars' worth, it was wrong. I was going into bad debt and was trying everything to get out. I was caught, of course, before I could even get the necklace out of the house. Ruby caught me. I gave the necklace back and tried to explain, to make amends. I told them why I did it. I pleaded with them to forgive me. Ruby did, but Reginald wasn't having it. He didn't fire me or press charges, but things changed. After Jackson was taken, a mean streak came out of him. Working for that family became pure hell, I tell you. Pure hell. I ended up quitting."

"I'm sorry for that," Carson said.

Georgia saw that he was sincere and wondered how many times he'd had to apologize for his dad and stepmother's behavior. Maybe he'd only just begun, after being gone for so long. He knew how his father was, the kind of man he'd become. In that regard, he related to the ex-housekeeper.

"Why would Reginald want to talk to me?" Evita asked. "I told the police all I knew, which wasn't much. I didn't see anyone take the child."

"How long did you work for him and Ruby?" Carson asked.

"Just a few months. From just before they were married and Jackson was born until…" Her voice trailed off as she was reminded of the stolen necklace. "Anyway, he was a different man before Jackson was kidnapped."

"He never told any of us about Jackson or the kidnapping," Carson said.

Evita nodded, still taken back in time. "He was so full of love for Ruby and that baby. I don't think either one of them planned to have a child, much less get married, but I do think they were meant for each other. It was awkward at first, the two of them so young and barely knowing each other. I said it was hell working for them, but not until after the kidnapping. Reginald doted on them both. I've never seen a happier couple in my life. Then the child was taken and a dark cloud passed over them both. They started fighting. Reginald stayed away from home a lot. He turned into an awful man, someone unbearable to be around. He had it all and then his whole world changed."

Georgia noticed how Carson sobered, his gaze falling to the shot in front of him. He hadn't known Reginald like that. Ruby had told her what their relationship had been like. Good. And then with Jackson gone, it had been exactly as the housekeeper said. It must have bothered Carson to realize his father had once been a good person. Full of love that he shared with Ruby. Something Carson had never seen in his entire life. Now he was hearing of it, and had only his mind to imagine what his father had been like, what the man beneath the sorrow had been like.

"I remember when I accidentally broke a family heirloom, one of the few things Reginald cared about that had come from his parents. It was an old statue." She swatted her hand through the air. "An ugly, dreadful thing, but he kept it proudly displayed. He was upset when I broke it, but he reassured me and told me it was okay and he knew I didn't mean to break it. I felt horrible, but he was a true gentleman about it. Attempting to steal the necklace tried his patience. And then after Jackson..." She shook her head. "Lord, he was a completely different man. He became a bitter, bitter man. I wasn't there when he and Ruby divorced, but I bet he was the one to end it. Poor Ruby was so distraught and full of guilt. Reginald never comforted her. Just blamed her."

"Ruby is my stepmother," Georgia said. "It would mean a lot to her to find Jackson."

"Oh, honey, you don't have to tell me that. I feel her pain. There was nothing anyone could do. Just sit back and watch Jackson's disappearance tear them apart."

Georgia thought she might be dramatizing a bit too much.

"What happened after Jackson was kidnapped?" Carson asked.

"I couldn't take it anymore. One day Reginald yelled at me for not being able to find a hat of his. I had put it away in the closet. He was so unreasonable. I yelled back at him and quit. When another client of mine called for a reference, he gave me a scathing one. I wasn't hired. No other opportunities came up. That's how I ended up here. All I have to be grateful for is that I'll never have to live for the whims of the wealthy. I live for myself."

Georgia could sympathize with this woman. She felt the same about wealthy people—certain wealthy people. The ones like Reginald, who let greed take control of their morals, who blamed, who expected average people to bow down to him as though he were a god. Bow or be ruined. That was Reginald's mentality, at least from her vantage point.

"Are you sure there's nothing you remember that you haven't told the police?" Carson asked. "Anything you may have seen?"

She shook her head. "No. If I did, I would have said something. Jackson was an innocent child and I had nothing against Ruby."

Only Reginald.

"Did you ever meet Reginald and Ruby's neighbor?" Georgia asked.

"I saw her a few times. I never spoke to her, though. She kept to herself. Came and went from whatever job she had and went into her house. I saw her get the mail and take care of her yard and that's it. She was a real recluse."

Georgia glanced at Carson, who shared her sense that the ex-housekeeper would be of no help. Why Reginald had thought she would be remained a mystery. Maybe it was a desperate reach.

"I feel sorry for her," Georgia said as they walked to the limo that pulled out from the curb, the driver having seen them. "She had nothing but good intentions toward Reginald." Except when she stole the necklace.

"By then, he was a changed man."

Tortured by the disappearance of his child. Yes. Georgia could understand that, but… "He didn't have to give her a bad reference."

"That was the father I grew up knowing."

Georgia could see how that troubled him. He had a father he'd never known. The real Reginald had been the man Ruby married.

Feeling a strengthening connection between them, she stopped attraction from taking over. He was nothing like his father. The only resemblances were physical and his nature to get in and get a job done. He made things happen as his father had. His father had done it in a corporate setting. Carson had done it in the military. They were both doers. She'd argue that Carson would also be a doer in a corporate setting. He'd gotten Patsy's attorney to back off. She didn't know how, but he had. If he'd used ruthless tactics the way his father would have, then he'd done it with a heart. He believed Ruby deserved the inheritance and had done what he had to ensure the right thing was done.

But allowing feelings to grow for him disconcerted her. She wasn't sure how to handle this.

* * *

They had to wait for Ruby's old neighbor to come home. Georgia sat in a rental car with Carson, parked along the side of a dirty street. Three teenagers with tattoos and backward hats and chains hanging down their pants had walked by, adopting the swagger of gangsters as they walked down the sidewalk. This was the reason they hadn't taken the limo. The limo would have drawn too much attention. Maybe they wouldn't have a limo by the time they finished.

A little unnerved by the elements of the neighborhood, Georgia dug into her orange purse and pulled out one of many clothes catalogs she received by mail. She also had her electronic reader with her. There was always something in her purse for moments like these.

Putting the thin catalog on her lap, she began to look through it.

"Shopping?" Carson asked.

She slid a look his way, not having thought ahead to what he'd perceive of this. "Just looking."

"You bring that with you?"

"For something to do, yes." Her eyes caught on a cute vintage blue dress. She had lots of accessories that would make it really pop.

"If you find something, I'll buy it for you. Pick out what you want."

She shut the catalog. "No."

"Come on. I dare you to find three outfits in there and let me buy them for you."

She laughed lightly. "I can buy them myself. I'm not poor."

"Okay, then I'll take you somewhere you can't afford."

"Carson…"

"Seriously. It will be fun. Let's do that after we talk to Ruby's neighbor."

He did not strike her as a shopper, not even a little bit.

He chuckled at what must be her wary look. "What does your house look like?"

Why was he asking her that? She could tell he was setting her up for another money talk. "Like a house."

He chuckled again, deep and warm. "I bet it's really nice."

Yep, he was digging for material items she loved and wouldn't admit to loving. "It's nothing like your ranch."

"Not as big. But just as nice."

"I didn't spend what you probably spent." Not even close.

"I didn't spend anything. Patsy and my dad did."

She wished he'd stop being a normal man, a normal, sexy, hot man. Special Forces man. Oh, how that turned her on. He wasn't just in the military. A man could be in the military and never train for special warfare, never risk his life on top-secret missions, fight the enemy in small, deadly teams. Carson was exceptional.

"I'd love to see it sometime," Carson said.

He wanted to see her house. She doubted anything would take him to Florida, but it so happened that she had pictures on her phone. Proud of her home, her sanctuary, she dug out her phone and opened her photos, scrolling to the ones she'd taken after picking up new rugs and throw pillows for her den—yes, she bought things for her house. What woman didn't?

She handed him the phone. "It's a three-bedroom condo I rent."

He began scrolling through the pictures. "I was right. It's nice."

The interior was the way she liked it. "I'm saving to buy a cottage someday."

"A cottage?"

The photos showed how she decorated that way. Simple, fresh, colorful. "With patio doors that open to a beach." She dreamed of owning a beach house someday. And someday she would. She didn't need millions to do it, either. Just a big down payment. She tucked away as much as she could each month.

When he didn't say anything, she turned to look at him. He wore a wry but fond look, and she predicted what he'd say before he said it.

"And you think money is bad."

"Too much money makes people bad."

"Just for that, I'm taking you shopping."

She laughed as a car drove by and pulled in front of one of the row houses with steps going up to a door. All of the houses needed new paint on this street. Most had brick lower levels and wood siding on the second.

An overweight woman with short, curly dark hair and thick glasses got out of the old Honda. Carrying a paper bag and a purse, she waddled up to her steps.

"Penelope Johnson?" Carson called as they approached.

The woman stopped at her door, turning her head to see them, most of her body facing the door. "Can't you see the no soliciting sign?" She pointed to her door.

"We aren't here to sell anything." Carson stopped at the foot of the stairs, Georgia beside him. "We're here to talk to you about an old kidnapping case. You used to live next door to Ruby and Reginald Adair." He stopped while the woman searched her memory or seemed to.

"That was a long time ago," she said. "Cops came by back then and asked about it. I'll tell you what I told them—I didn't see nothin'." She turned to the door and started to stick a key into the lock.

"Please," Georgia said. "We know you were going through a hard time back then. But maybe there's something that will help us get a break in the case. Anything at all."

"What do you know about what I was going through?" The woman straightened from the door and turned her head to see them. She did not take kindly to them poking around in her past.

"Your divorce. Taking your son…it's public record," Georgia said.

Still annoyed, Penelope shifted to face them fully. "I haven't seen my son ever since about the time that child was kidnapped. My ex-husband took him from me, you see. I was a wreck back then, but I cleaned up my life and he never once let me see my boy. Now he's a grown man and doesn't want to see me. Do you know what that's been like?"

Georgia looked down at the paper bag the woman held. It was the kind from liquor stores and she could see the top of one of the bottles inside. Apparently she'd slipped back into old habits; maybe she no longer did drugs, but the loss of her son had driven her to drink.

"I'm sure Ruby does," Carson said. "She lost a son, too."

That eased some of the woman's animosity. "I don't even remember those people. I took money from my ex-husband to buy that house and I was in it less than a year."

Then she'd been arrested and lost everything. That's how she'd ended up here in this low-end neighborhood.

"What were you doing that day?" Carson asked.

The woman adjusted her purse over her shoulder, keys jingling in her hand. She seemed to contemplate something. Georgia didn't think she would talk to them at all, but something had stopped her.

"I was home with my boy." The memory softened her further.

Georgia felt a deepening empathy for the woman. She'd paid a high price for the sins of her youth.

"I did see something. I didn't remember it at the time the police questioned me. I had so much trouble going on. Years later it came to me and by then I thought it was no longer important. I still don't, but you may feel differently."

Georgia exchanged a look with Carson. Could they be so lucky?

"I saw Ruby's friend Loretta the day of the kidnapping. She drove by Ruby's house, real slow. She might have been leaving at that time or just driving by. I couldn't tell. But I thought it was strange that she did that because Ruby told me about the conflict between them."

"Who is Loretta?" Carson asked, exchanging a look with Georgia. This was someone even Reginald hadn't known about, or left any clues that he had.

But something was odd about Penelope knowing a friend of Ruby's. They hadn't been neighbors long. They couldn't have become very close in so short of a time frame.

"One day I went to the store and I saw the two of them. It was a real spectacle. Yellin' and accusin' each other of cheatin'. I asked Ruby if she was all right. Bein' my neighbor and all. She looked so upset. She told me who the woman was and what happened. She and Loretta used to be best friends. Their argument was just about a week before Jackson went missing. Maybe she went over there to apologize but decided not to and drove by."

Or she'd taken Jackson for revenge.

"Did you talk to Ruby much?" Georgia asked.

"No, not much. After her boy was taken, I was dealin' with the courts a lot. Besides, she didn't seem interested in getting to know the likes of me. I married a wealthy man, but I wasn't like him. Ruby had all her rich friends and never seemed to want to talk to me."

"She had rich friends after Jackson was kidnapped?"

"She had weekly gatherings. I got the sense that she was trying to keep up appearances, you see. When no one was around, though, I heard them fighting, she and her husband. Screamin' matches some of the time." The big woman shook her head. "Mmm-hmm. They had some whoppers."

That fell in line with what Ruby had told her. But the social gatherings. Why had she done that? To try to fit in? Hang on to her marriage? In the end, she'd even given up on that.

But more important, why hadn't she told her about Loretta?

"She probably did better than I did in her divorce. She was always wearing nice clothes, never did see her in jeans. Jewelry. And her hair was always perfect. Girl like that needs maintenance."

Georgia didn't say that Ruby had walked away from everything. Reginald had taken his parents' side and driven her out. Ruby hadn't taken a thing, and during the divorce, she didn't take any more than she'd gone into the marriage with as far as money went.

"I'm afraid that's all I can tell you," Penelope said. "Now, if you'll excuse me." She moved the bag higher on her hip, getting uncomfortable holding the bottles.

Carson thanked her and she turned to the door, slipping the key in and unlocking it, ready to begin another night drowning out memories and the reality of her life, no doubt.

Loretta, it turned out, didn't have any children. Carson had gone through his commander to find out where she lived, and a background didn't produce any suspicion that she might have taken Jackson, unless she'd somehow gotten rid of him right away.

She seemed normal, harmless even. She'd done well for herself. Single after divorcing five years ago, she was ready to start looking for a companion. Carson had learned all this over the hour they'd been here. Loretta's house was a three-thousand-square-foot bright and modern suburban home. She was a real estate agent and had stacked up respectable savings before the market crashed. Now she was back in the game, planning a trip to Cancún this spring.

His energy sapped by the draining effect of her unending chatter, Carson was ready for a nap by the time she said, "What was it you needed to know about Ruby? I haven't spoken with her in years. I did talk to her once, just before she moved to Florida. Tragic about Jackson."

"Ruby's neighbor said she saw you drive by the day he was taken. Do you remember?" Carson asked.

"Oh." Loretta's brow scrunched and she looked across her big, white and earthtoned living room. "I remember I had thought about going to talk to her. I ran into her at the market and we had words." She looked regretful now, her brow still scrunched but softer.

Carson sensed another long-winded dialogue coming. A glance at Georgia and she was bracing for one, too. He almost smiled. Her head angled slightly and her eyes were wary, as though anxious over whether she could tolerate so much needless prattle.

"Ruby and I were inseparable throughout high school," Loretta said. "We did everything together. Of course, back then, we were into all sorts of trouble. Stealing liquor from our parents. Sneaking out to go to parties. Ruby was a real party girl. I drank but not like she did. She was sure wild."

"What drove you apart?" Georgia asked, a clear attempt to get her to the point.

"I remember this one time." Loretta laughed, in her own world and oblivious to them. "Ruby had a crush on this boy who was a year older than us. He was having a field party. A bonfire. Back then it was okay to drink and drive. Can you imagine? People drove with six-packs in their cars and parked at drive-ins or other dark places to party and make out."

She laughed lightly, slapping her knee to the fond memory. "Anyway, we sneaked out again, and I drove us to this boy's house. His parents were gone. Music was playing. People were talking and laughing. There were about fifty of us that night. Ruby, oh, my gosh." She slapped her knee again. "She went right after that boy.

Drinking with him and eventually they disappeared. It was more than two hours later she finally came down." Loretta put her hand up by her mouth as though to whisper a secret. "She slept with him. Ruby was like that. She slept with a lot of boys. I don't know how she managed to escape a bad reputation."

"Ruby?" Georgia was taken aback, mouth slack, eyes shocked.

"She's different now?"

Georgia scoffed. "Uh…yeah. Not promiscuous. At all."

Loretta sobered. "Well, I imagine losing her son changed her quite a bit. The Ruby I remember was loud and full of rambunctious laughter. She loved the boys. And then she met Reginald."

"What drove you and Ruby apart?" Carson asked the question again.

"Oh. Yes. Sorry." She swatted her hand in the air. "I get carried away. Ruby slept with my husband. I married before she did. Mistake, that was." She wiggled her left fingers. "Divorced twice now."

"She slept with your husband." Georgia said it flatly, in total disbelief.

Carson didn't know Ruby very well, but the few times he had met her, she seemed old-fashioned, but open to flirtation. Maybe it had been the man who'd brought that out in her. Maybe there hadn't been another man to do that since Georgia's dad.

"Yes. But I was having an affair with someone. She probably thought I wouldn't care. Maybe I didn't. The thing that hurt was that my best friend would do something like that."

Any normal person would feel that way.

"I can't see her doing anything like that," Georgia said. "Innocent flirting is one thing, but…having an affair?"

"Well, she's a changed woman then. Ruby was not as innocent as you might think. Anything she tried, she tried at full speed. There was no slowing that girl down. I was glad to get married. I couldn't keep up with her anymore."

"She is definitely not the same."

"When she met Reginald, that was the beginning of a new adventure for her. Mostly I think his money attracted her. She'd show off whatever trinket he bought her. After they married, I think she came to truly care for him, and he her."

"When did the two of you have your falling-out?" Carson asked.

Loretta turned to him. "She slept with my husband before she met Reginald. I didn't know she'd met him until one of our mutual friends told me. I only heard about her through other friends after I found out about her affair with my husband. People said she was happy. And faithful. I believed she was happy. Ruby was always happy, even when she was sleeping with other women's husbands. Faithful? I have a hard time buying that. Maybe having a baby changed her."

"Losing the baby definitely did," Georgia said.

Loretta fell into somber thought, looking across her living room again.

"Did you take her son out of revenge?" Carson asked. He knew it was blunt. He intended to shock her. He wanted to see her reaction.

Her head whipped toward him, yes, shocked by the question. "No. Never. I was hurt by what she did, but I got over it. My husband and I ended up divorcing any-way. I would never take her baby. Plus, I never had the desire to have any children."

She seemed to be honest. Carson got no guilty vibes from her. "I had to ask."

The shock wore off and sorrow took its place. After a moment she looked at Georgia. "Will you tell her that I'd like to hear from her? It's been so long since my first husband and I were divorced and all of that happened. It's all in the past now. And if Ruby has changed, I'd like to get to know her again."

Georgia smiled. "Of course I will."

She turned to Carson. "I'm sorry I couldn't be of more help. The police came to see me all those years ago. Ruby must have told them about our estrangement. They did a thorough job investigating Jackson's disap-pearance."

"Not thorough enough," Carson said.

If they had, then Jackson would have been found.

Long after leaving Loretta's house, Georgia was dis-tracted by the revelation that her stepmother had been so different as a young woman. It was more than grow-ing up, learning from mistakes. Her mistakes had been huge. Sleeping with her best friend's husband? Who would do that? Penelope had also hinted to a darker character. Ruby seemed to love the rich life, and hav-ing friends in the same class as the one she'd married into. Had she felt she'd hit the jackpot? Was that the kind of woman her stepmother had been when she'd met Reginald?

The Ruby she knew was charitable and loving. Maybe losing Jackson had humbled her. But before that, she seemed to have been the opposite. And she'd never told her about Loretta.

Georgia didn't like how that made her feel.

"Are you all right?" Carson asked from the back-seat of the limo.

"Yes," she answered halfheartedly.

"What's wrong?"

"Ruby…the way she was when she was young. Loretta. I…" She couldn't wrap her mind around it.

"So she was a wild woman. Lots of people outgrow that."

"Yeah, I know, but…it's almost like she fell for Reginald because he came from an affluent, wealthy family."

"Did she ever tell you that?"

"No."

"Why does it upset you so much?" Then he seemed to catch himself. "Never mind. Driver, take us to the Ocean District."

"Yes, sir."

What was the Ocean District? Before she could ask, he said, "I have just the thing to cheer you up."

Carson got out of the limo in front of a boutique where the lowest price tag was around two thousand dollars. He might be pushing it too soon, but the whole shock over Ruby loving Reginald's money warranted this foray. Getting out of the limo, he stopped the driver from opening the door for him or Georgia. He walked around to the other side. She hadn't moved to get out. Opening the door, he leaned down and looked at her profile, waiting for her to turn her head.

"Carson…" She'd protested all the way here.

"Just get out of the limo, Georgia. You need a dress for tonight."

"I have a dress."

"Not the kind that's in here." He thumbed behind him toward the boutique. This was the kind of place that took appointments. He hadn't had time to do that, but it would be just as good this way. "You'll be the most beautiful woman at the party."

"I don't need to be the most beautiful woman at the party."

"Just look around. If you don't see anything you can't resist in there, we'll go back to the inn." All they had to do was get their things. Kate had invited them to stay at her estate tonight.

After a few blinks of her amazing green eyes, she slid her slender legs out of the limo and even gave him her hand. People passing along the sidewalk noticed them. A limo had a way of doing that. He couldn't be sure she felt lucky to be the one they noticed.

"Haven't you ever rented a limo with your friends?" he asked.

"We all pitched in to get one for my best friend's bachelorette party."

"Did you like it?" He opened the boutique door for her, a light-colored stone building that had been converted to a shop from an old house.

"It was a great night." She stepped into the shop and then looked back at him. "But not because of the limo."

He let her get away with that as he watched her grow aware of the boutique. The owner had decorated the shop cottage style, with benches and wicker furniture and pottery here and there. Clothing racks were arranged around the furniture and two dressing rooms hidden by silky drapes swooped up like window coverings. Accessories were displayed strategically by clothes that matched in color. He couldn't have planned it better if he'd have known the shop would be this way.

Georgia wandered the shop, making a big show of disinterest. But when she came upon a rack of dresses with some eye-catching accessories displayed on the shelf above, she reached out and slid the hanger for a better look.

Hook.

She slid more hangers and removed a dress that was her size. It was a stunning beaded black cocktail dress. A mini. Spaghetti straps. The clear beads swooped beneath the neckline and above the skimpy hem.

Her head lifted, and she took in the accessories.

Line.

She fingered a necklace and then another. Snatching some earrings and a bracelet, she took those and headed for some clutch purses in a display case.

Sinker.

"Which one can I get out for you, miss?" the woman behind the counter asked.

Georgia pointed. "That sparkly black one."

"Ah. The Leiber."

"Leiber… as in Judith Leiber?" Georgia asked.

"The one and only," the clerk responded as she took out the purse and handed it to her.

She lifted the dainty price tag and then dropped it as though it burned. Then she stepped back, coming out of the trance she had been under.

"I—I'm sorry." She put the dress she carried and the accessories onto the counter. "I won't be needing these."

Carson let her walk toward the door, catching her vacant look as she passed.

Going to the counter, he took out a credit card. "Can I have these delivered this afternoon?"

The woman smiled. "Of course, Mr...." She looked at his card. "Adair."

"Is your girlfriend a little shy about you spending money on her?"

"*Shy* isn't the word I'd use." He was probably in for a fight when he got to the car.

"Well, I'm sure she'll warm up to the idea soon."

He wrote down the address to Kate's estate for her.

"Are you taking her to a special event tonight?"

"Yes, a fund-raiser at this address."

She looked down at the piece of paper. "At Kate Winston's house?" She looked up at him. "*The* Kate Winston?"

"Yes."

"Well, your girlfriend is a lucky girl, isn't she?"

"I hope that's how she feels when she sees these." He gestured to the items on the counter.

The clerk handed his card back. "She's crazy if she doesn't."

"Stubborn," he corrected her.

The clerk laughed politely. "Would you like to include a card?"

"Yes."

She gave him one and he wrote something quick on it and sealed it inside the envelope. Handing it to her, he said, "Thanks."

"Any time."

He felt her awestruck gaze follow him out the door. Climbing into the limo, he saw Georgia sitting all the way on the other side, close to the window, arms folded, eyeing him with displeasure.

"I have to ask you to stop doing this," she said.

"Doing what?" He was toying with her, he had to admit.

Her eyes narrowed into slits. "Throwing money in my face."

She was pretty upset. "I'm not throwing it. I'm showering it."

She blinked a few times, and he wondered if she was having trouble stopping a laugh.

"And not in your face," he said. "I just want you to enjoy the things I give you and the places I take you."

"We aren't even dating."

"Then let's go on a date. Tonight. Be my date for the fund-raiser." He couldn't believe he'd said it. She was so anti-Adair that she'd be a risk to pursue. But then, isn't that what appealed to him? She was a tough catch. A challenge. He was on a new mission.

She stared at him, stunned. "What?"

"A date." Maybe she needed some warming like that clerk had said. "I promise to be a gentleman."

"I think we do better as friends," she said, crossing her leg over her knee and bobbing, still with her arms crossed.

Why did the idea of a date with him make her so fidgety? Was it all about her anti-Adair philosophy? Maybe her defenses were crumbling and that's what made her uncomfortable. And if that was the case, then she liked him.

"We're going to the party together. We may as well call it a date."

"You can call it what you want."

That was fine by him. Date it was. He was looking forward to this.

"You don't seem like the kind of guy who'd go on dates," she said.

"What do you mean?"

She shrugged and her arms loosened, hands in her lap now. "You seem like you'd head straight for the bedroom."

That almost made him laugh. "I get their names first."

She slid a suspicious look his way. "Have you ever been in love?"

He'd had affairs and brief relationships, but nothing that lasted. "No."

"What kind of woman attracts you?"

Why was she asking him that? For someone who claimed to have no interest in Adair men, she seemed awfully interested. "I suppose someone who shares a lot in common with me. Isn't that what everyone looks for?"

"Sure. But would you look for someone in the same class as you or would it matter?"

Ah. Now he could see why she'd asked. "At the risk of sounding pompous and proving your opinion of my filthy-rich family correct, yes, it might matter."

"No wonder Ruby didn't fit in."

"Are you picking a fight or just trying to convince yourself that tonight won't be a date?"

"I'm just curious."

Curious if she was out of the running? Curious if he was pompous? "If a woman has money, I know she isn't after *me* for money."

"She still might be. She might be greedy."

"Have you met anyone like that?"

"I dated someone who had money."

"And did he turn out to be pompous?"

"I don't know if that's the right word. He liked his money. He liked showing it off to me. But he was nice, I guess. I couldn't really tell much about his personality because the money got in the way. It defined him."

"You broke it off?"

"Yes. But it wasn't ugly. We parted friends."

"A diplomat, are you?"

"No. A relationship needs to work on a fundamental level. Money can't play into it."

"Well, Georgia, it appears we agree on something."

She smiled, a warm smile that lit up her dark green eyes.

"Now it's your turn," he said. "Have you ever been in love?"

That made her go rigid. She turned to look out the window. "No."

The way she'd reacted to the topic suggested otherwise. She had the look of a woman who'd been hurt.

"Why haven't you?"

Now she shrugged. "It's not important to me."

She sounded like him, but she had different reasons. What else would shy her away from him? A broken heart? Maybe that had more to do with her distance than his money.

Chapter 6

Georgia finished showering and left the bathroom that was attached to her room at Kate Winston's estate. The place was everything she'd expected. Lavish. Extraordinary. Well beyond her means or anything close to what she'd ever be able to afford in her lifetime. Wrapped in a towel with another one twirled atop her head, she went to the bed where she'd laid out her outfit for tonight. She had packed a few dresses but none were cocktail caliber. She went with a formfitting black knee-length that showed a modest amount of cleavage. Her breasts were a nice shape for a D-cup. She didn't like showing them off and this dress was the most revealing of all her clothes. She had to admit she'd packed it for this very reason—in the unlikely event that she attended an event or dinner with the wealthy Adairs, she'd be prepared.

She had to pinch back the regret for not letting

Carson buy her that stunning dress today. The boutique was like nothing she'd ever seen. The mall that she frequented at home didn't compare. She doubted she'd found online sites that rivaled the character of that place. She could have gone hog wild. She almost had. Until she'd seen the price tag on that Judith Leiber clutch. After her breath had hitched, she'd struggled for composure. Talk about being slapped back into reality. She couldn't allow Carson to spend that kind of money on her. That rebellious voice inside her argued the first-class flight cost more. And clothing was… well…so much more personal.

We may as well call it a date.

He was going to consider tonight a date. She tingled inside the way she had when he'd said it in the limo.

She lifted the cocktail dress that everyone with any kind of fashion sense would know wasn't anything special.

"Maybe I should come down with a stomach bug," she muttered to herself. Her head said, *And miss a great party with a hot man*?

A knock on the door interrupted her inner debate.

She glanced down at her towel-covered body. What if it was Carson?

"Miss Mason?" a woman asked. "I have a package for you."

A package? The woman must be a member of the house staff. Georgia went to the door and opened it a crack. The woman held a box.

"For you," the woman said with a smile.

Georgia was instantly wary. "Who sent this?"

"A deliveryman just dropped it off. He said this is from the Silver Button Boutique."

That's where the smile came from. Georgia made no fuss when inside her nerves scuttled with excitement, dismay and, ultimately, unbelievable delight.

She took the package and thanked the woman and retreated into the privacy of the room where no one would see the big smile spreading on her face.

Trotting to the bed, she swiped her old, cheap dress aside. It fell onto the floor and she put the box down. The towel around her body fell off as she tore at the packing tape, pulling the lid open.

There was a card on top of tissue-wrapped items underneath. She opened the tiny card.

I hope you have shoes. You ran away before I could get your size. I'll be waiting in the front entry. C

She bit her lower lip to keep from squealing like a fourteen-year-old. Then, one by one, she lifted the items she'd picked out at the boutique.

"I'm *so* glad he can't see me now."

She held up the new dress in front of her, tickled beyond capacity. She thought she'd burst with pleasure. She wasn't even going to look for a price tag on it.

Laying the dress on the bed as though it were an ancient museum piece, she took out the other items, each wrapped in pretty tissue paper. Last came the purse.

She held that up in front of her. It was probably more expensive than the dress. The intricate detail of it magnetized her. The stitching. The tiny beads. The front clasp.

"I'll give this back to him," she said. She wasn't going to need a purse tonight anyway.

She placed the purse back in the box, feeling a little mournful. Self-discipline was a bitch.

But, oh…

She looked down at the dress. She was going to look fantastic!

Trotting back to the bathroom, she spent extra time doing her hair and face. When she finished, she relished dressing and then admired the end result in the mirror.

The small, beaded black cocktail dress drew the eye and kept it. She went with no necklace because the scooped neckline of the dress was enough. She only wore simple black earrings and a matching bracelet. She was…sexy. But elegant. If Carson wanted a date, he was going to get one.

All ready, she hesitated at the door. Why was she doing this? Why had she agreed to go with him to a party at a mansion? She was dressed up. For him.

No. For the party. She was dressed up so she'd fit in at his aunt's mansion.

With a big sigh, she left the room and headed for the front entry. Her heart raced. She felt warm as she glided down the hallway, delighting in the way the smooth, soft movement of the expensive dress felt on her skin.

At the top of the stairs, she spotted him down below in a suit that fit his form impeccably. The way he took her in with his eyes sent tingles all through her, glimmering blue eyes infused with the heat of his reaction to the sight of her.

He didn't say anything, just watched her step down the stairs. He had to feel good about the fact that she'd caved and worn what he'd had delivered to her. Now she knew why he was so slow leaving the boutique. With anyone else, she'd feel cornered. She wasn't supposed to be ready for this—for feeling like this in response to a man. It was the first time in a long time that she'd felt anything close to romantic interest.

At the bottom of the stairs, he held out his hand and she laid hers on top of his. Behind him, double doors were open to a crowd and jazzy music that was balanced with the level of noise.

"You look stunning," he said.

She smothered the warming effect of his flattery. "Thanks for the dress."

"I'm glad you decided to keep it. And wear it." He surveyed her whole form. "Where's the purse?"

"Don't ruin our date, Carson." She sent him a mega-watt smile that shut him up the way she'd intended.

He chuckled, a deep, sexy sound that made her want to forget he was an Adair.

This was nothing like the way Ruby had been treated after Jackson's kidnapping. The Adairs had held her lower income against her. Carson treated Georgia with respect and held her as an equal to those around him. Or so it appeared. She hadn't known him very long. Men put on their best face when they first met a woman. The details didn't emerge until much later. She'd experienced that herself.

She decided not to dwell on all her doubts. Not tonight. Tonight she was going to enjoy herself, and being with Carson, even if he was hell-bent on proving to her that his family wasn't the haughty aristocrats his grandparents were.

Slipping her arm through the one he offered, she walked with him into the ballroom. Chandeliers hung from the high ceiling, ornately trimmed in white. Windows lined two walls, the sheer curtains swept aside to reveal a lighted terrace and garden outside. A table along the adjacent side was full of items for purchase. They'd be auctioned later. Waitresses and waiters walked around with trays of champagne. There were two corner bars, and another long table near one wall of windows full of food and a chocolate fountain.

People turned as they entered. Georgia was aware of the extra time some of them spent checking her out. A few men were a little more appreciative than a casual notice. And some of the women seemed envious. Maybe they knew the dress she had on was expensive. Maybe they thought Carson had found himself a rich girl. Georgia didn't like that idea. Just wait until they heard she was a librarian.

"Carson, is that you?"

Georgia turned with him to see an older woman approach. Petite and Georgia's height, her sapphire eyes sparkled amid fine wrinkles and soft eye makeup. Her short brown hair had a hint of gray and wasn't styled into anything special for this occasion. Her gown was something of a marvel, though, long and flowing ivory with sequins crossing the bodice.

Beside her was a man of around sixty looking dapper in a tuxedo with a red bow tie and a full head of graying dark brown hair. He was in great shape but had a ruddy complexion and wasn't quite as tall as Carson. What Georgia noticed most was the way he held the woman's hand and the loving way they looked at each other.

"Kate." Carson leaned in for a brief hug. Then he introduced Patrick, Kate's husband of one year.

"It's a pleasure to meet you," Georgia said, shaking Patrick's hand.

"Georgia is Ruby's stepdaughter from Florida," Carson explained.

"Ah." Kate moved to take Georgia's hand in a casual shake. "Yes, I've heard much about the kidnapping. I'm so sorry your stepmother had to go through that. I can sympathize."

Georgia had no doubt, after being duped into thinking her baby had died, only to discover years later that the child had lived and was killed in a car accident. This woman knew the tragedy of losing a child.

"I'll be sure and tell her about your charity. She'll be thrilled."

"I wish she could have made it. I didn't get a chance to get to know her when she was married to Reginald."

Was she sincere or just practiced at being a gracious host?

"Carson tells us you're an avid reader," Patrick said from slightly behind his wife.

Georgia looked at Carson. How much had he told his aunt about her? It seemed they'd had quite a conversation. But he gave nothing away.

She held up her hand. "Guilty as charged." Lowering her hand as Kate backed up to stand beside Patrick, both of them smiling, she said, "As soon as I learned to read, nobody could stop me. I'm afraid it made me a bit of an indoor girl." She'd been at the top of her class in English.

Kate laughed lightly. "You could have discovered worse habits. And that's what personal trainers are for."

Or gyms. Or a good old-fashioned bicycle.

"Reginald talked about how much Carson loved to read," Kate said, oblivious to how alien a personal trainer would be to a woman like Georgia. "You two seem to have a lot in common."

She wouldn't go so far as to say they had *a lot* in common. Many people liked to read. That didn't make her and Carson special.

"Uh-oh." Patrick elbowed Carson. "Look out."

Carson grinned and didn't seem bothered by the teasing.

"You both went after careers rather than hitch up with someone and settle down," Kate said. "You each had something life-changing bring you together. And you're both still single. Imagine that."

While it was true that Ruby's unexpected inheritance and Carson's discharge from the military were life-changing, Georgia didn't believe fate was at work here. "Carson and I just met, and I'm only helping him search for Jackson."

Feeling Carson looking at her, she caught him eyeing her strangely, as though he thought she had only said that to cover up the truth. What was the truth? That this was a real date? That they did have a lot in common? Maybe he thought that way. He was the one showing her how much she liked the things his money could buy. What he didn't understand was that she didn't like what money turned people into.

"It doesn't matter if you just met. I can see you make a fine couple," Kate said.

"Kate…" Carson was doing damage control, trying to protect Georgia. That was sweet and it eased her rising tension.

"Kate is extra protective of her nephews," Patrick said. "Ever since Reginald was killed…"

"Sorry," Kate said. "It's true. And I so want Carson to find Jackson. It's such a tragic story."

Much like hers. Georgia could hardly fault her.

"She's also good at recognizing couples who fit together," Patrick said.

"Maybe you aren't ready to hear that." Kate looked at Georgia. She thought Georgia wasn't ready to hear it. Well, maybe she wasn't. And maybe she never would be.

"How are you faring now that you're out of the Marines, Carson?" Kate asked. "Whit told me you weren't taking it so well."

"He isn't," Georgia said, and then realized she probably shouldn't have piped in. Carson looked at her with warning.

"I'm handling it just fine."

"So, you're going to take over your father's place at AdAir Corp?" Patrick asked.

"That I haven't decided."

Kate frowned. "What else would you do?"

Georgia followed their conversation, having thought the same thing about Carson.

"I haven't figured that out yet."

The bite to his tone made Kate look from him to Patrick and then to Georgia, who tried to keep an I-know-exactly-what-you're-thinking look off her face. She didn't think she'd succeeded. Kate smiled and turned to Carson. "Well, something tells me you'll get some help in that regard."

This woman was incredible. And scary. Did she really see that much into her and Carson? That there was something cooking between them? The notion both excited and terrified her.

"There aren't many men who are capable of being the kind of soldier Carson was," Kate said. "He was among the best of the Special Forces, you know."

"Yes, I've learned that about him."

"Smart," Patrick said.

"Mmm-hmm." She slid her gaze to Carson. He was taking this glowing praise stoically. His experience as an elite soldier did impress her, probably too much. Impress didn't cover the way she felt about him in that light. Heated her blood might get a little closer.

"Strong and brave, too," Kate said. "For all his daring secret missions."

Kate was a proud aunt for sure.

But then she said, "You could do worse in a man."

The shock of that observation rippled through Georgia. Kate had deliberately led up to this baiting. She thought there was something worthy brewing between them and she'd just pointed that out—quite expertly—to Georgia.

"You're right," Georgia said, not seeing any other option. Disagreeing would not only be insulting, it would be a lie. "I could do much worse." She already had. Which was precisely why she was never going to make another mistake again. Not when it came to men. The wrong man could turn her life into a disaster. She'd barely recovered from the last one.

"I'm going to a spa tomorrow, something I sometimes do after events like this," Kate said. "Why don't you join me?"

"Me?" Oh, dear God. A spa? With a former vice president? The spa was a formidable temptation, though. She could afford to splurge on that.

"Yes. Just you and me. I'd love to get to know the woman who lassoed Carson Adair's heart."

"Kate…" Carson warned.

Patrick chuckled and slipped his arm around Kate.

"All right, all right. Don't listen to me. You'll see what I mean in due time anyway." She patted Carson's shoulder. "You enjoy the party. I've got to go mingle and make sure these people hand over a good chunk of their money." She turned to Georgia. "You. Me. Tomorrow afternoon. Two o'clock."

Georgia almost said, *Yes, ma'am.* But Patrick whisked Kate away as she waved a temporary goodbye, leaving her alone with Carson.

"She's very forthright," she said almost to herself.

"She wants to get to know you better."

She turned to his sly look. "Because she recognizes we're a couple?"

"This *is* our first date," he said.

She had to stop from allowing herself to believe that was what this really was. How foolish would she be to entertain the possibility that she could fit in with a family like this? Carson and Kate may be normal, as he'd put it, but there were plenty others in the mix who could inflict agony. All because of money. And her lack of it.

"Carson."

Georgia followed the sound of the female voice and saw a woman in a silky black dress that V'd well below her breasts. Diamonds decorated her chest and wrists and dangled from her ears. Her blue eyes were as light as Carson's and her jet-black hair was coiffed into an elaborate bun, wisps left to hang and tickle her shoulders. She must have a headful of long, shiny hair.

"Noreen?" Carson seemed startled to see the woman.

Of course he would know her, a beautiful, wealthy woman. Was this the type of woman he'd look for? He'd said he would because he'd know she wouldn't be after his money.

"I called Kate to see if she'd heard from you and she invited me to her charity event," she said. "I thought I'd come and see for myself that the rumors are true. You've left the military?" Her eyes roved all over his body. Was she sending him silent messages?

"Yes. I was injured." He'd seemed happy to see her, but this wasn't a topic he liked.

"Oh, you poor thing. That must have been terribly devastating. But you're back. I can't say that I'm sorry about that." She smiled, big, white teeth flashing.

Georgia looked for an escape. Not knowing anyone here, she was stuck with this woman pretending she didn't exist. She obviously would love to snag Carson as her man.

"I've been thinking about you a lot lately," the woman said. "About just after high school, wondering how things might have been different had you not gone away. I understand why you did, of course, but when I heard you were back in San Diego, I couldn't help myself. I had to come."

Georgia began to bristle over the woman's audacity. Did she know who Georgia was and decided she didn't matter? Ruby's stepdaughter couldn't be important enough for Carson.

"Noreen, this is Georgia Mason, my date."

Noreen finally turned to Georgia. "Oh. Your date?" She looked confused.

"Hi." Georgia offered her hand in greeting.

Noreen took it, but there was little warmth in her

striking eyes. "You're Ruby's stepdaughter, aren't you? The one who's after Reginald's inheritance?"

Annoyance burned in Georgia. Who did this woman think she was? Someone *rich*, that was for sure. She withdrew her hand. "Ruby is my stepmother. You're right in that regard."

"Ruby wasn't after any inheritance. My father left a portion of his worth to her in his will. It's rightfully hers," Carson said.

"Oh. Well, if you say so. It's hard to tell what's the truth in the media." She laughed, a fake laugh that was more for show.

"I'm sorry, Carson." She laid it on thick some more. "Of course it's her rightful inheritance. She was once married to Reginald. So, tell me, how is Ruby doing? It was just terrible what happened. And so long ago."

"She's doing well."

"Good, good." She glanced at Georgia. "So, when did this happen?" Her hand moved to indicate him and Georgia.

Carson slid his arm around Georgia, pulling her to his side. "This is our first date."

Georgia was happy he'd labeled it that now—even if it wasn't really a date.

"Oh." She nodded as she scanned Georgia's body, noticing the dress in more detail. "I thought Ruby married a construction worker. Your father."

Georgia did not feel like talking to this person. "He ran a roofing company."

She put a diamond-bedecked hand over the gap of silk on her chest, and Georgia was certain it was on purpose so that she'd see the money dripping from her fingers. "He was a roofer?"

"Entrepreneur. He owned the company."

"Oh. So he did well for himself." Down went the hand.

Georgia stole a glimpse of Carson and saw his amusement. He was staying out of this, letting her find her own way against a piranha like Noreen. Didn't he see that this was what she strove to avoid? Poisonous rich people like Noreen?

"He's dead," Georgia said, keeping her calm, "and no, we weren't wealthy. But we weren't starving, either."

"Oh."

If she said *Oh* one more time…

"And…what is it that you do, dear?"

Georgia was going to relish telling her. "I'm a librarian."

"Oh." Noreen looked at Carson as though she couldn't believe he'd picked such a low-hanging fruit.

"Georgia loves books as much as I do," he said to Noreen.

"Well, yes, and no wonder she became a librarian." She turned to Georgia. "Where is your stepmother? I would think she'd have to go to San Diego to claim her inheritance. Is that how you met Carson? Did you go with your stepmother to San Diego?"

"I took a leave of absence to help her. She stayed in San Diego while we came here to follow up on some leads Reginald uncovered before he was killed."

"Ah." Noreen glanced around the ballroom, looking uncomfortable.

At least she'd used another word.

"Well," Carson said. "It was nice running into you, Noreen. Georgia, would you like something to drink?"

She could have hugged him. "I'd love one." Anything to get away from this woman.

"If you'll excuse us." He gave Noreen a bow of his head.

"Of course." Flustered, Noreen stepped aside, and Carson kept his hand on the small of her back as they walked to one of the waiters holding a tray of glasses filled with champagne.

"Why did you take a leave of absence?" Carson asked her as he handed her a glass.

She hadn't expected him to ask that. And she realized she didn't have to tell Noreen. It had just slipped out. "For Ruby."

Sensing him assess her and accurately deduce that she didn't need to take a leave of absence to help Ruby with her inheritance. Some time off would have been enough. So why had she?

Before he could ask her, a man in his fifties approached.

"Robert." Carson shook the man's hand. "It's been a while."

"Ten years or more. I hear you're back for good now. Going to run your dad's company?"

"Robert, this is Georgia Mason."

"Hello," she said.

"Well, hello there." He gave her a once-over as though she were caged in a stock show.

Another one? Georgia looked around at all the poised and prim aristocrats and couldn't pick one from the other. Nice? Or snooty? She began to feel out of place.

Carson and Robert went into a long talk about EBIDA and stock shares. The topic of earnings before interest, tax, depreciation and amortization bored her to tears. She listened to Robert brag about his rising revenue and the new house he and his wife were building in Scotland. The yacht trip they'd just taken. He barely gave Carson time to talk. He was much more interested in discussing his possessions.

Georgia thought of home. How she longed to be there now, away from all this pretentiousness. If she and Carson took this date seriously and gave a relationship a try, how could she expect not to have to endure more evenings like this? She wanted nothing to do with any of it. If she never ran into another Noreen or Robert ever again in her life, she'd consider herself blessed.

"It's always interesting to listen to you, Robert," Georgia heard Carson say, "but I've got some people I'd like Georgia to meet."

Robert looked a little miffed as Carson steered her away. Had Carson noticed her withdrawal? He couldn't protect her from the people who surrounded him, the ones who were bound to be in his world. People who would never pop into her life. Her simple, humble life that she was beginning to miss.

Carson took her over to a good-looking couple. The man was as tall as Carson and had light brown hair like Carson, only it was longer—not difficult when compared to a military cut. His hazel eyes were strong and sure and full of love for the woman who stood beside him. Georgia saw the diamond ring on the woman's ring finger. It was beautiful but understated. She was fairly tall, five-nine or so, and had auburn hair that was up in a bun, and her smiling light green eyes were full of life. This was what happiness looked like.

"Georgia Mason, this is Thad Winston and Lucy

Sinclair. Thad is one of Kate's sons and a damn good crime scene investigator. Lucy is his wife. Are you still nursing over at Duke?"

"Nice to meet you, Georgia." Lucy took her hand. "I am still working there, but—" she turned to share an intimate look with her husband "—we're having a baby, so I'm thinking about taking a break for a while."

"She's going to be a kept woman," Thad said, earning a teasing glare from Lucy. After a chuckle, he said to them, "Lucy has to feel like she's making her own way, even though we can afford her not working."

They both had normal jobs. Yet they must have money, being Kate Winston's family. She glanced over at Carson, sure that he'd introduced them to her for a calculated reason.

"Congratulations on the new baby," Georgia said.

"Sophie is so excited," Lucy said. "She wants a baby sister."

"Kate told me you adopted her," Carson said. "She's a lucky girl."

"We did," Thad said proudly. "She's our daughter. And we're the lucky ones."

"Precious daughter," Lucy said. "Best thing that ever happened to us." She looked at Georgia. "But hey, enough about our boring life, how great that you're back, Carson. I mean, I was sorry to hear from Kate about Reginald, and that you had to quit the Marines, but it looks like it might turn out okay for you." She said the last with a glance at Georgia. "You brought her with you to search for Jackson?"

"I'm here for my stepmother, Ruby."

"Oh." It was a much different *oh* than what had come from Noreen. Lucy must have gotten another impression about Georgia, one that had her here for Carson, not Ruby. "I didn't know about her until Kate told us what happened." She looked at Carson. "Are you doing all right? With your dad and all…"

"As good as I can. Finding Jackson will help."

That, and forgiving his dad in the process. Georgia was pretty sure Carson wouldn't be able to let go of his military career until he accepted what had made Reginald the way he was. When he did that, he'd be able to run AdAir Corp without feeling as if he'd become his father—the father who had turned away from his kids and whose reputation bordered on tyrant.

They talked for a while longer and Georgia thought she'd found a true friend in Lucy. By the time they moved on to some other guests, she struggled to keep her guard up.

"Come here." Carson took her hand and led her to the dance floor, which was a space in the middle of the ballroom where people had gathered.

The DJ played a slow song, Georgia only then realized. "Carson." She began to resist.

He drew her against him. "This is a date, remember?"

She sucked in her breath as her body pressed to his and her hands went to his chest. She tipped her head back a bit to look up at his face, so close to hers. His blue eyes sparkled with mischief and more. The mischief helped assure her this wasn't a real date.

She followed his lead, acutely aware of his hand on her lower back and the way his other took one of hers. She slipped her hand up his chest to rest her hand on his shoulder.

As they swayed to the beat, she felt his every movement, his rock-hard muscles. Special Ops soldier muscles. Why did he make her so hot?

"What did you think of Thad and Lucy?" Carson asked.

"You know what I thought. They're wonderful."

"See?"

"You're wonderful. Kate is wonderful." She left it for him to assume by omission that there were others who were not wonderful.

He grinned. "You think I'm wonderful?"

She'd stepped right into that trap. "You know what I mean."

"No. I'm not sure I do."

"You're a nice man. If I'd have met you on the street I wouldn't have guessed you were Reginald Adair's son."

"Oh. For a minute I thought you liked me."

She smiled. Another man might have gotten defensive. "I do like you. It's impossible not to." The tone of her voice was seductive, a pure reaction to his flirtation, and the truth in the last that she said.

His gaze fell to her lips and when it traveled back to her eyes, no humor remained. There was a distinctive shift in energy between them. An unexpected blaze. Attraction that had been there from the start blossomed out of control. They stopped dancing.

Music faded away. People surrounding them, talking, laughing, joined the white noise. Nothing stood between them, no family members, no past hurts or cautions.

When Carson's head came down, Georgia tilted hers up enough to accommodate his kiss. Soft. Warm. He only pressed his lips to hers at first. But that quickly intensified into a brushfire of sensation. He kissed her harder and she welcomed him. Then he withdrew. She felt empty and full of regret that something so powerful and lovely should end so soon.

Blinking herself back to clarity, she grew aware of where they were. No. This couldn't happen. Not here. Not ever. Not with him. Stepping back, she saw that he was just as thunderstruck by the strength of the kiss.

She caught sight of Robert talking away with another man, who nodded mechanically. A pair of women watched the dance floor, and Georgia realized they were watching her, head tipped up and eyes judging. Did they know Carson? Did they know who she was? In an instant, she didn't care. She was on a collision course with a life that Ruby had tried and failed to hang on to. And the intimacy dredged up memories she'd rather not ever think of again, memories with a man she thought she'd spend the rest of her life with but who'd turned out not to love her after all. She'd been a possession to him.

Upset, Georgia walked off the dance floor and picked up into a jog to get away as fast as she could. She left the estate through the front doors. There were several limousines parked in the driveway along with a couple of taxis.

She ran toward one of them and then realized she had no purse.

"Georgia!"

It was Carson coming after her.

She ran to the first limo. It wasn't Carson's. What was she doing? She couldn't commandeer someone else's limo.

"Georgia," Carson said, a lot less urgent. He was right behind her.

She turned around, leaning against the back door of the limo, and reluctantly looked at him. Her whole body still shook from their kiss. The internal chaos that stirred was too wild for her to corral.

She looked toward the estate. The need to flee was so strong she felt irrational. She had to get away from here. Now.

Chapter 7

Carson saw the wildness in Georgia's eyes and in the way her hands flattened against the sleek, black limousine and didn't step any closer. She was about to run. She was a vision in the dress, a stunning creature. Leaning against the limo, she was so beautiful it stole his breath. Some of her dark red hair had come free of her hairdo and now fell untamed along her face and décolletage.

There had to be more going on to cause her to react like this. More than her issue with rich people.

"Kate's limo is right there." He pointed to the limo ahead of this one. "Why don't we go somewhere and talk."

She started to shake her head.

Taking a chance, he stepped forward and reached for her hand. "Come on. It's okay."

She eyed him and then looked toward the estate again.

"I'll get you away from here." He took her hand and gently coaxed her to go with him.

She didn't fight him, some of the wildness leaving her eyes. That kiss had sure spooked her. He wanted to know why.

At the limo, the driver had already spotted them and had the door open. He mouthed *thank you* to the man, who gave no indication that he'd seen or appreciated it other than a discreet nod.

With Georgia in the backseat, he sat next to her, seeing how her chest rose and fell with each agitated breath.

"Cooper Point Park," Carson told the driver. It wasn't far from here.

He watched over the next few minutes as Georgia's breathing calmed. By the time they reached the park, she'd regained control.

"I'm all right, Carson. We can go back."

"We're here. Might as well show you the homestead."

"Homestead?"

He got out of the limo and waited for her. The limo parked in front of the historic nineteenth-century house. It was closed at this hour, but still a spectacular sight.

There was a walking trail with a bridge over a stream where a pond drained. There were picnic tables along the way.

He walked next to Georgia, careful to give her some space.

"I don't fit in with those people," Georgia said.

"That isn't why you ran." It was too extreme of a reaction.

She stopped, and he did, too, facing her. "What?"

He took in her genuine confusion. "I kissed you."

Georgia resumed her trek along the path, and Carson easily stayed next to her.

"What is it?" he asked. "And don't tell me you don't fit in."

"I don't fit in."

"There will always be people you don't like. It doesn't take being associated with my family to run across people like that. And anyway, that's beside the point. You ran for another reason. You were fine until I kissed you."

She looked over at the old homestead, lights illuminating it in the dark. "I don't want to be a part of the way you and your family live."

"You base too much of your beliefs on what Ruby experienced," he said. "You've spent so much time protecting her that you can't stop. You've taken it too far. Let go."

She kept walking and didn't say anything, but he didn't think she agreed.

"You love her like she's your real mother, but you need to start living your own life, Georgia."

"I do live my own life."

She was happy being a librarian, but she could do that anywhere and she didn't need her limiting ideals that stemmed from being raised by a spurned Ruby.

"Why haven't you settled down with anyone?" He'd asked her this before, but he hadn't gotten down to the crux of what made her the way she was, what held her back.

"I haven't met anyone."

As she said that, she averted her gaze. And the sound

of her voice, so tentative, held no conviction. She *had* met someone. She'd talked about seeing someone but they'd parted friends. This had to be someone different.

Putting his hand on her arm, he stopped her, then used both hands to turn her to face him. "What happened? Who is he?" He hadn't asked her one question that she'd asked him. "Someone you loved?"

"No. Well…I mean, I did love him, but it didn't work out."

"He broke it off?"

She stared at him awhile, and he suspected there was a lot going on in her head right now. Whoever the man was, the breakup had been messy, not friendly like the rich man she'd told him about.

"It was mutual. I hoped it wouldn't end, but I can see now that it was inevitable."

He wouldn't press her for much detail. He could see it was painful for her to talk about it. "How long ago?"

"A few months."

Not much time had passed. Not enough to move on with someone else. Not that he was contemplating that with her. He thought of the kiss. Was he?

"I'm sorry I ran off," Georgia said. "The dress. The party…" She looked toward the homestead again and then back at him.

And then the kiss. She didn't have to tell him that had been the thing that pushed her over the edge.

"He was a friend from college and we started dating," she said. "That was a mistake. When things came to an end, I lost a man I loved and an old friend."

Things hadn't gone as she'd expected. Georgia needed everything in her life to go as expected. Taking care of Ruby may have done that to her. Georgia had the weight of the world on her shoulders. If she unloaded some of it, would she be so devoted to Ruby? It wouldn't mean she loved her any less if she put herself first a few times.

Funny, how he wanted to be the one to show her that was okay, to make her aware of what she was doing.

"Let's go back to Kate's," he said, and when her face fell with dread, he added, "Not to the party. Tomorrow you can go to the spa and then the next day we'll go back to San Diego. We're not going to find Jackson here any easier than we will there."

He watched her come close to backing out of her day with Kate, but then the strong Georgia returned and she simply nodded. She felt obligated. But Carson knew Kate would make her feel at ease, which was exactly what he wanted after the party.

"You might love the spa, you know," he said as they walked back to the limo. He'd have no mercy on her.

When she sent him a tiny smile that softened her, he was sure that all she had to do was admit wealth had nothing to do with her reluctance to be intimate with him. He began to have reservations as to his motives for trying so hard to win her over. Was it the challenge? Was it only that he meant to show her how wrong she was? Or was it hot, intense attraction?

The next day, Georgia went with Kate to the spa. It was all she could do not to get on a plane, go get Ruby and go home. She couldn't understand why she hadn't told Kate she wasn't going to the spa with her. But as she walked toward the Halcyon Spa, she was happy she'd changed her mind. She could use a little pampering. She had never treated herself to something like this before.

Inside the stone building, light brown blocks of tile spread over a relaxation lounge filled with ivory cushioned chairs and recessed lighting. A woman appeared through a doorway.

"Kate O'Hara," she greeted, leaning in for a two-cheek kiss.

"Nellie, this is Georgia Mason."

"Welcome to Halcyon Spa. I'm normally not so informal with my guests, but Kate and I go way back."

"We went to school together," Kate said. "Georgia is a librarian in Florida."

"Oh, that's wonderful. You're a reader, are you?"

Not expecting such a warm greeting, Georgia stammered. "Uh…well, yes. The library where I work is nearly a hundred years old. It's beautiful."

"Books and old architecture. Does it get any better than that?" Nellie said.

"Yes," Kate said. "With a hot-stone spa treatment."

Georgia laughed with Nellie.

"Well, let's get you started then." Nellie led them to another room with beige chairs, a hot tub and two massage tables.

There were dressing rooms for privacy. Georgia went into one silk-curtained stall and Kate into the other. She undressed to her underwear and then slipped into the robe that hung from a wooden hanger.

She stepped out at the same time as Kate, feeling a little awkward.

"Your first massage?" Kate asked.

"Yes."

"You'll relax in no time." Kate went to one of the tables and unabashedly removed her robe, picked up the blanket that was neatly folded on the cushioned table and wrapped it around her. Then she got onto the table stomach-down.

Georgia did the same at her table, wrapping the blanket around her, doing her best to preserve her modesty.

"They'll start with your back and you'll be purring," Kate said.

"I could use some tension release." Georgia thought of Carson and wondered if he could provide another kind of tension release. She also wondered what it would be like to get a massage like this with him instead of Kate.

She grew warm just thinking about it.

The masseuses entered the room and began to work their magic.

Kate was right. As soon as the woman's kneading hands sank into her back, she felt as though she could fall asleep.

"I saw you run from the party last night." Kate's voice sounded drugged with relaxation. "I don't mean to pry, but I talked to Carson and he told me about Ruby, how upset she was after she and Reginald split up."

And all about how she'd walked away from his money and the emotional anguish she'd suffered.

"I can see why you'd be so protective of Ruby, but do you feel like she needs to be protected from Carson?" Kate asked.

"No." Georgia kept her eyes closed, lulled by the massage.

"I saw Carson talking to Robert at the party," Kate said. "I bet that was taxing. He loves to talk about himself."

Georgia smiled into the face rest of the massage table. "Yes, he does."

"He's about to go bankrupt, you know."

Georgia opened her eyes, wishing she could see Kate. "Really?"

"He lies about his money. He's about thirty days from losing everything. His wife has a gambling problem and cheats on him. They're going to get a divorce."

"I would have never guessed."

"And Noreen?" Kate said.

"Ah, Noreen." Georgia smiled again.

"She's been after Carson since they went out in high school. Did you think she comes from money?"

Georgia's smile fled with that question. "Yes. Doesn't she?"

"Oh, no. Her father was a firefighter and her mother waited tables at a truck stop."

Georgia fell speechless while the oddness of that sank in.

"It's true," Kate said. "Noreen has been trying to snag herself a rich man her entire life. She called me as soon as she heard about my fund-raiser, asking if Carson would be there. She knew he'd been discharged and was waiting for an opportunity. Carson is too kind to her. But I suppose he feels sorry for her. She's desperate."

"How does she get invited to parties like the one you threw? Don't you have to have a lot of money to donate in order to attend?"

"Yes, but we've always given Noreen special consideration. She's more of a friend of the family."

One who'd forced her way into that friendship, plowed into it. And Kate's family was too kind to turn her away.

"She didn't know about you or I doubt she'd have come to the party," Kate went on.

"Why not?"

"You have Carson."

"I don't *have* Carson. Last night was a date, that's all." And not a real one. She still refused to think of it that way.

"It was more than that. I'm no fool, Georgia Mason." She laughed softly. "I know love when I see it."

Georgia scoffed. "Carson and I aren't in love."

"Not yet. But you will be."

How could this woman have so much insight? She tried to predict the future and she had no way of being sure what that future held. She was only voicing her hope. She loved her nephew. Why wouldn't she want him to be in love, especially Carson—who'd shut himself off from the world he knew and gone off to the Marines?

After falling speechless again, Georgia relaxed and shut her eyes. The masseuse worked on her shoulders now and it felt heavenly.

"People aren't who they seem sometimes," Kate said, drowsy with relaxation.

And sometimes they were. Reginald. Or had he been as he seemed? Carson struggled with that same concept. Kate challenged Georgia's bias. Carson did, too. They were ganging up on her.

"That's not the only reason you ran off, though, is it?" Kate asked. And when Georgia didn't answer, she said, "It's because you have feelings for Carson, isn't it?"

"I do like him," she admitted.

"But…?"

"Yes, but." She wasn't going to talk about that.

Kate didn't probe further. She'd done what she'd intended, and that was to get Georgia thinking about the source of her bias. It came from Ruby and her overprotection of her. Her defenses went on high alert around the people who'd hurt her so deeply.

After the massage, Georgia glided into the nail salon, where state-of-the-art chairs lined one side and a water fountain kept her mood serene.

They were seated, both in a bubble of leisure.

A woman entered the room with a tray holding two glasses. "Your complimentary glass of champagne."

Kate took the first one, and Georgia took the second. They'd drink champagne while getting their nails done. Georgia could get used to this. It was almost as satisfying as shopping.

She could also live without it.

More than two hours later and after being treated to a European facial, Georgia walked out of the salon a new woman. When she returned to Florida, she was going to get her nails done on a regular basis.

The limo pulled in front of the salon just as Georgia noticed a man sitting in a car that was backed into a space that faced the salon. She couldn't see his face clearly but knew he was looking at them.

An uneasy feeling came over her. Had the man who'd shot at Carson followed them to North Carolina? How would he have known they'd come here? Maybe it was just a husband waiting for his wife. The car didn't look expensive. Just a sedan of some kind.

"Something wrong?" Kate asked.

After a slight delay, Georgia shook her head. "No." She got into the limo.

As the driver drove out of the parking lot, Georgia looked back and saw that the car was following them.

Carson paced the huge living room at Kate's house later that day. His aunt had just told him that someone had followed them until Kate had told the driver, who'd sped up. As soon as he'd done that, the man in the car behind them had turned off onto a side road. There had been no plate on the front of the car. He was seized with fear that whoever it had been knew where Kate lived and that he and Georgia were here.

"He didn't see us come here," Kate said. "My driver is trained for this."

He stopped pacing. "We should leave. Tonight."

"Carson, don't overreact," Kate said.

Georgia didn't think he was. "No. We should leave. It might be dangerous if whoever followed us knows where you live."

"I'll alert Security," Kate said. "It's tighter than ever since I was shot. You don't have to worry. No one is getting in here."

Carson relaxed because she was right.

"Can we get tickets this soon?" Georgia asked.

She wasn't thinking. "I can have a jet ready in two hours," Carson said. "I arranged for one to take us back to San Diego." By the time they packed and made it to the airport they'd be right on time.

He saw Georgia staring at him. He'd planned to take her back in a jet. More pampering. He could tell she was reaching her boiling point. Good. That's what she needed.

Just then, Patrick came rushing into the room. "Kate!" He went to her.

She stood, and he took her into his arms.

"Are you all right?" he asked, leaning back to inspect her.

"Yes, Patrick. I told you over the phone."

"You told me someone followed you. With Reginald's murder…" He breathed an anxious breath. "You're going to send me to an early grave, woman."

She laughed softly and kissed him. "I love you."

He smiled and relaxed. "My Kate."

Turning back to them, Kate said, "I hate to see you leave so soon. We would love to spend more time with you. We don't get to very often."

"There will be plenty of other times now that I'm back in the States."

Kate turned to Georgia. "Good. We'll all look forward to seeing you both in the near future."

He and Georgia went up to get their things and then met out on the side of the estate, where the same limo was waiting. After saying goodbye to Kate and Patrick, he and Georgia sat in the back of the limo and left.

Carson searched the road after they passed through the guarded gate and saw no sign of a suspicious car. It wasn't until they reached the road that led to the highway that he spotted something. The opposite direction led to the salon where Georgia and Kate had gone. A car was parked on the side of the road, waiting. Sure enough, as soon as the driver saw them, he drove into the traffic.

Carson knocked on the window dividing the front from the back, and the driver pressed a button that slid it open.

"I saw it, Mr. Adair," the driver said.

"Let him follow us. I want to know who he is."

"Yes, sir." The driver left the window open.

When they reached the airport and drove to the tarmac and parked, Carson watched the other car turn around and begin to drive away. He dashed from the limo and ran as fast as he could with his limp, trying to catch a glimpse of a license plate. But the car sped up and disappeared around a corner.

Walking back to Georgia, he saw the limo driver unloading their bags from the trunk and led her to the waiting plane.

"Did you see who it was?"

"No."

"He didn't seem to care that you saw him."

No, he hadn't. That was bold. Well, he hadn't cared whether he'd been seen in the parking garage, either.

"At least Kate is safe."

"Yes." Georgia smiled.

She liked Kate. Who didn't like her? No one who knew her.

Georgia took a moment to absorb the posh accommodations of the private jet. There was even a bedroom in the back. The middle looked like a living room with a bar and there were rows of leather airplane seats toward the front. She chose a two-seater leather chair across from a sofa and buckled in. An attendant asked her if she'd like something to drink, and she declined. Her mood was somber. Was it seeing the man following them or something else? Like being on this plane with him.

He left her alone, picking up a tablet and searching through what books had been loaded. Not concentrating fully, he was more aware of how Georgia kept glancing over at him as she pretended to look through her ever-trusty catalog. She was itching to take him on.

Once the jet took off and ascended to a flight elevation, Carson released the buckle at his waist and resumed his halfhearted search for a book.

"Carson?"

He looked up from the tablet. Her tone was soft and tentative, as though she was really trying to keep calm.

"I need you to stop this game you're playing with me," she said.

She thought it was a game? Was it? It had started out that way, but now he wasn't so sure. Now he thought he really wanted her to confess that her opinion of the Adairs was off.

"You didn't like the spa?"

She wasn't humored.

"It's not a game to me," he said.

"Stop spending money on me."

"Kate paid for the spa."

She angled her head in reprimand. "This has nothing to do with how much Ruby suffered. It's…"

The date.

"I'm not your girlfriend," she said.

Not yet. The thought came unbidden. And it wasn't disagreeable. "What's wrong with us being that way together? Let's date and see what happens." It had a dangerous feel to it, something he missed from the military. Dating Georgia could be his adrenaline rush. But if she walked away in the end, what then? How would he feel? It was a risk, but one he was willing to take. His heart pumped with renewed excitement.

He could tell that suggestion had stunned her. Why was she so surprised?

"Are you afraid?" he asked. "Is it your last relation-ship?"

With that, she looked away.

He went to her, sitting on the chair beside her. "Who was he?"

After a few long moments when he watched fleeting regret cross her eyes, she said, "An old friend. Drake Foerster. We met in college in an English-composition class. His degree was engineering."

"And yours was English?" He smiled.

She smiled back but with only a hint. "He had a girlfriend at the time, and I wasn't interested in get-ting involved. I dated every once in a while but only to have fun. Drake and I would study together in the library. We went for coffee, lunch, sometimes mov-ies. We talked a lot. What I didn't know until much later was that going to college was freeing for him. He grew up in a poor house, the typical tragedy. Dad left when he was born, mom was a drunk and a drug ad-dict. Brother is in prison.

"Drake was on his way to a good life. It was after college that he told me that. By then we were very close. He said he broke up with the girl he was seeing in col-lege. He was going to marry her but changed his mind. I guess she was too much like his mother. She was drinking too much, he said. And told him she didn't want kids. It was important to Drake that he have kids and give them the childhood he never had." She stopped talking and bent her knees up to wrap her arms around her legs on the oversize leather chair.

"He sounds ambitious."

She nodded, but there was a general sadness about her, as though she mourned the loss of him.

"He had a rough childhood and changed his life by going to college," Carson said. "Why did he wait so long to tell you about his past?"

"He told me some things, just left out enough to make it seem normal. I knew Drake in a way no one from his childhood did. I knew the man he tried so hard to be. And I fell in love with that man. Especially after I learned he was available. We made it clear to each other when we did start dating that cheating was wrong, and we respected each other too much to cause hurt."

She gazed through the oval window across the plane, three times the size of those in a typical commercial plane. "I thought he was going to be my guy." She turned a wry smile to him. "Maybe I should have considered how his childhood affected him."

"How did it?" He stretched his arm across the back of the chair, Georgia's head in front of his elbow.

"He was ashamed of where he came from. He was insecure. He didn't like me going out with my friends and questioned me when I came home late from work. That was new from when we were friends. He called me constantly and if I didn't answer he got upset." She stopped talking, looking away again.

"What did he do when you went out with friends?"

"Nothing. He just said he wished I'd stay with him. But I could sense that it bothered him. We talked it over and he got better about it. He just had to learn to trust me."

"So he did trust you."

"Yes."

"Did you trust him?"

"Oh, yes." She nodded, lowering her legs.

"What happened between you? It seems like you loved him and he loved you."

Biting her lip, she lowered her head and rocked a couple of times on the chair. This was a delicate topic for her. A troubling one.

"I loved him more as a friend than a lover. I couldn't pretend otherwise. That hurt him. We haven't spoken since."

"How long ago was that?"

"Six months."

So, things hadn't worked out. That was life. She had lost a good friend. That's what hurt most. The breakup had ruined their friendship, a long and true friendship. He brushed some of her dark red hair off her face, his fingers gliding over her soft skin.

"I'd rather not talk about that anymore," she said.

"Okay." He continued to run his fingers along her brow, the feel of her silky hair keeping him coming back for more. In a selfish way he was glad she'd been the one to break it off.

Still, he had the sense that there had been something else that happened between her and this Drake character. Maybe he'd have the guy checked out.

For now, he just wanted to kiss her.

Leaning in, he moved his fingers to her jawline and turned her toward him. Then he pressed his mouth to hers.

She flinched a little, drawing back. But he kept kissing her, determined to win her over, to rid her of the ghosts that still haunted her. He felt her tension ease and moved back.

"At the party," Carson began, the kiss deepening his voice.

"Yes?" She sounded as aroused as him.

"When I kissed you…" He kissed her again, softly, briefly.

"Yes." This she rasped on a whisper. He wanted to hear her say that when they were naked together.

"Is that why you ran?"

"It was a game to you."

He kept kissing her chastely. "No game. Let me show you how real this is, Georgia." Waiting for her, seeing the passion burning in her eyes, he kissed her harder. When their breathing joined the whine of the jet engines, he scooped her up and brought her onto his lap.

Looping one arm around his shoulders, she placed her hand on his chest and bent back over his arm as he kissed her. She groaned when he trailed down her neck to the opening of her white scoop-necked dress. Her beaded silver sandals thumped to the floor and her bracelet slid up her arm.

When he returned to her lips, she was ablaze with lust that matched his. Instinct made him stand with her.

The attendant turned back toward the cockpit and serving station, discreetly sliding the curtains across the roof for privacy.

Chapter 8

Carson took Georgia to the back, where a small bed-room offered a double-size bed and slender storage areas built into the sides. He laid her onto the mattress and crawled over her, bending to kiss her more and stealing glances down her luscious body.

Putting one knee and then the other between hers, he spread her the way he yearned to see her. The hem of her dress slipped up her thigh. He ran his hand along the skin, all the way up, pushing the material to her hip.

"Your legs are so beautiful," he rasped. Then kissed her reverently. "You're beautiful everywhere."

As he ran his hand up the side of her body and cupped her breast, he felt her begin to stiffen.

"Wait." She pushed his chest.

Bewildered, Carson lifted himself off her and looked down at her scared face. Why was she frightened?

"Please, stop."

Rigid with desire, wanting her with a ferocity that gnawed at him, Carson got off the bed. No sooner than he did that, Georgia scampered off it and hurried out of the room.

Standing there fighting raging passion, he was slower to follow.

Georgia was appalled over what had almost occurred on Carson's jet. She unpacked her clothes from their trip, stuffing underwear back into the drawer. As she did, she noticed some were missing. She'd only taken what she needed to North Carolina. Was she mistaken? She sifted through them all again. Yes. She was missing two pairs. Had the maids taken them to wash? That must be it. She didn't recall leaving them out, but what else could have happened to them?

Leaving her room, she made her way downstairs to look for Ruby. She had a lot to talk to her about. She still felt betrayed that her stepmother, who was her real mother in every way except biological, had kept details of her past from her. She seemed like a stranger now. How had she changed so much?

She also thought it might be time for her and Ruby to go home. There was really no reason for them to stay any longer. Carson could let them know if anything turned up on Jackson's kidnapping. She couldn't help him with that or the shooting and neither could Ruby. But she felt so much dread in making that a reality. Going home. That had her at odds with herself. The day at the spa with Kate had temporarily painted a rosy glow on the feelings for Carson that seemed to have popped up out of nowhere.

Downstairs, she walked through the house and found

Ruby just entering the ranch house, laughing—no, *giggling*—as she closed the front door. When she turned, Georgia saw how flushed she was and felt her stomach turn. Was this the Ruby of pre-Reginald days?

"Oh, Georgia!" She rushed forward and flung her arms around her. "I heard you were back. I asked Hayden to drop me off early so I could spend some time with you." She leaned back. "How was the trip? You didn't call. Did you and Carson find anything?"

Georgia figured her expression said a lot.

Ruby stepped back and her face fell. "Nothing?"

"You've been spending a lot of time with Hayden."

"Those leads went nowhere?"

"Let's go somewhere to talk." Georgia found the living room empty and decided this was as good a place as any in this giant house.

She chose two armchairs before a big window and sat with Ruby.

"Nothing?" Ruby asked. "Nothing at all?"

This was the Ruby Georgia knew. The fragile Ruby. The loving Ruby. It softened her sense of betrayal.

"I'm sorry, no. We're no closer than we were before we went there."

"That's so disappointing." Ruby's head hung low.

Georgia gave her time to recover before saying, "Tell me what's going on between you and Hayden."

Ruby sniffled, fighting back tears. The subject of Hayden helped to brighten her. "He's been taking me places. It's still very innocent. He is such a gentleman. You don't have to worry, Georgia. In fact, you worry too much about me."

"What do you like about him? He's the Adairs' neighbor."

Ruby studied Georgia a bit. "Yes, I know. I never dreamed I'd take an interest in someone like that again. But it just happened. And I'm not even sure it's going to go anywhere."

"Does he spend a lot of money on you?"

Ruby laughed lightly. "He's taken me to dinner and to some museums and even an amusement park. Nothing too extravagant. In fact, he's rather frugal with his money. I get the impression he isn't as wealthy as the Adairs."

That made Georgia feel marginally better. Maybe Ruby wasn't turning into her old self.

Someone came through the front door. Carson had gone to AdAir Corp to help Whit. Maybe he had arrived home.

The burst of excited anticipation made her tense. So did the way she looked toward the living room opening and the rush of heat when Carson appeared.

But he looked stressed, as though he'd had a rough day. If she lived with him, she'd get up and make him feel better.

"Hi," she said instead.

The way she greeted him smoothed the hard lines on his face, and he grinned. "Hi." He turned to Ruby with a nod.

"We were just talking," Georgia said. There were still some things she needed to discuss with her stepmother.

"Meet me in the kitchen when you're finished," he said.

"Okay."

He looked at her a moment longer, the heat of it warming the room, at least to her it had warmed. Considerably.

When he disappeared from the doorway, Ruby fanned herself with her hand. "Well. It seems I'm not the only one who's been basking under a man's sun."

"Nothing's going on between me and Carson," Georgia said.

"Mmm. That's not obvious, Georgia. I just saw the way he looked at you and you at him. There's plenty going on there. More than what's going on with me and Hayden. He lost his wife, so he's taking things very slow. You and Carson look like you've been intimate already. Have you?"

"No!" Georgia feared she sounded too defensive.

"It's okay, Georgia. He isn't Reginald."

No, only his *son*. "Why didn't you tell me about Loretta's husband?" she asked, needing to get to the bottom of this.

That gave Ruby some pause, the excitement over her stepdaughter finding love doused. She studied Georgia's face. She must see how it bothered her because she blinked rapidly a few times and stuttered incoherently before finding her voice. "That was so long ago, Georgia. It had nothing to do with you and me and your father." She shook her head. "I was a little wild, I suppose. I didn't see it that way back then. I just always looked for opportunities to have fun."

"Sleeping with your best friend's husband was fun?" She couldn't keep the disgust out of her tone. Discovering her stepmother—her mother in every way that mattered—had not been the woman she'd idolized in childhood and respected and loved in adulthood was still a shock.

"Oh, Georgia." Ruby reached over, coaxing her for her hand.

Georgia didn't offer it to her. She needed an explanation.

Ruby let out a disgruntled breath. "No. It wasn't *fun*. It was a mistake. At the time, Loretta was already finished with her husband. She'd asked him to move out and he'd been in his own place for several months. The divorce was in process. She didn't love him. She was the one who ended it. I found out later that he slept with me to hurt her. As for me? I have no excuses. I had always found him attractive. I convinced myself that Loretta wouldn't care. He was available. But she did care. Even though she didn't love him anymore, the idea that I would sleep with someone she had been married to destroyed how she felt about me."

Georgia leaned back against her chair, growing more relieved.

"I was devastated when Loretta told me she never wanted to speak to me again. People say it was Jackson's kidnapping that changed me. It wasn't. It was that *and* losing Loretta's friendship. She taught me how to be a better person. I think that's why Reginald fell in love with me. It wasn't a game anymore. It was real. And it was good. For a few months."

Until Jackson had been kidnapped.

"Loretta said she'd like to talk to you sometime," Georgia said.

Ruby looked at her, a happy gleam lighting her eyes. "She did?"

Georgia smiled. "She wants you to call her."

"She does?" Ruby didn't believe it.

Georgia nodded. "I have her number."

"Oh." Ruby looked across the room, contemplating what it would mean to reunite with her old friend. "We'd have a lot of repairing to do." She turned back to Georgia. "But I'd like to try."

Georgia only nodded, happy she'd talked to Ruby but still plagued by what could happen to her and Ruby. Before coming to San Diego, she'd been convinced that she and Ruby should tread carefully around anyone with money—particularly the Adairs. Now Ruby was enjoying a rich man's attention, and Georgia was enjoying Carson's. What did that say about her? That she was a hypocrite? Or had she just been wrong all this time?

Carson found his sister in the kitchen in her pj's and a robe. Her long, dark brown hair was tangled and her blue eyes bloodshot. She poured a fizzing soda into a big, ice-filled plastic cup. Beside that, there were three slices of pizza on a plate. Cold.

He opened the refrigerator. "Been in bed all day?" Taking out a bottle of flavored sparkling water, he let the refrigerator door close.

"Movie day."

He twisted the cap off the water. "All by yourself?"

"Yes." She picked up the cup and gulped. "I had a late night."

She had been having a lot of those. He took in her disheveled state. Even tired, her beauty could not be diminished, but it wasn't like her at all to behave this way. What happened to his sweet sister?

"Where were you?" he asked.

Holding the cup with both hands, she drank some more soda. "I went to a party with Mitch and then we went to breakfast."

"You're seeing a ranch hand?" He threw the cap into the trash compactor.

"No. We're friends. We've been friends for a long time. You know that."

He did. But she had never gone *partying* with him before. She didn't *party*. Then something else came to him. "I thought you had a charity event scheduled for last night."

"Yes. Whit's assistant handled it for me."

"You made his assistant do it?" Carson was taken aback. "I bet that was a huge imposition for her."

Landry's head jerked back. "She was okay with it."

"She probably did it out of sympathy. You're falling apart after Dad's death and Mom's going after Elizabeth."

Landry looked down at her pizza and went to the refrigerator. "I'm starving."

"Landry." He watched her take out some dip and then go to the pantry for a bag of chips. "What's going on with you?"

"I'm okay." She picked up her plate and tucked the dip under her arm and grabbed up the bag of chips with the same hand that held the plate. Planting a kiss on his cheek, she took her soda and started to leave the kitchen.

"No, you're not, Landry." When she stopped and looked back at him, he continued, "You're acting strangely. Both Whit and I have noticed. You've been different ever since Mom ran off."

She angled her head in protest, adjusting the dip under her arm and balancing the cup of soda.

"What's wrong?" he asked. It was time she talked about it.

Lowering her head for a few seconds, she turned and deposited her picnic items onto one of the kitchen islands. After a few more seconds, she lifted her head.

"Everyone is so convinced Mom tried to kill Elizabeth. And that she might have even killed Dad." She shook her head. "Really? Mom? How can anyone think she'd do such a thing?"

"I do think her motive to kill Dad is weak, but she did try to kill Elizabeth, Landry. I know it's hard to accept, but she did."

He could see her struggle with that. She had a hard time wrapping her mind around her own mother trying to kill someone.

"Why do you think she ran?" he asked. "She's guilty."

"She ran because everyone is crucifying her."

Carson walked over to her and took her hand. "Landry, this is hard for you. She's our mother. We grew up with her. Nobody wants to admit their own mother is capable of murder, but ours is. You have to stop denying that. It's affecting your life."

"It is not. I'm fine." She gathered up her food and drink again. "Mom didn't go off the deep end and kill anyone."

"Mom has probably been off the deep end for a long time. She's guilty, Landry. Why is it so hard for you to see that?"

Landry jerked her hand free. "She's our mother, Carson!"

Carson decided to back off for now. He could tell when a woman had had enough. Pretty soon emotions would take over. He wouldn't upset her more than she was.

"Why are you badgering me, anyway?" she lashed out. "I was having a nice peaceful day until I ran into you!"

"Movie day." He pointed to her armful of food. "Junk-food-in-bed day because you were out all night partying? Since when do you do that? Since when do you shove your charity work onto somebody else? Somebody who has a family and has to work every day?"

Her head fell in contrition. She realized now what she had done.

"I'm sorry. I just…"

Can't deal with the drama Patsy had created. "It's okay. I'm here for you if you ever need to talk."

She lifted her head. "Thanks, Carson. You were always there for me."

He put his hand on her shoulder. "We'll get through this. Whatever the outcome, we'll get through it."

The Landry he knew and loved returned briefly. She smiled and leaned in for another cheek kiss, her bag of potato chips crunching.

When she drew back, she said, "I love you."

"Promise me you'll take care of yourself."

"I am."

"No more late-night partying."

"Mmm." She nodded noncommittally. "Maybe."

"Landry…"

"Oh, stop. You're always taking care of us. You should take care of yourself for a change. Starting with that woman out there." She pointed toward the living room and waggled her eyebrows. "I've seen the way she looks at you."

"We're not talking about that."

Her face lit up and she adjusted her hold on the dip again. "You like her."

"Stop it, Landry."

"What's stopping you?" She gave him an elbow to the ribs. "She's pretty."

What was stopping him? Her mystery, for one. His uncertain future, another. Or were those excuses? "I barely know her," he ended up saying.

Landry laughed a little. "You and Whit."

"I'm not getting married."

She just chuckled some more, turning with her junk food.

"Enjoy your picnic." He headed for the living room. "I'll be checking up on you, so behave."

"Okay. You do the opposite," she called.

As he stood in the kitchen, Whit entered.

"I just saw Landry. She looks a wreck."

"Yeah."

"But happy. What did you say to her?"

"I scolded her for being too wild and asking your assistant to do her charity work for her."

"She did that?"

"Yes."

"I'll have a talk with my assistant. I'll tell her next time Landry does that I ordered her to say no."

"Thanks." Carson sipped his water. "What brings you here?" Why wasn't he at home with his wife? That was why he had to fill in for him today.

"I needed to ask if you could you cover for me tomorrow morning, too. Can you? I've got some plans with Elizabeth until about noon."

Whit was trying to ease him into a full-time position. Carson didn't need a confession to know that. But like the last time he'd asked, it ate at him. Whit had turned their dad's office into his office. Every time he sat in there, it took him down memory lane and filled in gaps with the image of a grieving Reginald.

"You're doing this on purpose," Carson said.

Whit frowned in confusion. "Doing what?"

"Asking me to cover for you. You're grooming me to take over."

"I am not. Elizabeth is pregnant. She requires a lot of attention."

And she'd only require more once the baby was born. "I don't want to run AdAir."

"No?"

Carson looked away. He wasn't sure what he wanted. Getting to know his dead father was torturous, but it was also bittersweet. His curiosity kept him going back for more. When he was in his office, he seemed the most connected to him.

"Just the morning, Carson. It's no big deal. If we have to hire externally, we will."

Seeing Georgia appear in the entrance to the kitchen, he told Whit, "Okay. I'll be there."

He didn't want to argue in front of her.

"Thanks. My assistant will be there to help you."

Carson watched him go.

"You could suffer worse calamities," Georgia said, teasing him.

"I don't mind covering for him."

"Yes, you do."

He walked toward her. "Just for that, I'm taking you to dinner."

Georgia should have said no. But here she stood in front of the mirror, looking ready for a five-hundred-dollar dinner. And tingling on the inside because Carson was taking her. Was it a real date? What if she secretly let herself consider it so?

Hearing her phone ring, she went to her purse and took it out. Seeing the name on the screen, she went still. Drake. Should she answer it?

He hadn't tried to call her since she broke up with him. The way things had ended, she wasn't sure talking to him was a good idea. Severing all ties felt like the right decision. But why was he calling?

"Drake?"

"Georgia." He sounded relieved. "I wasn't sure you'd answer."

She almost hadn't.

"I just wanted to tell you that I miss you. You've been a good friend to me for so long. I really do miss you. I don't want to lose that, Georgia."

That was commendable, but could she ever go back to the way they were?

"I was wondering if we could meet sometime. Maybe for lunch or coffee. Nothing too cozy. Keep it casual. You know, like we used to."

For a moment, she was back in college, laughing and talking to him as if they'd known each other for a lifetime. How nice it would be to have that friendship again.

"I miss that, too," she said.

"Do you?" He sounded surprised.

Why was he surprised? Maybe it was his old insecurity popping out again. "Yes. You were my best friend."

"I can still be your best friend."

She hesitated, her insides rebelling against the idea of attempting friendship with him after what happened.

"No?" he coaxed.

"I…I don't know, Drake. I'm not sure we can be

friends like that again." Friendly, yes, but close friends? She didn't think so. She saw him so differently now.

"I'm sorry about the way it ended, Georgia. We should have talked first."

Talked before he'd shocked her with a side of him she'd never seen before. "Yes, we should have."

"How about we meet for lunch tomorrow. Are you free? We'll talk then."

Everything in her recoiled. "I—I can't. I'm not home. I'm in San Diego."

"Really? What are you doing there?"

She explained about the inheritance and Jackson's kidnapping but left out details. "Reginald's sons are carrying on with his investigation. They didn't know Jackson was kidnapped or that he even existed until the reading of the will."

"No kidding. That's amazing. His sons, huh?"

"Whit and Carson." After a lengthy pause, he asked, "When will you be home?"

"I don't know. I haven't made definite plans."

There was a long silence on the other end. "Well, it so happens that I've got a business meeting there in a couple of days."

Drake's job brought him to San Diego a lot. His company's headquarters was located there. She didn't say anything, lest she encourage him to ask to meet while he was here.

"You're spending a lot of time there. Is there a problem with the inheritance?" he asked.

She appreciated that he'd respected her need for distance. And he understood about Ruby. Of course, he would. He knew all about her heartbreak. "No." She didn't feel like getting into the mediation meeting and what Carson had done for Ruby.

"Then what's keeping you?"

"Ruby. She's getting hopeful Carson will find her son."

"Is she doing all right?" he asked.

"She needs me."

Drake chuckled with affection, a familiar sound from long ago. The nostalgia stung, though, now that they were no longer friends the way they were back then.

"My Georgia, always looking out for others and never herself."

She breathed a laugh and almost told him he reminded her of Carson.

"How are you faring with all those Adairs around you?" he asked.

Also like Carson, Drake was aware of her annoyances. "They aren't so bad."

"No?"

"Ruby is seeing one of their neighbors."

"Ruby? Where are you staying?"

She hesitated. "At Carson's ranch."

There was another lengthy pause, and Georgia felt sick that he might be jealous. "Why are you staying there?"

She didn't feel as though she had to answer that. But this was Drake. The old Drake, insecurities and all. "He invited us. While we look for Jackson..." She offered no other explanation.

"Do you like him?"

She faltered before saying, "He's been very kind to us. He isn't like his father."

"So you do like him."

She didn't respond.

"Georgia Mason is falling for a rich guy," he teased with a chuckle. "Who would have thought? Not me."

"I'm not falling for him. I'm here for Ruby and nothing else."

"So defensive," he continued to tease, and then he chuckled again. "It's okay, Georgia. I want us to be friends again. That's why I called you. I didn't like it that we broke up, but now I've had some time to think and I know what's most important to me. You. Your friendship. We gave it a try romantically. It didn't work out. Let's not let it ruin our friendship."

She smiled until she remembered what happened to break them up.

"Think it over," he said in her silence.

Her tension eased. "It's good to hear from you, Drake, but I have to go."

"All right, darlin'. Call me when you get home."

"I will."

Disconnecting, she stared at her phone awhile, not at all sure she would call when she returned home. Was it possible they could be friends again? Thinking of that awful night that had changed everything between them, she had major doubts. In fact, she was beginning to think she never wanted to go back to Florida. That maybe it would be best if she started over somewhere else. Like…here.

Snapping out of that fantasy, Georgia left the room. Moving away would only mean she was running from her past. She had a home and a job she loved back in Florida. No one and nothing was going to chase her away.

Chapter 9

Carson took her to Frederick's, a resort restaurant renowned for its fine-dining experience. Georgia didn't want to admit she loved it. The ambience. The silky cream-colored gown Carson had left out for her—along with accessories that included a feathery shawl. And food she'd never tried before. It all began with a coddled farm egg with caviar and capers. Next came sea bass in a green-curry broth with thinly sliced cucumbers. King crab–filled dumplings with a hint of orange and basil arrived third, and the grand finale before dessert was pan-seared salmon on a bed of sautéed spinach, garnished with shallots and sun-dried tomatoes and a beurre blanc sauce drizzled over the top.

"Admit it. You could get used to this," Carson said with a grin. Both of them leaned back against their chairs, content and full of great food and pampered by exceptional service.

"You do this a lot?"

He shook his head. "Never."

Really? She supposed that was due to the fact that he hadn't been here since he joined the Marines. She didn't want to like him even more than she did now. He was normal. Like her. An ordinary person. Except he had money. Lots of it. And once he acclimated to his new lifestyle, how would he change? Or would he? Carson struck her as a man who did things his own way and wasn't easily influenced by others.

"What do you like to do in your spare time?" she asked. "Besides read."

"What would you like to do with yours if you could afford it?" he asked rather than answered.

"I asked you first."

He thought a moment. "I don't really know."

"What did you like to do when you were in the Marines?"

"There wasn't much to do. When I was on assignment, which was pretty much all the time, I went out with the guys and played pool." Something else came to him, Georgia saw in the way his eyes grew more alert. "I did love to see the way the locals lived. Get out into the country and eat at pubs in villages. Tour historical sites."

She'd love to do that, too, if she could afford it. But one really great trip in her lifetime would be enough. She didn't need excess.

"One of my favorite trips was when I traveled from where I was stationed in Germany to Ambleside, United Kingdom, and visited Beatrix Potter's hilltop home."

"Beatrix Potter?"

"I read a lot of biographies. Hers was one of them. I

admired her courage to live according to her own rules. She went against her parents and had ambitions only most men were accepted to have."

She could see him having an affinity for people like that. He was no different when it came to defying his parents.

"I love rare books," she said. "I can't afford to collect the ones I'd really like—Beatrix Potter among them."

"That's the one thing my father did that I loved, too," he said.

"Reginald collected old books?"

"He did. I used to read them and he'd get really mad at me. I used to hate him for that, but now…" He went off into memory. "I've begun to go through his books and have been thinking about carrying on his collection."

"That sounds lovely." She smiled with how much she liked that. She would be an avid book collector if she had the money. "Does he have Beatrix Potter?"

He shook his head. "Amazingly, no. I think he might have if he'd have thought of it. I can see that was one more thing I never noticed about him. His book collecting. One more thing that made him human."

"Your dad was human?" She breathed a laugh.

"You wouldn't have guessed it if you ever met him."

Georgia didn't have to meet him. She had gotten well-acquainted with the man through Ruby.

"Jackson changed him," Carson said.

"It would change any parent. Can you imagine losing your own child? Not knowing if they were dead or alive? It would be pure torture."

He nodded solemnly. "I wish I would have known while he was still alive."

"Why? How do you think that would have changed anything?" Reginald would have been the same man. He still would have shut everyone out, including Ruby. To Georgia, that was unforgivable. Selfish.

"I would have tried to get to know him more. Maybe I wouldn't have joined the military."

"You'd have worked at AdAir?"

"If I was close to my father?" He considered that awhile, looking over at a waiter pouring wine into a glass at a neighboring table before turning back to her. "Maybe."

Wow. Georgia was impressed. It took a noble man to admit his shortcomings, and Carson had nearly done that. Joining the military had been a form of rebellion. But if he'd been close to his father, he might not have been inclined to run away.

"You wish you would have known him better," she said.

He nodded. "Most of my life I thought of him as a cold, ruthless tyrant who didn't love us. Any of us. Patsy, either. I remember wondering why he didn't just leave us. I thought it was because he didn't want to pay Patsy. She'd take too much from him. But that wasn't it."

Reginald had simply been unhappy and resigned to the fact that changing who he lived with wouldn't matter.

"Losing his son doesn't excuse him from treating everyone else poorly," she said. "I can understand why you wish you could have had a better relationship with your dad, but he made the choice to alienate himself. He didn't have to do that. He could have chosen to show his love." But he hadn't. "He lost any hope of happiness by choosing that path. He must have lived in the past."

"In the past and in the shadow of his parents. They treated him much the way he treated us growing up."

"Some people survive by living with what's familiar."

Carson grunted. "Loneliness is familiar. Maybe you're right."

"I wouldn't spend too much time feeling bad for never knowing your father. If he really knew you, he'd be proud of the man you've become. He'd be proud that you made your own way in life."

"He'd think he won if I run AdAir."

"The ruthless tyrant would. But the dad before Jackson's kidnapping wouldn't. He lost touch with the father in him."

Carson met her gaze with soft appreciation. His regard slowly changed from healing talk of his father to an awareness of her. The way he took in her face heated the moment.

Georgia was relived when a decadent chocolate torte arrived for dessert and she had something to occupy herself. She ate a few bites while she wrestled with how much she was beginning to like this man. How easy it would be to forget her original assumptions, to compromise her beliefs and see what happened. What if she just enjoyed him? What if she stopped trying to protect her future and just lived in the here and now? With Carson. She could decide later where they were and how she felt and make a decision then. Nothing may come of this. Carson could get bored with pampering her and then a side of him she wasn't seeing now might emerge and ruin everything.

"Not very good?"

She looked over at him and then down at her barely

touched dessert. "It's delicious. Everything was delicious."

"What were you thinking just now?" he asked in a low, deep voice, an intimate voice.

"That I'd be a fool to fall for you."

He studied her. "Maybe I'm the one who'd be a fool... falling for you."

Was he falling for her? The heat returned between them, making Georgia look down at her dessert.

"Are you ready to go?" he asked, his voice low and gruff, as though he struggled as much as her.

Grateful, she nodded and he helped her into her shawl before they walked out of the restaurant. A valet summoned the driver of the limo that had taken them there. The excessive show of wealth should repulse her. Instead, it was a fitting end to a wonderful evening—a drive home in a princess carriage. Everything she'd previously thought about rich people—about the Adairs— wasn't true tonight.

The driver got out of the limo and started to walk around.

Carson tugged Georgia's hand. She stopped and faced him. With the warm gleam of his eyes, he seemed as content as she felt.

"I had a nice time tonight," he said.

"I did, too." Truth rang in her tone.

"I won't tease you about that." He grinned, sexy and full of affection.

Her heart flopped into more excited beats.

"I started out taking you here on purpose, but now I can't recall when I've enjoyed being with a woman more."

Her breath caught for a second.

"I'd like to do this again, Georgia."

"Oh...I..." She may as well melt right here.

He slid his arm all the way around her, pulling her close. And then he kissed her. It happened before she could react. His mouth over hers sent tingles of shocking pleasure all the way through her, spiraling down to her core and brewing desire she wasn't expecting.

"Gun!" someone shouted.

Carson lifted his head and then swung her around before she could look to see who'd called out. He brought her down onto the stone driveway and covered her body with his as a shot exploded. The limousine blocked the bullet. Georgia heard it hit the other side and glass shatter.

A woman screamed.

Hearing footsteps as though someone was running, Georgia sat up as Carson's weight left her. He crouched low to peer over the hood of the limo. Kneeling behind him, Georgia grew aware of stinging pain on her knee and palm. The silky cream-colored gown offered little protection.

Carson turned toward her. "Wait here."

She held her stinging palm as he ran off with an uneven gait. Standing up, she watched him go down the driveway. A valet was chasing another man. He must have been the one to shout out.

"Are you all right, miss?" the limo driver asked.

Still stunned, she nodded.

"Police and paramedics are on the way," he said, holding a cell phone in his hand.

The sound of squealing tires said the gunman was getting away. Seconds later, Carson walked into sight, his limp more pronounced than before he'd gone running. The valet driver was behind him.

Sirens sounded.

Carson reached her and took her hands. "You're hurt." He looked down at her dress, where blood had seeped through from her knee. He helped her to her feet and guided her to the front-passenger seat of the limo.

"I'm all right," she said as she sat down.

The driver retrieved a first-aid kit and handed it to Carson. He rummaged inside and found some alcohol wipes. She sat still as he treated her hands. Both palms were scraped.

Fire trucks and police cars arrived before the ambulance, and a throng of onlookers had gathered, some from the street, some from the restaurant.

Carson lifted the hem of her dress to expose her knee. He was gentle and considerate of her modesty. She winced as he applied the alcohol. Next came a big Band-Aid.

"Are you folks okay?"

Georgia looked up to see a firefighter standing there. "Yes."

"Was anyone hurt?"

Carson shook his head.

A police officer approached. After introductions were made and the officer wrote their names down, Carson explained what had happened.

"The gunman shot at you?" the officer asked.

"Yes."

"Why do you think he was shooting at you in particular?" the officer asked.

Carson told him about the shooting in the parking garage. "He shot right at me again this time. The bullet hit the back window. I was walking to Georgia's left. If someone wouldn't have shouted, 'Gun,' and we hadn't gotten down, I would have been hit."

The questioning finished up and she and Carson were allowed to go. The limo driver had arranged for another car to drive them to the helicopter pad.

Georgia's magical evening was gone. She wondered if it had gone when Carson had kissed her. Because foolish or not, she *was* falling for him.

Two days later, Carson was back at AdAir Corp, sitting behind his father's desk again. He'd been busy ever since the shooting outside the restaurant. He'd studied all the video surveillance at the ranch and spotted a suspicious car drive by the entrance in one of them. That alone wasn't significant, but Carson thought the car was the same as the one he'd seen the shooter get into and race away. None of the camera angles gave him a clear view of the driver. One would have, but the man was wearing a hat and a hoodie. He was about the same build as the unidentified man they'd encountered in Myanmar. Not taking any chances, he'd bolstered security at the ranch.

He'd reported the car to police and given them a copy of the tape. Now he had an hour to call his commander before his meeting with the vice president of Human Resources. Sergeant Major Copeland must have something new because he'd called this morning and left him a message.

"Carson," Sergeant Major Copeland boomed into the phone.

Carson sat in AdAir's SCIF. "Sir."

"We got a big break yesterday," Copeland said.

Carson leaned back in the leather conference table chair. Finally. Something to go on. How big would it be?

"We've tracked the man in Myanmar to the Philippines. Nothing came up there on him, but we also checked passengers who flew from there around the time of our mission. We did background on all of them and three came up suspicious. Two men were traveling together on false passports. They ended up having connections to an emerging terrorist cell. Homeland Security apprehended them and brought them in for questioning. They were able to prove they weren't in Myanmar at the time of the mission. Both had hotel reservations in Davao and the hotel was able to corroborate."

"That leaves the third man," Carson said.

"Stephen Chow," Copeland said. "His father was a businessman working for a US corporation in China. His parents moved him to the States when he was around five. The father traveled a lot and the mother died of cancer when he was a teenager. He's had brushes with the law, the usual adolescent things. He drops off the radar as an adult. He's thirty-one now."

"He traveled to Myanmar under his real name?" Carson pressed the speaker button and stood so he could walk around secure conference room.

"No. We only found a round trip from the United States to the Philippines and back."

"Around the time we were in Myanmar?"

"Yes. Do you want to hear something even more chilling?"

Carson waited for Copeland to continue.

"He lives in San Diego."

Carson stopped pacing. "What?"

"He *recently* moved there, as in, right after the failed mission."

"Really." Carson started walking again. "You have an address?"

"I've got a lot that I'm sending over the SIPRNet."

Secret Internet Protocol Router Network. "What else do you know about him?"

"Not much. I was hoping you could go in and get that for us."

A flash of excitement coursed through him. It would be like being in the Marines again. Working for the mission.

"If he's after the missing data and thinks you have it or can get it for him, this could be dangerous for you."

That didn't scare him. "If he's after the missing data, then there is no other choice. I have to find the data and I have to stop Stephen." He thought of Georgia. Stephen had seen her with him. That was a new feeling for him. He had never had to worry about anyone other than himself on missions like this. Now he was determined to see to her safety.

"We need to know his connection to the organization in Myanmar. Why did he start smuggling technology to North Korea and is that all he's doing?"

Carson had been thinking about the data a lot. "Stephen must have been the one who was supposed to deliver the data." Then the mission had gone bad and everyone had scrambled to get out of there alive. "If he doesn't have the data, who does?"

"That's what I need you to find out, Carson."

That was his intention all along. "We've had some incidents since I left North Carolina."

"The lead detective told me about the shooting. Is your lady all right?"

Why had Copeland phrased it that way? *Your lady.*

"She's a strong woman. She'll hold up just fine." And in that instant he knew it was true. Georgia was no kept woman. No trophy wife. No sheltered, frail thing. The opposite of Ruby, who struck him as someone who needed constant care. Another reason why Georgia was the way she was when it came to her stepmother.

Georgia was pampered only when Carson pampered her, and he was of the opinion that she needed a lot more of that. Someone to take half the burden. An equal work share in a relationship.

"I think the car that the gunman got away in is the same one I saw on my surveillance video," Carson said. "The police believe it's the one that was reported stolen a few days ago."

"What about the car involved in the shooting at AdAir Corp?" Copeland asked.

"The rental was found abandoned in a parking lot of an out-of-business retail store."

"Hmm." Copeland fell silent while he thought. "The shooter stole a different car for the second attempt?"

"That's how it appears. My guess is the police will find that car abandoned, as well."

"Let's hope he's overconfident."

If he was confident enough to smuggle technology to the North Koreans, he was confident enough to keep a stolen car hidden.

After talking to Copeland, Carson left the SCIF and walked up to his father's office, shutting the door and going to sit behind the desk. His phone rang and he saw that it was Whit's—no, the new executive assistant Whit had hired. His boldness was getting irritating. He'd hired an assistant for Carson.

"Yes?" he answered.

"You have a delivery, sir."

"Please call me Carson. I'm not formal about office protocol." He might be in a suit, but no one should mistake him for his father's ilk.

"Sorry, sir…er…Carson."

"What kind of delivery?" he inquired.

"It's from the police department. It's a box of things they don't need for your father's murder investigation anymore."

That stunned him for a second. "I'll be right out."

He opened the office door, which, he realized, he kept closed too much. The short, skinny girl with thick black hair had trouble meeting his eyes. Whit had introduced them, but he'd barely spoken to her. She was probably bored out of her mind.

"Abby, isn't it?" Carson said.

She looked at him and nodded.

"I know I've been in my office with the door shut and not here much. I've been a little preoccupied. My brother hired you and I'm not accustomed to having an assistant."

"Oh, don't worry about that, Mr. Ad— Carson. All the assistants work together here. There's plenty of work."

"Oh. That's good, but if you have some downtime, don't think you can't take care of personal matters. I can't stand corporate environments. There's more to the bottom line than a workaholic mentality. Productivity increases the happier the people are."

She smiled.

"Will you set up a luncheon with all the administrative staff? Include Whit and the head of HR. I'd like to get to know you all more." His brother was going to feel his pain on this one. And if he was going to drag him into the office, then things were going to be run the way he liked. Nothing like his father. Not that Whit wasn't a good boss. He was. But Carson wanted his ideas on corporate culture communicated.

Abby's smile grew bigger. "I'll get something on your calendar."

"I don't look at my calendar."

"I know. The calendar is more for me. I'll make sure you're aware of when the luncheon is scheduled."

"Thanks." He picked up the box and walked back into his dad's office. *His* office now. He was about to swing the door shut when he looked at his assistant and then some others working in cubicles. Leaving it open, he went to stand behind the desk.

His employees were human beings who had personal lives that mattered to them. His father hadn't cared about that. He'd only cared about making money. Well, Carson was going to make more money than he did—by making sure his workforce was happy when they walked into work, that they were glad to be at work.

Carson opened the top of the box. There wasn't much. Notepad. Pen. Several documents. There was another box, this one sealed. He took that out and used a pocketknife in the middle desk drawer to open it. Inside, something had been carefully wrapped in packaging paper. Removing the paper, he found a ceramic bowl—the one he'd seen in the picture on his dad's desk. Carson picked that up and turned it in his hands. It was old. An antique. Asian, he'd guess, with its pretty blue-and-white intricate pattern and its smooth, daintily curving shape. He didn't know that much more about it. Putting it down on the desk, he stared at it, wondering what his dad had liked about it.

Did tyrants like art?

He supposed anyone could. No matter how brutal or harsh. But this piece must have cost a fortune.

Sitting down, he placed the bowl on the desk and called his brother.

"When did Dad start collecting art?" he asked Whit when he answered.

"I don't know. He's been going to antique auctions for years. Why?"

The idea of his dad at an antique auction chipped away a tiny bit of his perception of the man. "I never knew that about him." He'd never paid attention to his book collection, either.

"You were gone by the time he started taking an interest in that. He didn't go often. It wasn't a passion or anything. He donated everything he found to his favorite gallery downtown."

"He *donated* everything?"

"It was a tax write-off. You aren't starting to think he had a redeeming side, are you?"

Carson grunted. "No." Even his book collection didn't make him redeeming. He hadn't collected them for anyone other than himself. Or had he? He'd had the ceramic bowl on display in his office. And if he collected rare books, why not art that caught his fancy? Not everything had been a tax write-off.

After a brief pause, Whit said, "Finding out about Jackson does change how you see him, doesn't it?"

"A little." A lot. He was glad to hear Whit was dealing with the same emotions over their dad's death.

After another brief pause, Whit asked, "How are you liking the office? Getting settled in?"

Recalling his interaction with Abby and the meeting he'd asked her to arrange, he struggled with a moment of angst. Was he getting settled in? It had felt good to start injecting some of his influence in this company. To make it better than his dad had. Maybe that was where he got his satisfaction. It was a form of rebellion. But did he want to take the helm of this monster?

One step at a time. He had to track down Stephen Chow. Jackson had to be found. And a murderer needed to be brought to justice. The rest would have to wait.

"I talked to my commander today," he said, a perfect segue.

"Change the subject if you want. I know you're loving it there."

Ignoring that comment, Carson told him about his conversation with Copeland and what he was going to do.

"Be careful," Whit said, not worried. He knew Carson was capable. "And enjoy your day at work."

"Next time you ask me to cover for you, I just might say no." Because his brother was doing this on purpose, acclimating him to the corporate world.

"All you have to do is make it yours, Carson. You don't realize it yet, but you were made to be a leader of a company like AdAir."

"I don't see how you can say that." He was a marine, not an executive.

"You came to the company with Dad when you were

a kid, up until you were a teenager, and saw him for what he was. Then you ran. It's in your blood, Carson."

Remembering the days he'd come with his dad to work, Carson resisted the truth in what his brother said.

"I'll talk to you later, brother." Carson ended the call, but he couldn't shake what Whit had made him start thinking.

He'd idolized Reginald. What innocent child didn't look up to their parents? He'd loved the corporate machine. He'd watch everyone do their job and when he was older, he'd seen how each one contributed. But then he'd also seen how his dad kept pushing for more. More, more, more. Always more. Revenue never rose high enough. That was a screwed-up way of running a business.

He looked down at the desk and stared at the bowl.

Carson sat down, wondering if Whit was right. He could run this company differently than how Reginald did. Whit had brought back pride in the service they provided. Carson could continue doing so, not skimping on resources to make revenue look better, but by taking action with honesty and integrity.

Carson picked up the bowl and studied it some more. It was a beautiful piece. Had his father appreciated that about it? Or had the price been right?

He knew someone who'd appreciate this art. Georgia. He imagined giving it to her and smiled. She'd put up a fuss and then secretly cherish it. It was perfect for her and her dream of owning a cottage-style house someday. He wanted her to have this. He wanted her to have it and many others like it. With him. The idea of that rocked him so much it shook him. How good it felt.

Getting up, he left the office and stopped at Abby's

desk. "Could you please look in my office for some papers on the ceramic bowl that's on my desk? Anything you can find that will provide proof of its worth and heritage."

"Of course." Abby stood.

From there, he headed back down to the SCIF and badged through the door. A security administrator got up from her desk.

"Can I help you, Mr. Adair?"

"Just here to pick up something from the SIPRNet."

She made sure he signed in before going into the room where the secure computer systems could be accessed.

He went to a computer terminal and logged in. Finding the email from Copeland, he opened it and began to read.

Stephen Chow lived in Albuquerque before moving to California. In Albuquerque, he worked for a technology company unrelated to nuclear, but he had a girlfriend who was a physicist at Hendricks Laboratory, renowned for its cutting-edge, top-secret weapons research. It was believed that was where he obtained the information he tried to sell to the North Koreans. He had been married and had a daughter. The affair with the physicist must have ended that. The ex and the daughter now lived in Kansas City, Missouri. As a child, he grew up in the slums of New York and, judging from his arrest record, belonged to a gang. Assault. Resisting arrest. Theft. He'd done a year in prison and got out on parole. There were photos of him from previous investigations involving drugs and gun sales. Another file told all about one of his close friends, a drug dealer who was shot and killed two years ago during a raid.

There was nothing in the files that revealed any association with terrorism or anyone from North Korea.

Carson wondered if going to talk to his ex-wife would be worthwhile. Police must have talked to her already, but had they asked her about his taste for terrorism?

Picking up a small photo of Stephen, he studied the man's face. His light brown hair was trimmed short and feathered to the sides from a middle part. Dark brown eyes held no emotion, no humanity. He read in the file that he was six feet tall and a hundred-ninety pounds. Trained in martial arts. He could probably use a gun. When he'd seen him in Myanmar, he'd worn a scarf over half his face.

Carson flipped the photo over and put it on the desk so that he could write Stephen's San Diego address and his ex-wife's address there. When he finished that, he put the photo into his wallet.

Hearing the door open behind him, he quickly minimized the screen showing the last of the information he'd read and turned his head. The security administrator stood there.

"Sorry to interrupt, Mr. Adair. Security is in the lobby asking for you."

Chapter 10

Carson reached the lobby to find four security guards surrounding a young boy of about thirteen sitting on a chair. One of the guards saw him and took him aside.

"He claims a man paid him to come in here and deliver this."

Carson took a sealed envelope from him. "Get a plastic bag or something"

The guard went to do as he was asked while Carson opened the envelope and took out a piece of paper. He read the note. Just two lines: *I'm going to kill you for ruining my plans. If you care about the woman, you'll back off.*

The last threat angered Carson. Why involve Georgia? She hadn't done anything. She was a defenseless bystander, her only fault, if one could call it a fault, was being seen with him. That made him more determined than ever to get Stephen. The guard returned with a clear storage bag, and Carson carefully slipped the note and envelope inside.

"Don't touch these and don't let anyone else touch them." He handed the bag to the guard. "Have you called police?"

"Yes, sir." As soon as the man answered, Carson heard the sirens.

"Give that to them."

"Yes, sir."

Carson approached the boy, who looked scared out of his mind. He had light gray eyes and thick black hair that needed a good cutting. Carson knelt before him.

"What's your name?" he asked.

"He said his name is Rubin Gonzales," one of the guards said.

Carson looked up at him and the others. "Thanks for taking care of this. Would you mind giving us some space? The police will be here any minute."

The guards backed away, albeit slowly and reluctantly. Clearly, they would rather stay and listen.

Carson faced the boy. "I'm Carson. I hear someone paid you to deliver a note to me."

The boy looked toward the front doors as though contemplating making a run for it before the cops came.

"You're not in any trouble," Carson said.

The boy turned back to him.

"What you did isn't illegal. All I need to know is who paid you."

"He didn't tell me his name." The boy opened his damp palm to reveal a hundred-dollar bill crumpled there. "He just handed me this and an envelope and said the money was mine if I took the envelope in here and gave it to the security guards inside."

"Where were you headed?"

"Home. My mom and I live in an apartment near here."

The apartments near here were pretty upscale. "Your mom must do pretty well for herself."

"She's a lawyer."

"Are you going to be a lawyer someday?" As he talked, Carson retrieved his wallet and removed the photo of Stephen Chow.

The boy made a face. "No way. I want to be a vet."

"You like animals, huh?"

"Dogs. We can't have any in our apartment."

"Yeah, that makes it hard." Carson showed the boy the photo. "Is this the man who paid you?"

The boy looked at the photo as Carson saw police appear outside the door, lights flashing as their cars came to a stop in the parking lot.

"Maybe," the boy said. "He wore a hat and a hood and sunglasses. But that looks like him." The boy pointed to the photo where the man's chin was.

"His face looks the same?" Carson asked, to be sure.

"Yeah. Who is he?"

Carson straightened. "I'm going to give you some advice, Rubin. Don't talk to strangers and don't take money from them if you don't know what they're paying you for. You could get yourself into a lot of trouble, maybe even get yourself hurt."

"Yeah. I'm sorry. I told the guards I was sorry, too."

The police entered the building, and Carson stepped back as they surrounded the boy and the guard with the envelope handed it over to an officer. Another officer came over to him just as he spotted Georgia enter the building, looking chic and sexy in a white shirt, flaring beige jacket with toggled black buttons and a black circle skirt with thigh-high boots. She had been out there and Stephen might be watching. No. He was being paranoid now. Stephen was long gone. He'd delivered his warning.

Seeing Georgia wait near the door, he answered the policeman's questions and walked over to her.

"What happened?" she asked.

He told her about the boy and the message as they went outside. He searched all around for any sign of Stephen and saw none. Waving away the limo driver, he asked a valet attendant to bring him a corporate car.

"What are we doing?" Georgia's gaze drifted from his face on down his body. When she was looking in the vicinity of his waist, her eyes popped round and her lips parted with a soft inhalation.

He looked down and saw his gun—a big gun. His suit jacket had blown open in the breeze to reveal it tucked into a discreet holster. One thing he'd taken home from the military was a detailed knowledge of weapons, and extensive experience in using them. This one was his favorite. The M45 MEU(SOC) was a modified Colt 1911.

Her eyes lifted. "What are you going to do with that?"

"Hopefully nothing," he said.

The valet attendant drove up with a Mercedes sedan. A little flashy but they'd blend in better than they would in a limo. Taking the keys from the attendant, he opened the passenger door for Georgia. Closing the door after she was inside, he went around to the driver's side.

"How long have you been carrying a gun?" She seemed to recover from seeing the weapon and realize it wasn't all that shocking. He was trained to use this pistol.

"Ever since someone shot at me." He caught sight of her legs. The dress had hiked up above her knees and showed off the slender beauties.

"North Carolina?"

"I picked one up on my way to see my commander." That had spared him from having to deal with security at the airport.

After entering Stephen Chow's address into the GPS, he started driving.

"Where are we going?" she asked.

How much should he tell her? He'd just left a SCIF where he'd learned all about his top-secret enemy.

"My commander gave me a lead," he finally said.

"More secret ops details you can't tell me about?"

"He gave me a name." She may as well know. "Stephen Chow." He could tell her that much.

She paused. "So…we're going to go get him?"

"We're going to watch him. See what he's up to, see if he's into any terrorist activity."

After a while, she asked, "Isn't that dangerous?"

He looked over at her, sexy as hell with her beautiful, inquisitive eyes and exposed knees. "For him, yes."

Georgia couldn't stop looking at Carson across the table from her. He was in a sleek dark suit, his buzz cut giving him a clean look. James Bond, only better. More personality filling the suit. They had come to this café to watch for the man named Stephen. Surveillance. Dangerous surveillance.

For him, yes…

He'd said that with such powerful conviction earlier

that she was wet with desire. His Special Ops expertise fascinated her. But why should seeing him armed with a gun be so erotic? It was strapped so neatly to his torso as though it belonged there and had been there many times before, as though the gun were part of him. And wasn't it? He'd worked Special Ops in the military. He'd used weapons of many kinds and was probably good.

Carson turned from the window and sipped his coffee. "He's leaving."

"Really?" She looked out the window, only to earn a playfully reproachful look from him for being too obvious. "Oops." She was no covert operative.

"Let's go." He dropped more than enough cash for their coffee, and she followed him out the door.

When he took her hand, she didn't protest. He put on his sunglasses, and she knew he was looking only with his eyes for the other man. A car drove into the street. Carson let her in the passenger side of the Mercedes and got behind the wheel. She lost sight of the car that Stephen must have gotten into, but Carson hadn't.

He made a turn, slowed and then sped up. He was keeping careful distance. Stephen drove onto a residential street that led to some big lots. These were very nice houses on the southern edge of the city.

Cresting a hill, Georgia saw the other car turn in to a driveway.

Carson pulled to the side of the road. There were lots of palm trees here, but nothing blocked their view. She saw the car come to a stop in front of a stone home with panels of windows filling the front. She could see a wraparound porch and the ocean in the distance. The house wasn't on the beach, but one would have an easy walk there.

The man got out and looked around but not very observantly.

"Aren't you worried he'll see you?" she asked.

"He hasn't yet, which tells me he isn't expecting me." He took out his gun and did something to it, readied it to fire. "Do you want to wait here?"

He was giving her the option? Not knowing where he was or what was going on was scarier to her than going with him to face whatever peril he'd cause. Besides, she was safe with this soldier.

"What are you going to do?"

He typed in the address of the house into a text message and sent it to someone, his commander. Georgia could see the screen from here. Copeland, it said.

"Ask him why he's been shooting at me." He was so cavalier that it eased her fear some.

She got out of the car. He walked over to her. "I'm a little concerned over your shoes."

She had on some three-inch boots. "They're fine. I can run in them if I have to."

Hearing a car, she turned with him to see Stephen leaving already.

Carson slipped his arm around her waist and brought her snug against him. "Make it look good."

They stood in front of the neighboring house, the Mercedes parked just ahead of the driveway. That's all she had time to notice before Carson kissed her.

She put one hand on the back of his neck and left the other on his muscular shoulder, right on the ball of it. She could feel the sinew move as he ran his hand up her back. Fiery tingles attacked her abdomen and in a split second she was hurled into oblivious passion. The invitation to make it look good lowered her defenses.

This was okay because it was acting. She gave her all to this kiss.

When Carson finally lifted his head, he was breathing faster and his eyes were hooded with desire.

"Where is he?" she asked, just as breathless.

"I don't know."

She smiled and then he released her. While he jogged around to the driver's side, she got in. Revving the Mercedes, he raced down the street. She looked over at him as he maneuvered the car in and out of traffic, the swerves smooth and sure, his face hard with concentration, his hand on the wheel firm but not tight. His legs were slightly open. She still felt his lips on hers.

Over the next hill, Georgia saw Stephen's car turn for the freeway. Carson slowed the Mercedes and kept a discreet distance again.

A few minutes later, after more glances at Carson and a body that wouldn't cool down, she noticed the car ahead took an exit. Georgia saw a strip mall with only one shop open, the rest of the units empty. A closed restaurant. A vacant office building. Weeds grew up from the cracks in the parking lot. This was a bad part of town.

Carson turned onto a narrow, poorly maintained street, veering around a deep pothole. She didn't see the car ahead.

"Where did he go?" she asked.

"He turned in to an abandoned warehouse lot a few blocks back."

She twisted to see where that would be. The warehouse must be on the opposite side of the street.

Turning around, Carson drove toward the warehouse, pulling to the side of the street a block from there. Georgia could see it now. It looked much like the strip mall and office building. Abandoned.

Carson backed the Mercedes up and drove down an alley that ran along the edge of the warehouse parking lot. Trees and a six-foot chain-link fence divided the lot from the alley. At the end of the lot, another alley, this one gravel, ran along the back. Backyards and garages and sheds lined the opposite side. Carson pulled in front of one of the garages, backing in so they faced the warehouse.

Someone had opened a tall, double-wide overhead door, and two men stood there talking. Stephen's car was parked in front of the building beside another one. There was an SUV on the other side of the big door.

"Which one is Stephen?" she asked.

"The man with light brown hair. The taller one."

The other man with him wasn't that much shorter, but his stomach was fatter and he was going bald.

A delivery truck with no markings on the sides drove into the empty parking lot. Four more men appeared from inside the warehouse. She watched with Carson as the truck backed up to the open garage door. The driver got out, and Stephen and the fat man met him. They carried on a discussion.

The driver of the truck reached into the truck and came out with a backpack. He handed that to Stephen, who unzipped the top and inspected the contents. When he nodded, the fat man waved to the four standing in the open door. They went to work after the driver opened the back of his truck.

Georgia watched with Carson as crates were loaded into the truck.

"Drug dealing?" Carson said.

"What were you expecting? A nuclear warhead?"

He glanced over at her with a wry smirk. "My commander said Stephen Chow did jail time for drugs. If he's after the data he was supposed to deliver in Myanmar, I'd think he'd be busy trying to get it back."

He'd just told her something he probably shouldn't have.

When he looked at her again, she saw him realize that. "Talking to you is too easy."

She was beginning to feel that way, too, as if she could say anything to him and it would be okay. "Just don't tell me what the data is."

"That'd be treason for sure." He grinned.

"Your secrets are safe with me." She half hoped he'd tell her.

He didn't. Instead, he started taking pictures with his cell phone.

A half hour later, the driver of the truck slid closed the back door, and the four men disappeared inside the warehouse. Stephen waited until the truck was driving away before slinging the backpack over his shoulder. The bald man went inside the warehouse.

Stephen was about to do the same when he saw them.

Georgia went stiff with tension. *Had* he seen them? They were about forty yards away and there were trees along the chain-link fence, not thick enough to hide them, though.

"This Mercedes sticks out like a sore thumb," Carson said.

"Can he see us?"

"Yes, but probably not *who* we are."

"He could take an educated guess." Mercedes. Who else would be driving that?

Carson drove away from the garage, turning to go back down the alley. Stephen watched them until they turned toward the main road. Then he walked into the warehouse.

At the main street, Georgia saw that the truck was just now turning into traffic, which was heavy and backed up from two stoplights a block apart. Carson drove up behind the truck, a few cars back.

They followed the truck onto the freeway and up to the next exit. This neighborhood was much nicer than the last. The houses were around three- to four- thousand square feet and had neatly trimmed lawns and luxury vehicles in driveways.

"He makes a good living selling drugs," Georgia said.

Carson backed into an empty driveway where it looked as if the occupants were away at work. From here they had a good view of the truck driver's house. Two other men came out of the inner door of the three-car garage and began to unload the crates. The third stall was left closed, and that's where they stored the crates.

"What's he going to do? Sell it out of his house?" Georgia asked, and then she saw Carson using his phone, looking up the address.

"It's on the market."

Georgia looked toward the house. "Does he have a real estate license?"

"If he does, I have his name now."

His name would be listed with the posting.

"This is going to happen quickly," Carson said. "Unless the owners already moved."

"The house must be empty unless he arranged a showing," Georgia said.

A van appeared at the house, one of those tall, windowless white vans. It backed into the driveway and four crates were loaded onto it. Money exchanged hands. Carson got it all on video using his phone.

Over the next two hours, three more vehicles showed up, and then the sale must have been complete, because the driver of the truck paid the other two men and then everyone drove off.

Carson followed the truck again. The truck driver stopped at a storage facility, where he dumped the truck and got into a BMW SUV and left. Forty-five minutes later, they arrived at a beachfront condominium complex with a cut roofline and white pillars.

Carson parked and watched the man climb some stairs to an upper-level unit. Then he turned to her. "You might want to wait here. This could get messy." He worked with his phone, getting the recording ready. He was going to use it to make the man talk.

Georgia looked around. What if Stephen arrived and saw her alone? "I'd feel safer if I went with you."

He didn't argue. Together, they walked up to the door of the man's condo. After a couple of minutes, the door opened.

"Tyler Jones?" Carson asked.

The man looked from him to Georgia with a low brow that creased the skin above his nose.

Carson held up his phone after starting the video of the drug deal going down.

The man watched for only a few seconds and then turned to Carson.

"We have something to discuss," Carson said, parting his jacket to show him his gun. "Are you alone?"

Tyler reluctantly opened the door wider. "Who the hell are you?"

Carson stepped inside, and Georgia went in after him. He stopped and guided her to stand next to him and in front of a wall, away from windows or doors. The whole wall facing the beach was nothing but windows, but inside the open living room, an arched hall led to bedrooms, and the kitchen was adjacent to the far side of the living room. All the walls were white and there was very little adorning them. Big trim, high ceilings, dark furniture and plenty of light were enough.

"Someone who's going to turn this over to police if you don't tell me about your business with Stephen Chow."

Tyler met his look for several seconds. He wore dark green slacks with a white polo shirt. "You saw my business with him."

"What do you know about him?"

He gave off a sarcastic frown and spread his hands wide. "I buy from him."

"How did you meet him?"

"We hang out at the same club." He told them the name. "He goes there after every big deal. He's probably there now."

"Has he ever talked about his interest in North Korea?"

That lifted Tyler's brow. "What kind of an interest?"

"Technology. Nuclear."

Tyler whistled with mock awe. "Stephen?" He chuckled. "He's a little weird but…nukes?" He chuckled some more. "He ain't that smart."

"Why do you say he's weird?" Georgia asked.

He looked at her and shrugged. "He's all into politics, always talking about how this country is failing and nobody's doing anything about it. It's more than an opinion, you know. He's obsessed. The guy's delusional."

He turned to Carson. "That why you're after him? He do something against the country?" Tyler laughed, a gravelly sound. "Plan a bombing or something?"

Neither she nor Carson returned his humor.

"What happened with his job in Albuquerque?" Carson asked.

Georgia looked at him. What job?

"I didn't know him then. My business with him is recent. He did mention he quit some technology company where he was a janitor and then moved here."

"Do you know why he moved here?"

Tyler cocked his head. Stupid question. Southern California. Drug trade.

Stephen hadn't talked about the data. Tyler wouldn't be able to help Carson. They left him calling after them, asking, "What are you gonna do with that video?"

Two Peaks wasn't a strip club, but the cocktail waitresses barely wore any clothes. Carson noticed Georgia's shock as they entered and found a table. It didn't take long for him to spot Stephen. He sat with two women with dipping necklines. They smiled, one with a drink in her hand and the other on his lap with a hand on his chest. He was talking to another man at the table, who was with another woman. She wasn't making a spectacle of herself.

"Wait here," he told Georgia.

"And have one of these hoodlums hit on me?" She got up from the chair. "No, thanks."

Carson put his hand on her lower back, more of a message to say that they better not hit on her.

Stephen saw him approaching, and instant recognition flattened his smile. He lifted the girl on his lap and put her on her feet. Then he gave both women an order that had them withdrawing and leaving the table.

His friend looked back but remained seated. That told Carson he was an important player in Stephen's dealings. He did say something softly to his woman, who kissed him and got up and left.

Carson stopped at the table. Stephen looked at Georgia beside him and then returned his gaze to Carson.

"It was you I saw today, wasn't it?" Stephen asked.

"What did you expect?" Carson wasn't the type to lie down and let things roll over him.

Stephen made a show of searching the bar. "Where's the rest of your SWAT team?" Then he tipped his head up with a drawn-out "Oh," and said, "That's right. One of them died."

Stephen had killed him. Carson held on to his cool.

"I could have had you arrested," Carson said.

"Well, why didn't you?" He lifted a drink and sipped, shrewd eyes on him. His friend stood from the table. He was a big man, about three inches taller than Carson. Problem was, he stood too close to Georgia. She sidled next to him as though uncomfortable.

Carson turned his head. "I suggest you step back."

"Or what?"

"Or I'll make it the last step you make for a long time." He'd break his leg.

The goon grinned lopsidedly, overestimating his brawn.

Stephen watched the exchange and then held his hand up, telling the man to stand down. "Mr. Adair here is ex–Special Ops. He's a big-shot MARSOC soldier. Don't upset him, Lucky."

Lucky didn't like being told to back off, but he did. Folding his arms, he took a step away.

"Now that everyone's place is established, why are you here?" Stephen asked.

"Someone shot at me in the parking garage of my company."

"Oh? Too bad they missed."

"And again outside of Frederick's restaurant."

"Missed again."

Carson waited for him to take this seriously. The length of time he took almost made him wonder if he hadn't caught on.

Then Stephen's eyebrows lifted and he pointed his fingers toward his chest. "You think *I'm* trying to kill you?"

He was playing ignorant. And why wouldn't he?

Stephen lowered his hands at that, calculation hiding whatever he was thinking. "Why are you here? You got what you were after in Myanmar."

Carson said nothing.

As Stephen watched his face, he began to realize the answer to his own question. "You don't have the data."

Still, Carson said nothing. Nether of them had the data.

"If I don't have it, why would I try to kill you?" Stephen asked.

"Revenge."

Stephen nodded. "I did want your head on a stake after that. You cost me a lot of money. My friends don't want to work with me anymore because of you."

There was a motive. Stephen had just handed it to him.

"You have to resort to drug dealing?" Carson took out his phone and showed him one of the photos.

"What are you going to do with that?"

"I haven't decided. Maybe it would help if you tell me what happened in Myanmar. What happened with the data you had?"

Stephen stared at him for a long moment. "I told you. I don't have it. And I'm not trying to kill you. If I were, you'd have been dead already. I would have killed you when I had the chance. Maybe in Myanmar along with your friend. I heard that you two were close."

"Who told you that?"

When Stephen only smiled evilly, Carson surmised it must have been the media. There had been a fair amount of coverage after he'd been injured in North Korea. News that one of his teammates had been killed had leaked out.

"You wasted your time coming here."

Carson didn't agree. "I came here to warn you."

After a deep laugh, Stephen said, "I'm scared."

He should be. But he wasn't thinking yet. Carson helped him out. "You're going to be arrested. And when you are, they'll ask you what I just did, only they won't listen to *I don't have it*. And after you tell them everything they want to know, you'll be sent to prison."

Traitor.

That wiped the smile off Stephen's face. If Carson knew where he was, so did the government. Would he try to kill Carson again? Would he run? He wouldn't get far because after today, Copeland would have Ops all over him.

Seeing Stephen's hand tighten on the glass he held on the table, Carson smiled, satisfied that he finally understood the predicament he was in. Satisfied, too, that he'd have some time to find the missing data. The only question was where would he start looking?

Chapter 11

Carson had to go in to work again today. Georgia had spent the morning reading. This had a surprisingly normal feel to it. Other than her opulent surroundings, she could be in suburbia somewhere and be utterly happy. The only thing that had ruined it was the message from Drake.

He had texted her to let her know he had arrived in San Diego for his business meeting and would be here for a few days. He'd also asked if she would be available to meet him for coffee. He'd said she didn't have to respond, just show up at three if she felt comfortable doing so. He'd also said not to feel obligated to meet him.

Making peace with what had happened did appeal to her, and this felt like a good opportunity to do that. She didn't have to bring him back into her life again. They could just talk, and she could let him explain why he'd done what he'd done. She did need to know that. She should just let him and then put the past to rest. Move on. Wherever that led her.

Those thoughts were what had brought her downtown to the hotel lobby where he'd told her he'd be for one hour. If she showed up, they'd walk to a nearby café for coffee.

Georgia entered the hotel lobby and spotted him right away. He sat on a chair in one of three seating areas, reading the paper.

Seeing her, he put the paper down and stood, smiling the way he used to, which put her at ease.

"Georgia." He stepped toward her and reached for her hands. "Thank you for coming." He leaned back to look at her. "Stunning as usual."

She'd worn a white shirt with crocheted bodice and sleeves with jeans and a tan floppy hat today. Turquoise loop earrings and a turquoise ring added just the right pop. Carson would have looked at her like that, too, only his look would have been much more appreciative and with a hint of amusement and affection. With Drake, it was pure animal attraction. She was a sex object when he liked how she looked. With Carson, it was the whole package. Her. Inside and out.

"Thank you," she murmured, not really meaning it. She didn't like feeling like a sex object.

"No, thank you, Georgia. I'm so glad you came. Let's take a walk."

As long as she stayed in public with him, she saw no risk. She slipped her hands free of his and preceded him out the door. It wasn't as if she'd go to his room with him. No.

The street was busy. People filled the sidewalks and cars clogged the street.

"I know I already apologized, but I still feel like more needs to be said. At least, that's the impression I get."

"Yes," she said. "That's why I came today."

The hint of a smile and softening of his eyes said he was glad. And hopeful. She recoiled against any hope he might have.

Their feet tapped the concrete sidewalk and other people passed them going the other way. Georgia sensed him working up to talking about a difficult topic. It was difficult. But it needed to be said.

"I should have known I'd shock you," he started out by saying.

"*Terrify* is a better word." She didn't go light on him.

He slowed to a stop, and she did the same. Then he faced her. "I'm so sorry about that."

"Why did you do it?"

"It's just…how I like it. I don't hurt anyone. Usually they're willing and enjoy it."

S-M? She subdued her frown of distaste.

"I should have known you wouldn't like it. That it would scare you. I just… You're just…you're the best friend I've ever had. You're important to me, Georgia."

The last of what he said didn't ring true. She didn't know why. Georgia started walking again. She wasn't comfortable being close to him anymore.

He walked beside her. "I know it won't be the way it was before."

How much else didn't she know about him? His sexual preferences were so far off what she'd assumed, she felt certain there was much more he kept hidden. And it all stemmed from the way he was raised.

"You didn't tell me about your childhood," she said. "Not everything."

He grunted. "Who'd want to talk about that? I wish I was from a different family. They embarrass me."

"You should have told me how you felt."

"Exactly why I called to apologize and why I asked you to meet me today. I should have told you a lot of things. I was afraid of scaring you away." He grunted derisively. "Guess I ended up doing that anyway."

She was glad he'd admitted that, but she still had reservations over how thoroughly fooled he'd had her.

He opened the café door for her and she was relieved to see it was busy here, too. He was making a real effort. The old Drake was coming out and working hard to earn her forgiveness. But there was something…off.

She walked inside and followed a hostess to a table near the front window. Sitting across from Drake, she listened as he reminisced on old times, not feeling the same as she had back then. Now she saw him as he really was, a man with a troubled past that made him more apathetic than she'd have ever imagined.

He watched her, looking at her mouth and into her eyes with a sorrowful kind of yearning.

Her uneasiness intensified. She hadn't felt totally relaxed since she saw him.

"Part of the reason I was the way I was with you is that I fell so hard for you, Georgia. I didn't expect to. I lost control."

He must have felt that way about her long before they'd decided to try dating.

"You're the most amazing woman I've ever met," he

said. "No one compares to you. It would be worth it to me to change so I could have you. Marry you, maybe. We could be so happy. We could."

What?

Coldness spread through her. Was he insane? Was she for coming here?

"Don't decide now," he said when he saw her revulsion. "Let's take it slow. I love you, Georgia. I think I've loved you ever since college."

Loved her?

Georgia fought back her nausea. "I don't love you, Drake. I told you that night was a mistake." A terrible, terrible mistake. She stood up. It was time to be stern with him. "I want you to leave me alone."

He obviously would never be able to look at her as a friend again. She shouldn't have come here. She should have known that he was too different from her. He wasn't going to let her go and she couldn't shake this feeling that he wasn't going to take it well.

At his crumbling face looking up at her from where he sat, she said, "I'm sorry I met you today. I don't mean to hurt you, but I don't think it's wise to talk to you anymore. Please don't call me or try to come and see me. It's over between us. We can't be friends anymore. I want to part ways amicably. That's why I came here. But if you can't do that…"

"Georgia." He stood with her.

"No, Drake. I've been patient with you until now. You haven't listened to me. Just leave me alone." She knew Drake wasn't the one for her. Especially after meeting a man like Carson. She deserved someone like him, minus the money. Or did that matter anymore?

Thinking of Carson, none of that seemed important. Which kind of frightened her.

"So this is it? You're not even going to give me a chance?"

"A chance for what?" He'd had his chance. He'd blown it.

"To make amends. To give us a real try, Georgia. We're good together."

Georgia rolled her eyes. "I have to go." What a disappointment. She'd mourn the loss of her college friend all over again, but it was not healthy to subject herself to him anymore. She started for the door.

Outside, he took her arm and swung her around. "I know all about the Adairs, Georgia. You told me, remember?"

What was he talking about? Why was he suddenly bringing up the Adairs?

"I also know Carson Adair is back from the Marines and quite available. You've always said you would never be with anyone like Reginald, rich and cruel. You saw what it did to Ruby."

"Yes, that's all true." She jerked her arm free. She couldn't argue that, but even as she said it, something in her rebelled. It didn't feel true anymore. Not the wealth part. Reginald, yes, but some wealthy people were good.

"I came here to stop you from making a mistake."

Like the one she made with him? And was he saying he'd lied to her? All that bull about only wanting to be friends had been a lie. He wanted her for more than that and it made her sick to her stomach.

"How did you know I was in danger of making a *mistake*, as you call it?" She marched down the street toward the hotel and the limo.

He walked beside her. "It was a hunch at first. Then I saw you with him."

"Carson?" She was taken aback. Stopping, she faced him. "When did you see us together?"

"Outside his company." He breathed in exasperation. "You and I are meant for each other, Georgia. I know I was too aggressive with you. I've been wanting intimacy with you for so long I guess the degree of my desire got away from me and I got careless."

Did he think he had to plan how he treated her? With bile rising in her throat, she walked as fast as she could toward the hotel.

Why had he gone to AdAir Corp? He must have gone there when he'd arrived in San Diego, determined to talk to her in person. To make amends.

"Georgia." He caught up to her.

"I'm going to call the police if you don't leave me alone!" she said without stopping.

"What?" He took ahold of her arm again.

"Hey." She protested against his grip.

Easing up, he pulled her gently to a stop. She was forced to look into his eyes, which were sincere. Or was he putting on a mask?

"It's me," he said.

She searched his face, not seeing the man she used to know, the one who'd been such a good friend. Now he was just desperate. She could think of no other word to describe him. Had he hidden that from her all these years?

"Who are you?" She didn't know anymore.

He blinked with a stab that delivered, and she felt him tighten his hand on her arm.

"I won't let you do this to us," he said.

"You won't *let me*?" she scoffed. "Let me do what?"

"Ruin us by letting that bastard take you from me."

"You can't make decisions for me. This is my life and you don't control it." She pulled her arm, but he wouldn't release his grip, which became painful. "You're hurting me." She pulled harder.

When he hauled her toward an alley, she saw a car parked there and began to panic.

"Drake, let me go." With her free hand she dug into her purse for her phone. She took it out as Drake opened the passenger door. "What are you doing?"

"Taking you home."

Georgia yanked hard and freed her arm. She began to call for help, when he knocked the phone from her grasp. It clattered to the ground.

"You're crazy."

Then she saw a man approach behind him, an uneven gait that she recognized. Carson.

Carson clamped a hand on Drake's shoulder and swung him around. Then he punched him with his other, square in the face. Drake grunted and stumbled backward, but then he charged forward.

Carson easily ducked a punch and then swung his leg around in a side kick that connected with Drake's head, sending him falling onto the pavement. From there, Drake stared up at him, disbelieving that Carson could fight so well. He was a trained soldier. A human weapon.

How could she be attracted to him at a time like this? Scared. Ready to run for her life.

Standing over Drake, Carson pointed his finger down at him. "Stay away from her."

With a trembling hand, Georgia knelt to pick up

her phone. Drake wiped blood from his lip as he watched her.

"I'm going to get a restraining order," she told him.

"Georgia." He started to stand. Carson planted his foot against his sternum and kicked him back down.

"Leave her alone or you'll have more than a restraining order to worry about," Carson said. Then he reached for Georgia, sliding his hand to the small of her back and guiding her down the alley.

Georgia glanced back to see Drake still on the ground, sitting up and watching them go, his brow low. She felt his anger.

It was several moments before Georgia could calm her nerves. That's when it struck her as odd that Carson was there.

"How did you know where I was?" And to come after her?

His limo pulled up alongside the curb.

"With everything going on, I asked the driver to tell me if you went anywhere. He called me when he dropped you off. I was worried so I had someone drive me here."

He'd known she was safe at the ranch, but if she left, Stephen could go after her. He hadn't anticipated an ex-boyfriend would be the one to threaten her.

"Why did you meet him?" Carson asked. "He's the guy you were with in Florida right?"

"I thought he wanted to make amends," she said. "I was wrong."

Really wrong.

Carson waited until he had Georgia home and comfortably sipping a fruity cocktail in a sunroom that had views of the ranch land before bringing up Drake. He had a lot of questions and he hadn't pressed her in the limo because she was still so shaken up.

She'd changed into dark tan leggings and a silky taupe shirt that fell below her waist, a taupe belt with dark tan buckle hanging loosely and leather riding boots. It was a cloudless day and the sun beamed low in the sky. He sat on the chair beside her and put his feet up the way she had hers, amused over how she basked in the sight of horses grazing in the setting sun.

"It's so beautiful here," she said.

"All that money can buy," he teased, grinning when she turned a scolding look his way, one that was tempered with twitching corners of her mouth. "You like it. Admit it."

"It is nice. But it isn't all there is to life."

Of course not. He'd break her of that if it killed him. In time she'd get to know him enough to realize that. In time…

More and more he was thinking that way with her. As if she'd be around indefinitely. Did he want that? With everything else going on, it might get complicated. The idea of seeing her romantically wasn't disagreeable. Only the timing was. And her bias over rich people. She was too judgmental. *That* he didn't like. He had fun with her over it, but deep down, he didn't think highly of her poorly informed opinion.

"Why did you meet Drake, Georgia?"

She looked at him unappreciatively.

"You were friends. I get that. And his background checks out. But you must have known there was something wrong with him. Why did you risk it?"

Her brow furrowed. "Background check."

Whoops. He'd let that slip. "I asked Whit to run one on him."

"Why did you do that?"

"I got the impression you were a little afraid of him."

When her brow smoothed and she looked out across the pasture, he knew he was right. She was afraid. And something had caused that fear. After they were friends. Long after, like maybe when they had become intimate.

"What changed after you slept with him?" he asked.

She looked over at him for a while, turmoil storming in her eyes. Standing, she walked out of the sunroom.

Why was she so upset over it?

Carson followed her. She left the ranch house and walked toward some outbuildings. Carson caught up to her and led her to the stable, where he asked one of the workers there to saddle up a couple of horses.

"You don't have to do this," she said.

She'd walked aimlessly from the sunroom and he'd guided her here. The way she'd looked at the horses gave him this idea. If he could get her comfortable enough with him, maybe she'd tell him about Drake. His need to know disturbed him a little. He cared too much. Or did he? He wished he was clearer on where his future was headed. He felt as though he were on a runaway train. Would he end up wrecking or stopping right where he was meant to be?

The stable hand gave him the reins of a docile quarter horse. "Have you ever ridden one of these?"

"Uh…yes. A few times." She took the reins.

"Then let me show you something." Taking the reins of a bigger horse, he climbed onto its back and rode out of the stable.

Glancing back, he saw Georgia following.

When she caught up to him, he sped up the pace into a smooth canter.

"What are you going to show me?" she asked with a loud enough voice for him to hear.

"You'll see."

"Where are we going?"

"Not far."

They reached some trees, and he slowed his horse to a walk. Moments later, he spotted what he was looking for. He pointed for Georgia.

"See that?"

She looked to where he indicated and, impressed, drew in a breath. It was a sizable tree house, one with lots of amenities. Suspended by support hardware in four large trees, there was a wraparound deck and a Jacuzzi underneath. A spiral stairway wound its way up one side of the tree house.

He got off his horse and Georgia got off hers.

"Wow," she said. "This is incredible!"

"It was featured on a home-and-garden show a few years ago. Not just for kids."

He led her over the drawbridge that took them from the top of a hill to the deck of the tree house. She was awed in a magical way. He held back a chuckle. She sure liked what money could buy.

He opened the door to the tree house and let her in. Although simply furnished, there was everything a person would need, including a queen bed, seating area and kitchenette. It was decorated like a cottage, white and color giving it a *pow*.

Georgia went over to the bench seat in a window with a view of the rolling landscape and sat.

He went there and sat next to her, on an angle like her.

"This is so beautiful. Did you play here?"

"It wasn't made for kids. But, yes, I've played here."
She looked at him and smiled.

"What did Drake do to you?" he asked, regretting
that it swept her smile away.

"It's too personal, Carson."

"I'm worried that it has something to do with why
he's here and why he came after you."

"He had a business meeting in San Diego. He comes
here a lot."

"All right, but he planned to meet with you, too.
Please, Georgia, tell me what happened."

After several seconds, she relented. "We started
to have a serious relationship. His...tastes were too...
shocking for me. And afterward, he showed a side of
him that made me nervous."

"For good reason. Did he force himself on you?"

"No. I was willing. But not for the...you know...
things he did."

"Did you tell him to stop?"

"Yes, and he did, but then he convinced me to continue." She averted her head in shame.

"He was always such a smooth talker."

She hadn't felt right about it and yet she'd done it. Her
eyes misted. The experience had scared her.

"Why did you let him?"

Slowly, she turned her head back to him, wiping
a tear. "I trusted him. And I couldn't believe he was
someone so different than the man I'd known for so
many years."

"But he was."

She nodded her head, lowering it. "He was my friend
up until then. My best friend."

Carson felt himself fall for her even more. For such a strong woman, she had a soft, sensitive side that required tender care.

"He didn't understand when I broke up with him," she said.

"That's because there's something wrong with him." There had to be. She hadn't accepted it until today. She'd lost a friend and couldn't come to terms with the discovery that he wasn't who she thought he was.

She lifted her head, no longer about to cry. "I know that now."

Carson cupped her face and used his thumb to catch the tear. "You're safe now."

She looked into his eyes and blinked warmly, as though those words were the most welcome sweetness he could give her right now. He made her feel more than safe.

He ran his thumb over her soft skin.

The glow of their untamable, unpredictable attraction intensified. Cupping her face with both hands, he leaned forward to kiss her.

She breathed in with the instant ignition of passion they generated together. It awed him, how much he felt when he kissed her.

"Forget about him," he whispered.

"Keep kissing me and I will."

Sliding one hand behind her head and the other down to her waist, he angled his head and pressed for a deeper taste. Then, cradling her, he lifted her onto his lap. She wrapped her arm around his neck and put her other hand on his face.

The feel of her lips on his roused him to do more. Standing with her, he took her to the bed. They'd gotten this far before, but he felt her need and it was different than on the jet. This time he'd take it slow with her, excruciatingly slow.

First he sat with her on the bed, still cradling her. She looked up at him uncertainly and he kissed her back into a dreamland. When her eyes were hooded with pure desire, he kissed her once more. She wasn't ready for the bed.

"Let's go in the hot tub," he said.

He watched her realize they'd have to go naked. Not sure she'd do it, a rush of lust swamped him as she stood from his lap and went into the bathroom. He removed his shirt, shoes and socks as he waited for her to emerge.

When she did, she held one towel wrapped around her and held another in her hand that she extended to him. He stepped forward to take it but made no fuss over taking off his jeans. Her gaze lowered as he stepped out of them and his underwear and then wrapped the towel around his waist.

He was slightly bigger than average. Nothing ridiculous. Nothing so big that it would be painful, but big enough to be noticeable…and feel good. He was going to make her feel really good. If she let him go that far.

He descended the spiral stairway after her. At the bottom, his feet touched the cool concrete around the hot tub. He removed the cover and turned on the bubbles. Then he watched as Georgia removed her towel, revealing her curvy body. Carson couldn't help staring. Her breasts were large, high and firm. Those slender legs stepped into the hot tub and bubbles concealed her.

Now she watched him.

He released the towel from around his waist and stepped in, going to sit beside her. She had trouble meeting his eyes. She was uncomfortable. Was she thinking about Drake?

He reached for her. "Come here."

Floating in the water, she moved to him as he guided her gently and slowly onto his lap. Her knees straddled him. Bubbles came up around her breasts, hiding her nipples. She had her hands on his shoulders, and he felt her grip him tighter.

"Carson…"

When she began to withdraw, he locked his arms around her.

"Shh." He looked up at her face, so full of worry. "Kiss me, Georgia." He wanted her to do it.

She hesitated, her bad experience threatening to dim her passion.

"Kiss me," he said.

She looked down at her naked breasts, nipples hardened and brushing his chest, and then back up into his eyes.

"You're safe with me." Seeing how that washed over her and drained away her tension, Carson restrained his rising urge to put himself inside her.

She put her hands on his face and brought hers close. "I know," she whispered, and then kissed him.

The warm, wet kiss was made warmer and wetter with the steam coming off the surface of the hot tub. Georgia's breathing grew rapid and her kisses more demanding. Carson didn't give her more than she was willing to give. He let her set the pace. He just kept running his hands up and down her soft body, up her ribs to tease her breasts and then to her back and down again, to tease her butt and run down her thighs.

She began to move on him, a slow back-and-forth grind.

He couldn't hold back a groan. She kissed his mouth in response and whispered his name.

He had her trust, and it was a precious thing. But still, he held back, guiding her mouth and hips.

She found him herself, using his shoulders to brace herself and easing down, taking him into her. He tipped his head back, surrendering to the ecstasy. She kissed his mouth full on and began to move up and down. She started out slow and gradually heated things up. Carson fought back an explosive orgasm until she cried out hers. Then, at last, he could let go. With the sun setting and streaking the sky pink and orange, his world changed.

He became aware of her coming down to reality.

"Let's dry off and go up into the tree house," he said.

"Okay."

He climbed up first. They dried in silence. When she reached to put on her clothes, he stopped her by taking her hand.

"Wait," he said.

"We should get back."

"Why? Let's stay here tonight." He tugged her toward the bed. "I can have dinner brought here."

"But…"

"Ruby won't be surprised or worried. You're safe here. Everyone knows that." And she should, too.

She went with him to the bed, and he wondered if that was how it had been with Drake. He'd coaxed her and then she'd regretted it the next day. Well, she wasn't going to regret this.

He used his cell to have an Italian meal sent to them.

While they waited, he made love to her again. He kept it slow and gentle. Her orgasm was stronger than the first time.

He studied her when dinner arrived, and she picked at hers. She avoided looking at him.

"Georgia?"

She lifted her troubled eyes.

"What's wrong?"

"Nothing." She smiled.

She wasn't telling him. Something was wrong, but she'd decided to keep it to herself.

And he suspected he knew what it was about, and it wasn't Drake. This time it was him. Was she worried she'd make a mistake? Did she still think he was poison just for being an Adair?

After dinner was cleared away and they watched a movie with barely any words exchanged, Carson pretended to fall asleep with her next to him.

He felt her ease away around midnight. He'd expected this. He listened to her dress and leave the tree house by way of the spiral stairway. Getting up, he went out onto the patio. Lights outside the tree house revealed her jogging through the trees. He didn't call out to her. Just ached that she'd felt the need to run. Something must have made her slow and stop. She looked back and saw him, as though some invisible energy had told her he'd be there. She stared for several seconds. Was she undecided? Oh, yeah. She was confused. And that confusion made her turn and run out of sight.

Watching her run away should make him think twice about pursuing her, let his rebellion take over. Instead, it only made him burn for her more. She wasn't running from him. She was running from herself. And he intended to melt all of her barriers away. See what remained when he finally penetrated her fully. It could be something phenomenal. Or it could tear his heart out if she ran again.

Chapter 12

Georgia had a hard time looking at Carson without her imagination going back to the tree house. She was mystified over how easy it had been to become absorbed with him. That she'd told him something so personal. And then had sex with him. Incredible sex. It had obliterated Drake from her soul. For that she'd be forever grateful. But what was she getting herself into here? Love? The blooming of it. And the man. He enchanted her. She was beginning to feel that she couldn't get enough of him. But did she know him? Past experience had shown her that she lacked the ability to expose people for who they really were. She was too trusting. Didn't giving Drake another chance prove that? She'd let him talk her into meeting him and look where that had gotten her.

More than anything, Georgia feared that feeling so much for Carson was dangerous. That had her rather shaken as she made her way down to the kitchen at the ranch.

Ruby was there, sitting at an island on a stool having a chat with the cook, who'd made her breakfast, as evidenced by Ruby's now-empty plate.

"There you are," Ruby said when she saw her. "You slept late."

She'd stayed in her room to avoid Carson. "Hi." She leaned in for a cheek kiss.

"Can I get you anything?" the cook asked.

"No, thank you."

"I'll leave you two alone, then." The cook turned and left the kitchen.

"Were you with Carson last night?" Ruby asked with a mischievous smile.

Georgia went to the refrigerator for something to drink. Dread, regret and fear all knotted in her core.

"Uh-oh," Ruby said. "I know that look."

"It's nothing, Ruby."

"Huh. Normally you'd have called me Mom if you weren't upset."

When Georgia turned with water in her hand, she saw Ruby pat the stool next to her.

There was no getting away from it now. Georgia went to sit beside her.

"You slept with him, didn't you?" Ruby said.

Georgia could only look at her.

"Mom…" she started to say.

Ruby smiled at her use of that word. But it was a grim smile. "Reginald was a lot like Carson when he was that age."

Great. Just what she needed to hear.

"Fighting his parents. Wanting to get as far away from them as he could."

Yep. That was Carson.

"It ended up ruining him."

"Jackson is what ruined him," Georgia said.

"His parents were just awful to me, as you know. They never accepted me into the family. That took its toll on him. And me, of course."

"Why are you telling me this again?"

"Because I wonder if it's different now. I've had time to get acquainted with Reginald's kids. They've been nothing but gracious since I've been here."

"What are you saying? That everything you told me isn't true? You never wanted to see any Adair ever again. You said so."

"Yes. My heart was broken. It's been broken for nearly four decades. And I've been blind because of that." She put her hand over hers. "I'm sorry, Georgia. I fear I've jaded you and you weren't the one who had to live that hell."

What was she saying? That she had forgiven them? That she was ready to risk her heart again?

"You've been spending a lot of time with Hayden," Georgia said.

Ruby's face lit with joy. She looked so radiant. "I never dreamed I'd meet someone like that on this trip."

"Maybe you should slow it down a little. Like I just said, you've been spending a lot of time with him."

"Like you have with Carson?"

Georgia didn't remind her that it was her fault she was spending said time with Carson. But then, Ruby hadn't told her to take a leave of absence. And Ruby hadn't forced her to come here.

"Maybe it's time we left," Georgia said. Before both of their lives were turned upside down.

Ruby's glow dimmed. "I'd rather stay a bit longer. Carson might find out who took my Jackson."

Georgia heard the hope in Ruby's voice and felt a familiar protectiveness rear up. She didn't want to see her stepmother hurt.

"Carson may not be able to find him," she said.

"Yes, but he might."

"Ruby—"

"Now, Georgia, you stop. I don't want to leave yet. If you want to go, then go. You don't have to stay and watch over me."

Leave her here so she could continue to spend time with a rich man? "Why do you like the rancher?" she asked. "Is it his money?" Ruby met her gaze as she registered what Georgia asked, seeming a little taken aback.

"No. It's not his money. Money is nice, but it's the man, Georgia. Why do you think money has anything to do with it?"

"What about Reginald?"

"I loved Reginald. I also loved his pedigree, but I'm not that girl anymore." Ruby searched her face and eyes. "Do you think that because Carson is rich that he'll end up like Reginald? A bitter, heartless man?"

"I think it's a possibility."

"Ah." Ruby nodded. "And you don't want to risk it."

Georgia lowered her head, looking away.

"You've already taken the risk, Georgia. You slept with him. You opened your heart to him."

She shook her head. "No."

"I don't believe you for a second." Ruby leaned forward, squeezing her hand tighter. "Let go, Georgia. Stop protecting me. And stop projecting the bad things that happened to me onto your own life."

In an instant, Georgia realized her stepmother was right. Carson had seen it about her, too. She protected Ruby and put herself second. It was time to put herself first.

"How?" Georgia asked. She had no idea where to start changing her life, only felt the rightness of doing so. Making a change. For the better.

"Give Carson a chance."

Georgia slumped against the back of the chair. Really? Should she? Did she even know what she wanted in a man? She'd been so on the lookout for snobby rich men that she hadn't given it much thought.

"Oh. Hayden took me shopping today." Ruby leaned down and lifted a paper shopping bag. "I found the damnedest thing." She put the bag on her lap and dug inside.

Her hand came out with a book. An old book.

"You told me you'd like to collect Beatrix Potter books and I found this one for a really good price."

Georgia was speechless. It was a first edition of *The Tale of Peter Rabbit*. The bindings and cover were in good shape. She flipped through the pages. No markings.

"It's signed," Ruby said, sending chills through Georgia. "Dated August 1927."

"Oh, my God," she breathed, going to the front and seeing the slightly faded signature of Beatrix Potter herself.

Ruby laughed her delight. "Your dad would be so happy to see you right now."

Georgia began to think clearer. "You can't afford this." Had Hayden bought it for her? If so, she'd have to give it back.

Ruby patted Georgia's hand. "Stop fretting. You've been entirely too anxious this whole trip, Georgia. Hayden bought the book for me so that I could give it to you."

"But—"

"No," Ruby stopped her protest. "You'll keep it and you'll be happy to do so."

There were times when Ruby showed some backbone and now was one of them. She would not take no for an answer and she would not allow Georgia to give the book back.

She got up from the chair and hugged her stepmother. "Thank you."

"See?" Ruby teased. "Money isn't always a bad thing."

Sitting, Carson held his cell phone in his hand. He'd just disconnected with Copeland, who'd informed him that his best friend's wife had called 911 last night during a break-in. The police were calling it a robbery. It hadn't been a robbery attempt. Copeland said the police arrived before the burglar could take anything, but both he and Carson were not so optimistic.

"Why is your commander calling you about a robbery at your teammate's house?" Georgia asked.

In another spicy southern California outfit, this one in shades of blue and green, she sat beside him at a booth inside a café where he'd taken her for breakfast before going into the office. There would be a change of plans today.

"I'm not sure yet." Could it be that Leif had some-how gotten the data before he died? How could any of them have missed it? Had they even thought to look? His personal things had been gathered and delivered to his wife.

Carson called Whit to tell him he couldn't go to the office today, and then arranged for the jet to be ready within the hour.

"What are you doing?"

"We're going to Oregon." Copeland had asked him to. His teammate's wife lived in a small town on the coast of Oregon.

After paying the bill, they left the café. The limo driver stood beside the back-passenger door and opened it when they appeared.

"Oh." Georgia stopped. "I forgot my jacket."

"I'll wait right here, sir," the driver said, closing the door.

He was about to turn with Georgia when a deaf-ening explosion shocked the air all around them. He pushed her, and she fell to the concrete sidewalk in front of the café. He covered her body with his. Pieces of debris rained down on them. People screamed. A car screeched to a halt.

Carson rolled off her and she twisted to sit up, look-ing at him in total shock.

"Are you all right?" He touched her arms and looked down her body. She was a little dirty but seemed okay.

She nodded. He looked for the driver and saw him lying on the sidewalk at her feet.

"Oh, no." Georgia scrambled to her hands and knees and hurried over to him, oblivious of any pain she was probably feeling. She bent over the driver.

"He's breathing."

Carson briefly shut his eyes in thanks and got on his phone to call for help, all the while searching the surroundings for anyone who might have done this. His enemy from Myanmar. When all appeared safe and help was on the way, he knelt with her. A crowd began to form.

"Stay back!" he hollered.

Moments later, sirens grew louder. Heat from the burning limo choked Carson. Georgia and a few others nearby coughed. It was a metallic, pungent smell. Thick black smoke rolled up into the air.

Georgia checked on the driver again. He was bleeding from somewhere on his head and he was still unconscious. But he was alive. She didn't move him. Carson would have stopped her if she'd tried. It was best not to.

Fire trucks arrived and paramedics rushed over to them. Carson took her hand and guided her out of the way. Police and an ambulance arrived next.

Georgia leaned against him. He could see her intense worry about his driver. "We have to go to the hospital with him. Call his family."

"We will." He took her hand when the driver was wheeled to the ambulance, finding Whit's assistant's number and calling to instruct her to notify the limo driver's family. She stayed calm and promised to do so immediately.

Carson helped Georgia up into the ambulance first and then climbed in after her, seeing news vans show up just as they were leaving. He held her hand and she sat close beside him.

"Who did this?" she asked, but she must already

know. Or did she? "Why is he trying to kill us if he thinks you have the data?"

An innocent man might have been killed.

"He must know I don't," he said. "This is about revenge. I'm back in the States. My teammates are harder to reach while they're on assignment."

In other words, he'd kill them, too, if he had the chance…when he had the chance. How many others would be hurt?

"I just want it to stop."

Carson would see to it that no violence ever touched her again. "I'll make it stop."

She lifted her head, close to tears, and blinked understanding when she saw his set determination.

The limo driver was going to be all right. Georgia sagged with relief, fatigued from all the drama and stress. All she wanted to do was sleep, but Carson was hell-bent on going to Reedsport to talk to Leif's widow. The trip exhausted her more. This jet ride was much different from the last. No frivolities other than the convenience of having your own plane. Just fast transport.

Now they were in a cab driving up to the widow's house. She lived in a modest two-story home on a wooded lot in Reedsport. The trees were so thick here that the neighboring houses couldn't be seen. Georgia heard kids playing somewhere nearby and a single car drive by on the street. Carson had called the woman who'd been married to his best friend. The conversation had been brief and she could hear the awkwardness in Carson's tone.

"Have you ever met her?" she asked as they walked up the sidewalk to the front door.

"Yes. But I missed Leif's funeral. I couldn't make it back in time."

Because he'd been shot. This might be an emotional encounter. Carson rang the doorbell and took a deep breath just before the door opened. A woman about Georgia's height stood there. Her son clung to her leg. He had to be about four or so.

"Andrew, go on and play," the woman told the boy. When he didn't move, his curious eyes absorbing the two strangers who'd come to his door, his mother said, "Go on, go to your room and watch cartoons. Your favorite is starting."

With that, the boy bounded off.

Georgia saw how Carson studied the boy, not looking away until they were inside the home. Did the child look like his friend? Did it remind him too much of his time with the man? And now he stood before his widow.

"Leif talked about you a lot," she said.

"I'm sorry I couldn't make it to the funeral," he said.

"Your commander said you were shot."

"Yes."

The woman's eyes lowered, and Georgia felt her wishing her husband had survived his gunshot wounds.

"I'm also sorry I haven't contacted you before now," Carson said.

"I didn't expect you to." The awkward way she clasped and unclasped her hands and looked around the room said otherwise.

"You must have questions that their commander didn't answer," Georgia said.

Carson looked at her as though he wanted to clamp her mouth shut. His mission was classified, but didn't this poor woman deserve some kind of explanation?

The woman looked at Carson with hope she didn't attempt to hide. "It has been difficult. Not knowing how…" Her voice trailed off.

Not knowing how her husband died. All she knew was he'd been shot in the line of duty.

"Did Sergeant Major Copeland talk to you?" Carson asked.

"He called. After the police left. It was quite a shock hearing from him."

She hadn't considered that the break-in might be related to her husband's death. And Copeland hadn't told her much.

"Who was it and what are they looking for?" she asked.

Georgia looked at Carson expectantly. He'd better give her something. The poor woman.

"When the mission went bad, the information that we were sent to intercept wasn't recovered. Recently, we've learned it's been missing all this time."

"So…" The woman thought a moment. "You think someone came here to get it?"

"Do you still have his personal items? The items that the military gave you after…" His death.

She stared at him, tortured with what happened to the man she loved. But then led them down a hall to the master bedroom. In the closet, she dragged out a box. It was in a place for easy access, and Georgia guessed she must go to that box at her loneliest times.

"Were you in here when the break-in occurred?" Carson asked.

"Yes. I heard a noise outside. When I looked out the window, I saw a man in all black in my yard. I went to get my son and locked us in the bedroom while I called for help. He was inside when police arrived."

"He never made it up here?"

"No. But police caught him on his way up the stairs."

So close to her room. She must have been terrified. But the box had been in the room with her, behind a locked door. The robber hadn't succeeded in getting what he was after.

Carson began to carefully go through the contents of the box. There was a baseball cap that he held for a moment, memories enveloping him, no doubt. He held a dog tag, then a T-shirt. He went through his pack. That was mostly empty aside from clothing. There were no weapons in the box except for a sheathed knife fastened to the waist strap of the pack.

"That was his dad's," Leif's widow said.

Carson removed it from the pack. "He had it with him everywhere he went."

Georgia saw how it hung from the pack. Once the waist strap was secured, it would have been easily accessible in a fight. Watching Carson inspect the knife, she saw that it had a pouch for a sharpening stone. If the data had been stored on a flash drive, it would fit perfectly there.

She knelt beside Carson and reached for the knife. Looking at her quizzically, he gave it to her. She released the button holding the stone-sharpener pouch closed, slid her fingers inside and felt smooth plastic. She brought out a black flash drive and held it in front of her, shock singeing her as she was sure it was doing to the other two, as well.

Carson took it from her, cursing.

"How did he end up with that?" Georgia asked.

Carson looked from her to Leif's widow. "The terrorists ambushed us. The man they were meeting drove up at the same time the terrorists did. He ran from gunfire. Leif must have chased after him." He looked over toward a window, and Georgia saw him getting lost in memory.

She pictured him fighting off terrorists, losing track of his friend.

"When the terrorists ran, I searched for Leif. He was lying next to a burning pickup truck. Stephen Chow must have shot him." He lowered his head in remorse. "I didn't see him go down."

Going to him, Georgia knelt beside him and put her hand on his back. He lifted his head, helplessness that was so uncharacteristic of him heavy in his eyes. Then he looked up at Leif's wife. "I'm sorry."

The woman stood there with silent tears rolling down her face. "Just get the man who killed him."

Carson's fist clenched where it lay suspended over his muscular thigh. "I will. I promise you. I will."

The woman moved toward the box, bending over to pick up the baseball hat Carson had held so long. Wiping her tears, she handed him the hat.

He took it, slipping it onto his head and grinning through his sorrow. "Thanks."

She straightened. "It's okay that you didn't make it to his funeral. I knew where you were. And I know how much Leif cared about you."

"He also had you and your son."

The woman shook her head. "He was where he wanted to be. He loved us, but he loved the Marines just as much. Don't kid yourself into thinking he was a family man. He was, but only when the military allowed it."

"He wanted to be here with you."

"Yes. Of course he did. He loved me."

And she'd loved him, too, enough to share him with his passion. Georgia stood up, Carson doing the same, reaching for the knife. When she handed it to him, he put the flash drive back into the pouch and fastened it shut.

"Do you mind if I keep this for a while?" Carson asked Leif's wife.

"Keep it."

It made great camouflage. No one had discovered it there when his things were being transferred.

"I'll make sure he gets credit for completing a successful mission," Carson said.

The mission hadn't been a failure as he'd originally thought. His best friend had seen to its success.

Carson spotted the car behind him as soon as they drove away from Leif's house. He turned a few corners to be sure and then sped up the rental. The car behind them sped up, too.

"What…" Georgia looked back. "Here? He followed us here?"

Carson found that extraordinary, as well. "He's not working alone." Terrorists worked in groups. Stephen could not have pulled off what he had in Myanmar by himself. He hadn't completed his delivery, but he'd gotten damn close. He'd planned how to steal the technology, stolen it and then managed to get it to North Korea's back door. No, he had to be working with others.

Swerving into the next turn, Carson revved the engine and drove fast—but not too fast—on Umpqua

Highway. It wound its way along the Umpqua River. He'd studied a map on the flight here so that he'd memorized every escape route from Leif's house in case something like this occurred. He could lure the driver of that car back there to a remote location and with strategic methods beat information out of him.

The driver wasn't Stephen. He'd studied the man in the rearview mirror. That confirmed his earlier assessment.

Georgia kept twisting to look back.

"Can't you go any faster?"

He glanced at her a few times as dawning came to him. She hated violence. He was about to use violence on the driver of the car behind them. Their rental could easily outspeed the one the other man drove.

Carson debated what to do. He looked in the rearview mirror. An opportunity wasted if he didn't lure the man.

He looked at Georgia again. There were dark circles under her eyes and she was breathing faster than normal. She was frightened.

He continued to drive as he had for a few miles as that filtered through him. He'd only had to think of what had to be done and then do it. Now he had another person to consider. A lovely person he cared about greatly.

"I'm sorry," he said.

She turned to him. "What?"

"I shouldn't have led him here."

"Here?" She looked through the windshield, then his window, then hers and then back at him. "What are you talking about?"

He downshifted with the touch of the gearshift and gave the car plenty of gas.

What he didn't anticipate, and what hadn't been on his map, was the construction that must have started that day. As they approached a bridge that was blocked down to one lane with a worker holding a stop sign in their direction, Carson slammed on the brakes as Georgia screamed.

So much for sparing her violence.

He maneuvered the rental through a fishtail and took a dirt road to avoid running over the worker, who had leaped off the road and fallen on the grassy side.

The road came to a dead end at a cottage, of all things. Carson parked. The car behind him hadn't appeared yet.

"What are we going to do now?"

Georgia was breathing really fast, and she gripped the door handle harder than she needed to.

"Georgia."

Her head jerked toward him.

"I've got this."

She started to take slower, deeper breaths.

"That's my girl." He took out one of the two pistols he'd strapped to his body when they'd arrived.

"What are we going to do?" she asked.

"We're going to get back to the jet, and then we're going to go home."

"That sounds wonderful."

He shoved the clip into his second pistol and held it as they stared at each other. The way she'd said that held deeper meaning, as though his home felt like her home, as though she wanted to go there with him.

A bullet shattering the back window jarred them from the heat.

"Get down!" Carson yelled.

He opened the door and started firing as he left the rental, rolling and rising to his feet to fire again. He got the driver of the car. But what concerned him was that there were two cars now. And the driver of the second vehicle was Stephen Chow.

Chapter 13

Carson was about to attack Stephen when he heard helicopters overhead. Running to Georgia, he opened her door and aimed his gun over the top of the roof. She stayed inside the car as Stephen tried to turn his car around, but vehicles appeared on the road and trapped him. Armed military men got out of the SUV with weapons drawn.

Stephen got out with his hands in the air, dropping his weapon. He was going to be arrested. Carson's teammate would have his justice. That should feel more rewarding than it did. While he was satisfied Stephen Chow would never be able to hurt anyone else, his friend was still dead.

Carson stuffed his guns away and gave Georgia his hand.

She took it and he pulled her out of the car as the helicopters landed. She watched with parted lips as men swarmed the clearing and Stephen was taken to one of the choppers.

Carson recognized Copeland as he approached.

Keeping his arm around Georgia, he guided her so that they faced his commander.

"Carson." Copeland nodded once and then looked at Georgia.

"It's good to see you, sir," Carson said.

"We had him tracked after the robbery attempt."

Of course he had. Carson smiled. "Thanks."

"He must have known you'd go there after you heard about the robbery."

"Because he knew who had the data. And if we didn't have it, that meant Leif still did." And where would his personal belongings be sent after his body was shipped back to the United States? Home.

"After you called, I got a search warrant for his house," Copeland said. "Found all kinds of incriminating evidence. He was actively trying to get duplicate data of what he lost in Myanmar. The girl he was lying to talked to us. It's enough to put him away."

Georgia's head fell onto Carson's shoulder. He looked at her and decided she was in dire need of some serious pampering.

When they arrived back at the ranch, Georgia slept in her own bed, too uncomfortable to sleep with Carson. She was so out of sorts when it came to him. Did moving on from always watching out for Ruby mean taking up with a new man? A rich man? She wouldn't fall in love with him for his money. She'd fall in love with him for who he was, his humble and heroic nature. His fun-loving way.

The next day she avoided him, only to discover that she didn't need to. He'd been at work all day. It was six in the evening and she was beginning to miss him.

"Why don't you bring him some dinner?"

Startled, Georgia turned to see Ruby enter the kitchen. It took her a moment to think clearly. Luckily she'd waited before bursting with excitement and putting a picnic together.

"We should go home. The shooter is caught. Carson will be able to concentrate on finding Jackson. He can call us to keep us apprised of his progress." If he made any. "You have your inheritance. There's no need for us to stay any longer."

Ruby was slow to smile. She'd spent that time assessing her, guessing, knowing. She walked toward her, coming to a halt before her, reaching out to brush some hair from Georgia's cheek.

"All of that is true, Georgia. But I'm not ready to go yet."

Georgia stepped back and angled her head, defenses rising. "Why not? We're imposing now. We should go."

Ruby laughed softly. "We aren't imposing. These are the most gracious, welcoming people I've met since your dad."

"You're falling for Hayden." Why did she feel so betrayed?

"Yes, I am, but it's still early. I want to rent a place here. Stay a few months. See where things go."

Well, she could afford to now. The biting comment stayed in Georgia's head.

"You know what I think?"

"What?" she snapped harsher than she intended.

"I think you feel so much for Carson that you're confused."

"Confused?"

"Yes. You don't know what to do with the way you feel. And I feel partly to blame."

Georgia looked away, well aware of what she meant.

"Let's stay. Just for a few more days."

"Mom—"

"I love you, Georgia," Ruby cut her off, defusing her in an instant. "I'm going to use your overprotectiveness in my favor one more time and insist we stay, at least until after the party."

"Party?" Another snooty party? "What party?"

"There's a big family reunion planned for this weekend. Saturday night. We'll meet everyone. You should be there, Georgia. You need to be there. You can see for yourself that all of these people are no different than you or I."

Georgia folded her arms and tipped her head to look upward. She felt trapped and yet the idea of staying longer, being with Carson longer, excited her.

"Yes, I know you went to Kate's fund-raiser and had a reaction to two of the attendees."

"How do you know that?"

"Two, Georgia. Out of how many? And were they part of the family?"

"Who told you?"

"I talked to Carson this morning."

"You did what?"

"He needed to know a few things about you. Imagine my surprise—and delight—when he said he already knew. He knows you, Georgia. And he's going to fight for you. Forget about all his money. What kind of man is he?"

She could argue that Reginald and Patsy were part of his family but she didn't. She understood what Ruby was saying. Carson was an incredible man who was overcoming past rebellion and getting to know his father, getting close to the man he once was and loving him for that. Patsy was another issue, but Carson was nothing like her.

Her heart won over her brain. "All right. Until after the party."

"Good. It's settled then." Ruby clapped her hands together. "Now. How about that dinner? Carson said he wouldn't be home until late."

Could she do it? Bring him dinner? Did she want to? *Yes.*

It would be fun. Spontaneous. Especially if he wasn't expecting it.

"Will you help me?"

Ruby's warm smile spoke volumes about her happy state. "I wouldn't have it any other way."

She may not, but how did Georgia feel? She was a jumble of confusion, fighting for sense and not sure she'd ever find it.

Carson finished reading over the latest launch-campaign management plan for AdAir Corps's next communications satellite. They were due to launch in two months. Sending the email with his final comments, he sat back on the chair and let out a sustained breath. He hadn't worked a long day like this since he was in the Marines, and boy, was it different work.

His gaze caught on the ancient Chinese ceramic bowl

as it often did. The piece had become a bittersweet reminder of who his father had been, the real man underneath the ruthless exterior.

Thinking of his father, he took out the folder with everything Reginald had gathered pertaining to Jackson's disappearance. He read through it all again with fresh eyes, searching for anything that he could have missed. The frustrating truth was there was nothing to go on and there hadn't been since his half brother vanished. He hated contemplating that Jackson was one of those real statistics where a murderer got away with his crime. It happened more often than most people realized. Those crime shows that were so prevalent on TV only covered the ones that were solved, the stupid criminals that made mistakes. When would he and his family have to face that Jackson may well be one of those victims?

But Carson didn't feel that Jackson was dead. It was a sense. He was alive. Somewhere. Carson just had to find him. He wasn't giving up until he did. He could not lose faith. Even though it seemed hopeless right now, faith would get him through. Faith would keep him searching.

A soft knock on his office door caused him to look up. Georgia stood there in jeans and a T-shirt. He grinned because that was so unlike her.

"What are you up to?" he asked.

She smiled back, turning to bend over and get a picnic basket. He got a nice view of her butt.

She lifted the basket and then shut his office door, making a show of locking it with a coy look his way.

"What have you got there?" He stood with a grin forming. She'd brought dinner. And her timing couldn't have been better. Not only was he finished for the day; thinking about his dad had begun to be a real downer.

"Something we middle classers all learn to love." She put the basket down on the table in front of a sofa across the office and began removing items. First came a table-cloth, very old-fashioned with red-and-white checks. It was even plastic.

She had him chuckling already. This was going to be an interesting dinner. He walked over to her, remov-ing his suit jacket and tossing it over one of the guest chairs in front of his desk. Loosening his tie, he sat on the sofa next to her as she brought out paper plates, the really cheap ones, and napkins. While she sliced Granny Smith apples, he took out peanut-butter-and-jelly sand-wiches and put them on their plates.

"PB&Js, huh?"

"Ever had one?"

"Many times in the Marines."

She looked at him somewhat in surprise and then warmth changed the look to something more steamy.

He removed his tie, seeing she noticed. "I'm not dif-ferent than you, Georgia. When are you going to accept that about me?"

She put apple slices on their plates. "You seem to be settling in nicely here."

At AdAir. In his father's office. Taking over for Reg-inald. "Yes. But not the way my father did. I doubt he ever felt settled when he was here." He looked over at the desk. He'd thought about a lot of things today. That's why he'd told Ruby he would be home late. He needed time to sort out his feelings and make some decisions regarding his future.

"No," Georgia said. "I talked to Landry before I left

and she said she's been hearing some positive things from the workers here. They all love you."

"They love Whit, too."

"Just take the compliment." She laughed at his humility.

"How did Landry look?" he asked.

"Beautiful. She was on her way out for the night."

"Again?" What was the matter with her? Why couldn't she snap out of her funk?

"Still skirting the compliment?" Georgia asked.

"My employees like me. Good. More evidence that I'm not my father." He didn't have to be a marine for that, either. He'd realized that today. He'd also realized that he enjoyed running this company and he was excited about seeing how he could make improvements.

And that realization had led to another. He took in her adoring face. "There's something I need to ask you."

At his serious tone, her adoration turned to wariness. "Okay…"

"How long were you planning on staying in San Diego?"

"I talked to Ruby about that. She doesn't want to leave yet. But there's really no reason for me to stay."

She didn't seem certain, and he'd use that to his advantage.

"Stay."

She hesitated. "For how long?"

"For as long as you're able." Forever.

"My leave is for six months."

"Then stay until you have to go back to work." That should be enough time for him to convince her to stay for good.

When she didn't respond, he said, "If you're not comfortable at the ranch, I can arrange for an apartment downtown." Her face showed disappointment. "And don't start thinking I'd be supporting you. I want to spend more time with you and it will be hard if you're all the way across the country."

"I don't know, Carson."

He took her hand and held it in his. "Don't be afraid."

"I'm not."

"You are." She was still clinging to her bias, even though deep down she knew it was only a crutch. "You don't have to take care of Ruby anymore. She's happy fooling around with Hayden. And you could be happy with me. If you let yourself."

"What are you saying? Carson…"

"You know what I'm saying." They didn't have phenomenal sex for no reason. He wanted to see where this led on this new path his life was taking, and he had a strong feeling that she was an integral part of making it feel complete. Meant to be. A good decision. All of that.

She began to fret, leaning away from him, tugging her hand free.

Carson slipped his hand along the side of her face and moved his head closer, drawing her gaze to his.

"Carson," she said breathlessly, a passionate whisper. Just like that he could turn a switch in her. In him, too. That's how much they desired each other.

He kissed her. Softly at first, but when her hands ran up his chest to his shoulders, the inferno roared. He kissed her harder and leaned forward until she lay on her back, fevered and all else falling away except this, the love they made together.

Kissing his way down her neck, he slipped his hand

under her T-shirt and felt her soft, firm waist, caressing her up to her breasts.

Her hands were busy, too. They were up under his shirt, feeling the contours of his lightly haired chest.

Devouring her mouth again, he then rose up to remove his white dress shirt. Georgia propped herself up onto her elbows to watch. Her doubt began to return, and he sensed she was about to withdraw. He came back to her, kissing her into sweet oblivion.

He tugged her T-shirt up, and she raised her arms to accommodate him removing it. Then he wasted no time unclasping the hook of her bra, baring her breasts for his tongue and mouth.

She arched her back with a groan.

Taking some of that groan into his mouth, he took his time there. She raked her fingers into his hair, ran her hands down his back to the waist of his slacks. She found the fastener and slipped it free, then slid the zipper down. Her hands went inside to his behind, and she pushed the trousers down. Then she slipped her hands inside his underwear, kicking off her shoes as she kneaded his tight butt.

Carson unbuttoned her jeans and pulled them off her, taking her underwear with them. When those were on the growing pile on the floor, he sat up to remove his shoes and the rest of his clothes.

Georgia lay on the sofa waiting for him, watching him, taking in his nudity. He kneeled between her legs, loving how her dark red hair fanned out on the sofa cushion and her green eyes smoldered with sexual hunger.

"You're so beautiful."

She wrapped her legs around his hips as he found her and slid in, her head falling back at the sensation.

"You make everything right." He moved back for a slow, deep penetration. She grounded him. It all made sense because of her. Settling down no longer felt dreadful, as if he would be falling in line with his tyrannical father's wishes.

Georgia hooked her arms over his neck and kissed him fervently with his declaration. In the heat of passion she she was all his. Would he be able to make her his at all times?

He showered her with passion the way he did costly things. He only hoped she wouldn't cost him his heart.

Thought left him and he had to move faster inside her. Deeper. She felt so good. The way her bare legs rubbed him, her fit stomach against his, the softness of her breasts. Full, parted lips begging for kisses.

She cried out as she reached her peak. He groaned and came. As the eddy calmed, he kissed Georgia.

"Tell me you're staying," he said.

Her eyes opened, still drugged in the aftermath.

"Stay, Georgia."

A soft smile pushed up her pink lips and she nodded.

"No, no, no." He kissed her mouth. "Not good enough. I want to hear you say it."

"I'll stay."

He kissed her harder, deeper, moaning with pleasure her yielding gave him. If only he didn't fear a silent voice finishing her sentence. *For a little while.*

Georgia lay against Carson on the sofa, a soft blanket he had in a closet draped over them. She fed him the last piece of PB&J and rested her head on his chest.

She hadn't let herself analyze what had occurred in his office. She only basked in the loveliness of being with him, of the astonishing way she responded to him. The part of her that turned to butter whenever Carson kissed her wasn't having anything to do with logic, practical thinking.

That made her toes tingle like the way they did when she was standing on the edge of a high cliff.

She had to be rational about this. About Carson. Did she want a man like him? Or did she really prefer to avoid him? Everything she'd grown up believing no longer held true. She had put Ruby first in all things. She loved her stepmother and didn't regret doing so. Meeting the rancher had helped Ruby. She was happy again, the way she was when Georgia's father was alive. She didn't need Georgia as much as she had after he died.

Georgia could live anywhere she wanted. She could get a job here. Keep seeing Carson. If they lasted, great. If not, she'd still be close to Ruby. Because it was clear that Ruby wasn't going anywhere. She was going to be with the rancher, at least for a while. Who knew what the future held for them both. It felt refreshing not to know and not to have to plan.

She couldn't plan who she'd marry. But she could plan for the next few months. And staying here with Carson made her feel happy.

Carson's phone rang.

"It's late," he said.

Something must be wrong. Reluctant to get up from the sofa and leave the cocoon they'd created, Georgia sat up as Carson jumped from the sofa and went to pick up his cell from the desk. He stood silhouetted by the single light they'd left on, a work of naked art.

But when his face grew ominous with apprehension, she stood with the blanket, wrapping that around her.

"What kind of alibi?" Carson asked the caller. When she came to stand before him, he said into the phone, "So what you're saying is the parking-garage shooter wasn't Stephen Chow."

Carson finished his conversation with the caller as shock singed her. If the shooter hadn't been Stephen, then who had it been? Carson's original theory that Reginald's killer had shot at him came back into play now.

Carson put his phone down. "That was Copeland."

"Who shot at us after dinner that one night?"

"Stephen doesn't have an alibi for that night, but he denies he shot at me."

"Do you believe him?"

"I don't know."

"If he's telling the truth, he may not have known the technology was still missing. Is it possible that he thought you had it until you started tailing him?" It had to be. Wouldn't he have known Leif had taken the flash drive? Possibly. "He might have run before you or your teammates got to Leif after he was shot."

Carson nodded. "And Leif put it in his knife holder before he died."

"And he died before he could tell anyone."

Carson stared at her, deep in troubled thought.

"Come on." She took his hand. "Let's go."

They dressed and left the office, Carson carrying the picnic basket.

Walking through the dark building was creepy. She could imagine what it must have been like for Elizabeth to walk back in and find Reginald's body. His then assistant was alone. Her then boss had been killed in a dark and deserted building, on a night not much different than this. She could also imagine Reginald's killer stalking them. This would be the perfect opportunity to try to kill Carson again. Her, too.

They made it to the private elevator. Carson kept a vigilant watch of their surroundings until the elevator doors closed. He'd sent the limo driver home after she'd arrived. At the main level, they walked through the dim lobby. The two security guards there made her feel a little better.

Outside, Carson waved for a taxi.

Carson's phone rang again, making Georgia flinch. "Landry?" He sounded frustrated and incredulous. "Where are you?"

After disconnecting, he turned to Georgia. "It's an active night. Landry is stuck at a bar. She didn't bring the number for the limo and she can't find a cab. He told the driver where to take them.

Moments later, the driver pulled up to the front door of a bar. Music played loud enough to hear it outside.

Landry stood at the curb, waving at the cab. When Carson got out to let her in, she seemed surprised to see him.

"You needed a cab," he said. "We had one."

"Thanks." She stumbled as she bent to get into the cab, and if it hadn't been for Carson, she would have fallen.

Landry sat in the middle, looking over at Georgia. "Oh, hi, Georgia." She smiled big. "You and my brother are out late. What were you doing?"

"We were at the office," Carson said.

"Ooooh, the office." She waggled her eyebrows. "Sexy place to do it."

"You're drunk again," Carson said.

"Only a little." She held her pinched fingers up for him, then turned to Georgia and laughed lightly.

"Landry, you have to stop this behavior. You're letting too much of your responsibilities go. What kind of reputation do you want to have?"

Her smile faded and she looked down at her lap. "Don't be mean, Carson."

"Mean? You're in self-destruct mode. If somebody doesn't step in and straighten you out, you're going to ruin your life."

"No, I'm not." Her voice was quiet.

"When was the last time you worked on your charities?" he asked.

"I… Not long ago…"

"You don't even remember?" Carson sounded disappointed and he was upsetting his sister.

"I'm sick of doing what everybody else expects of me!" She began to cry. "I wish I was more like you, Carson."

He put his arm around her. "There, there. It will all be okay in the morning. But right now, we're going to sober you up."

He told the cab to stop in front of a twenty-four-hour diner. Georgia was flabbergasted because it was so not rich-man. A diner? It was an old building and nothing to rave about, but they'd have hot coffee and a greasy breakfast.

After two stout cups of coffee and a bacon, sausage and egg breakfast, Landry showed signs of sobering. That's when Carson very deliberately told her about the call he'd received from his commander.

"What are you saying? That our mother is trying to kill you?"

"It's possible. She could have sneaked back into the country."

"That would imply that she killed Dad."

"Yes, it would."

Landry slapped her hand onto the table, enough booze still left in her to make her dramatic. "I refuse to believe that! Mom did not kill Dad! She wouldn't do it. Damn it, Carson, why are you going after her like this?"

"I'm not. I'm trying to make you be realistic. We don't know who killed our dad. But it could have been Patsy. You have to accept that."

"No, I don't!" She stood up and marched toward the exit.

Carson turned to Georgia, his frustration and concern clear.

"Is there someone close to her that she could talk to?" She waited while Carson took a few seconds to think.

"Rachel Blackstone," he finally said. "Her best friend. She's kind of a socialite, but she's a real giver, like my sister. Maybe a little lonely, too. Her parents died when she was young and she comes to see Landry at the ranch a lot. She's like extended family to us. Maybe she can reach her." He looked toward the exit. "We'd better make sure she gets home. I'll call Rachel in the morning."

Maybe someone who wasn't a family member could help Landry face the fact that Patsy was not a sane woman. She was a woman capable of murder. She'd already proven that by going after Elizabeth.

Chapter 14

Three evenings later, Georgia got out of the shower to find another cocktail dress on the bed. This one was a beautiful azure-blue that would look dazzling with her dark red hair. He must like her legs bare because it was above the knee like the black one. There were also diamond earrings, a necklace and a bracelet. Sparkly, silver high heels were placed on the floor.

She had to smile.

At Whit's suggestion, Elizabeth had planned a family reunion to try to inject some joy in the wake of Reginald's murder and Patsy's attempt to kill her. The thought was that if everyone got together, they'd all see they were still a family. Carson had joked with her that it would also show her that the good ones were left. A little bad humor since he'd implied that his parents were the only bad ones in the bunch.

Having already done her face and hair, Georgia dressed. The dress fit perfectly and the jewelry made her look more elegant than she'd ever seen herself. She touched the tasteful diamond necklace and almost didn't recognize the woman standing before the mirror. There was a content look in her eyes and yet her hair had a wild flare to it with the mousse she'd used. She looked hot.

Going downstairs, she found Carson waiting for her in a tuxedo. A feeling of déjà vu stole over her until he looked up and his eyes heated with intimate knowledge. He watched her come down the stairs and then took her hand when she reached the bottom.

Drawing her to him, he slid his hand around the waist of the formfitting dress that flared below her butt.

"Georgia," he rasped. "You're killing me." He kissed her.

She laughed and looked up at him.

"Maybe we don't have to go tonight," he said.

"How much did you pay for this dress?"

He smirked.

"We're going." She eased away from him and walked toward the door. Elizabeth had reserved a ballroom at a posh hotel. Many were staying there for the night.

In the car on the way there, Georgia was ever aware of Carson looking at her.

"Did you talk to Landry's best friend?" she asked for idle talk.

"Yes. She's going to watch Landry. Spend more time with her."

"Good."

"Let's leave the party early."

She laughed as the limo stopped in front of the hotel.

Entering the ballroom on Carson's arm felt strange but good. She felt secure with him, and with anyone she encountered tonight. Maybe she would fit in with his family.

"Carson." Whit approached with Elizabeth. Elizabeth looked radiant in a long black evening gown with her blond hair up in an artful bun. Her pregnancy was beginning to show now.

"Hello, Georgia," Elizabeth said.

"Hello." She smiled. "You look beautiful."

"Aw, thanks. I feel fat." She put her hands over her belly and made a face.

Georgia laughed but stopped short when she heard Carson say he'd spoken with Kate O'Hara about Reginald's murder and the dead ends they kept butting up against.

"Did she have any ideas?" Whit asked.

"She's going to send someone to help us."

"Really? Did she say who?"

"Not yet, but she's got connections we need right now. Police are going nowhere with the case and so are we."

"Good thinking on getting her involved."

Spotting Landry, Georgia watched her greet a few men and then head over to their circle.

"Carson tells me he had to go get you from a bar last night," Whit said.

Landry rolled her eyes. "I'm not drinking tonight." She looked at Carson. "I wish you'd stop worrying about me."

"I will when you start acting yourself again."

"I second that," Whit said. "All we have is each other now."

No more Mom and Dad.

Landry averted her face, sorrow drawing all traces of cheerfulness away. She so wanted her parents to not be what they were, victim of murder and possible suspect of it. But Georgia sensed a shift in her, that perhaps she was beginning to come around.

Spotting a woman she didn't recognize, Georgia was drawn to the man beside her. The woman leaned over to say something to him. Something about him kept her staring. On the tall side but not quite as tall as Carson, he had lots of dark blond hair styled to look unruly. He was fit like Carson, too. What was it about him that struck her?

"That's Emmaline Scott and her son, Noah," Carson said. "Emmaline is Reginald's older sister. She's been in Europe until about a year ago."

"He looks familiar," she said.

Carson turned a sharp look to her. "You know them?"

"Not her. Him." As she studied Noah, she realized what it was. "He has a cleft in his chin. Blue eyes. And his face…" Where had she seen it before?

She inhaled a startled breath when it dawned on her. "He looks just like Ruby's father."

After a beat of two, Carson said, "What?"

"Who?" Landry asked.

"Noah Scott?" Whit chimed in, exchanging a look with his wife.

Georgia had them all spinning with possibilities. Her own head was spinning. Noah Scott was the spitting image of Ruby's father. They had to be related. As she looked more, she could see a resemblance to Ruby herself. Could it be…

Georgia grasped Carson's forearm. "Is that Jackson?"

"What? Impossible."

"Just because he looks like your stepmother's father doesn't mean he's her son."

"Emmaline is Reginald's sister, so of course there'd be some resemblance to the family," Whit said.

"Ruby's father isn't related to the Adairs." Georgia turned to Carson. "He's Ruby's son." She felt it to her core.

Carson's brow slowly lowered, a brewing storm. "Listen to what you're implying, Georgia."

She wasn't implying. Noah Scott could very well be Jackson Adair.

"You said she's been in Europe until last year. How often have you seen Noah?"

"She's my aunt."

An aunt who may have kidnapped Jackson. He hadn't seen much of Noah. None of them had. "It's worth checking out, isn't it?"

"No." Carson was aghast at what she had instigated. "It's ludicrous."

Ludicrous? His tone and choice of word revealed a new side to him. Was this when she'd reach a point where the enchantment ended and the true Carson Adair emerged?

She met his furious eyes. "You'd shun me and not at least check?"

What about Ruby? Would he not stop and think what this could mean for her? She could at last have closure. If Noah was, indeed, Jackson, she'd be reunited with her long-lost son. She could live the rest of her days in peace, finally knowing what had happed to her baby boy.

"I wouldn't say shun," Whit said, "but what you're suggesting is too much. It's enough that we have to deal with our parents."

"Despicable," Landry said.

They were in denial. They'd already received more bad news in the family than they could take. But Georgia refused to let this go. If that was Jackson, she'd push the issue. "Kidnapping an infant is despicable," Georgia retorted. They were all ganging up on her. She saw how Elizabeth just stood there looking at her. Was she silently judging?

Not even at Kate's party did she feel as much of an outcast as she did right now. All three of them looked at her as though she'd been found guilty of something unspeakable.

She looked at Carson, removing her hand from his arm and stepping back. "You'll just dismiss what I've noticed?"

"Yes." He scoffed. "Don't you think one of us would have noticed our own aunt kidnapped her brother's son?"

"Emmaline has been in Europe until last year, but she gave birth to Noah there," Whit said.

"It would be hard to kidnap someone if you're overseas when the crime happened," Landry said.

Georgia looked from one to the other and lastly at Carson. He was disgusted with her. She looked at the rest of the crowd, at all the people dressed in expensive clothes, at the food that may as well be in a palace, and then down at herself, dressed just like them.

When her eyes lifted, she saw Carson's anger was dissipating as he read her thoughts.

"I don't belong here." She pivoted and walked fast toward the exit. Thank goodness her stepmother wasn't here yet. She wouldn't tell her about Noah. Not yet. Not until she did her own investigation. She didn't need Carson to do that.

"Maybe it is worth checking out," she heard Elizabeth say.

"Georgia!"

Oh, damn, Carson was coming after her.

She started running. Outside, she flagged a taxi. She didn't know where she was going. Anywhere but here. Back to the ranch to get her things, then the first flight home. No, she had to track down Emmaline and see if she had indeed been in Europe at the time of Jackson's kidnapping. Maybe Noah wasn't Jackson, but it warranted at least checking. Carson was more concerned with the embarrassment to his family.

"Georgia." Carson took her hand and spun her to face him.

She heard the taxi pull up. Yanking her hand free, she opened the car door.

"This has nothing to do with you belonging or not belonging," Carson said.

She got into the cab and told the driver the address to the ranch. But as she tried to close the door, she found that Carson wouldn't let her.

"Come back inside."

"No. We're finished, Carson. Whatever this was. It's over!" She pulled the door.

He didn't budge, his face hard with consternation. He was still upset over her speculation but didn't want her thinking she didn't fit in. How could he not think that? If ever there was a more blatant sign, this was it.

She couldn't rock the boat. She had to live by the Adair rules. Well, no, thanks.

"Let go of the door, Carson."

"Will you be there when I get home?" he asked.

"No."

"Where will you be?" He looked at the hotel entrance. "I have to go back in there. I can't leave like this."

"Of course you can't. They're your family."

"What do you mean by that?"

"Let go of the door."

"Georgia…"

She just looked at him, full of resolve. He saw it and stepped away, releasing the door so she could close it. When she did, it felt as if she'd just shut the door on her chance at happiness.

At the ranch, she folded all the clothes Carson had bought her but kept some of the accessories and shoes, especially the Judith Leiber purse. That she'd cherish always. In payment, though, she left him the Beatrix Potter book, along with a note tucked inside. The book was worth about what the things she was taking with her were worth, so it was an even trade. She could not leave here feeling as though she'd been a charity case to him. This wasn't about protecting Ruby, or any bias she'd developed from learning how abominably Ruby had been treated by the Adairs. This was about standing up for herself.

Touching the old book one more time, she put it on Carson's bed and left, rolling her suitcase behind her.

She'd told the staff to leave her alone and had asked for the taxi to wait for her. She'd call Ruby in the morning.

Outside, the driver helped her with her bag and drove down the lane toward the road. At the end, a car was parked, blocking the way. The driver stopped and Georgia saw a man standing outside the car. He had a gun. And it was Drake.

Georgia opened the back door.

"Stay inside, miss," the driver said.

She stood from the taxi. "Drake?"

He strode toward her, aiming the gun. "Come with me, Georgia."

"What are you doing?"

"You should have listened to me." He grabbed her arm. "Get in the car or I'll kill this man." He pointed his gun at the driver, who, clearly panicked, began speaking fast and incoherently.

"Okay, okay," she said. "Don't kill him. I'll go with you." She'd known Drake for so long, and yet she hadn't known him at all. She felt brave enough to go with him, but this crazy side of him was unpredictable. She could be walking toward her own death. But she couldn't allow him to kill an innocent man.

Drake produced a piece of paper from his jean pocket and handed it to the taxi driver. "Give this to Carson Adair."

The driver took it with shaking fingers.

Then Drake grabbed Georgia by the arm and walked her to the car. The engine was still running.

Forcing her into the backseat, he picked up a rope from the floor.

"Drake, you don't have to do this."

"Shut up."

He roughly tied her wrists behind her. She didn't struggle, fearing if she did that he'd kill the taxi driver, or her. She'd try reasoning with him first.

Getting into the driver's seat, he drove away from the ranch. Georgia twisted behind her and saw the driver on his phone, calling for help.

Facing forward, as much as she could with her hands tied behind her, she met Drake's eyes in the rearview mirror. He looked at the road.

"You were all I ever wanted, Georgia."

She kept quiet.

He scoffed. "I was crazy for not realizing I could have had you ever since we were in college."

"The same thing would have happened," she said. "I would have broken up with you."

"Then there's no other way. It ends tonight, for both of us."

That sent chills riding down her spine and arms. She thought back to the shooting the day she and Ruby went to AdAir Corp to settle the inheritance dispute. And again after she and Carson had dinner. The car bomb. Stephen had an alibi for at least one of those instances.

"It was you, wasn't it?" she said, bringing his eyes back to the mirror. "You shot at Carson. Twice." He'd tried to kill him. And then he'd put a bomb in their car. Was he trying to kill them both at that point?

Stephen claimed to have only shot at Carson after they left Leif's house. That had to be true. Drake was insane. He'd progressively gone more insane the longer she'd known him. He'd done a fine acting job up until they'd had sex. Then he could no longer hide the darkness in him.

"You lied to me," Drake said.

"About what?"

"You said you would never marry a rich man."

How wrong she'd been about that. "Not all rich men are bad, Drake. I've learned that. I was narrow-minded for thinking that of all rich men."

"You fell for him."

"No. I'm going back to Florida as soon as Ruby's son is found." She didn't dare tell him what she'd discovered tonight. The less he knew, the better.

"You fell for him!" he shouted.

Georgia couldn't suppress her flinch, cringing against the seat at the sheer volume of his voice.

His eyes were dark and evil in the mirror.

"I didn't. My suitcase is in the taxi. I was leaving when you blocked the driveway."

His eyes shifted from the mirror to the road.

Maybe she could play on that with him. Get him to think she wasn't in love with Carson.

In love with him?

She stayed focused. Her life depended on how she handled Drake. Carson's, too, since she was pretty sure the paper he'd handed the taxi driver was instructions on where to find her. He'd lure Carson to wherever he was taking her and then kill them both.

Carson was still at the party an hour after Georgia left. Whit and Landry were as upset as he was over the idea of Jackson being stolen by one of the family. They'd suffered enough as it was because of Patsy. How much more drama could they take? Landry, especially. He saw how the suggestion had her staring off in depressed thought.

He'd watched Emmaline. He'd studied Noah. Emmaline seemed normal. She smiled and chatted with every-one and now she was close to him and Whit and Landry.

"I can't take this," Landry said. "I'm going back to the ranch."

"I'll go with you." Rachel Blackstone had come to the party. Her wavy light brown hair was left down, falling to about her shoulders. Her green eyes reassured him that she'd take care of Landry.

"Thanks, Rachel," Carson said.

"Good night, Carson." Landry stepped forward to kiss his cheek. She hadn't drunk anything tonight, only water. Carson was proud of her.

"I'll see you tomorrow," he said.

She said goodbye to Whit. Elizabeth had wandered off to talk to Kate and Patrick O'Hara, who'd flown in for the festivities.

"Carson and Whit?"

Carson turned with Whit to see Emmaline stand-ing there.

"My, have you two grown. I saw Landry. She's leav-ing early."

"Emmaline. How have you been?" Whit asked.

"I should be asking you that. I can't believe it about Reginald."

Had she killed her brother when he'd discovered she was the one who'd kidnapped Jackson? Carson banished the terrible thought as soon as it struck him. Damn Georgia. Why did she have to be so adamant about something so unlikely?

"How's your hip?" Whit asked. "We heard you broke it."

"It aches but I can get around. You can't complain at my age."

She was around sixty-six with graying brown hair that she kept in a sleek bun.

"Could have been worse," she said. "I could have been in my seventies."

Noah appeared next to his mother. "Hey." He held out his hand for Carson to shake. After he did, he shook Whit's hand.

"You've been busy farming on the ranch," Carson said, trying not to stare at the cleft on his chin. He'd worked with him a little but saw less of him now that he was spending more time at AdAir Corp.

"Yeah, I like the hard work. The fresh air. Out in the open."

"It does grow on you," Whit said.

"I miss traveling, but I'm glad to have work," Noah said.

He'd traveled to many countries, having grown up in Europe. He had a lot of stories to tell. He'd lived a good life. It was impossible for Carson to believe he could be his secret half brother.

Not liking the way he kept searching for signs that he might be Jackson, Carson excused himself and said his goodbyes. He felt his phone vibrate and took it out as he left the hotel. It was the ranch number.

"Carson?" It was Landry. "You better come home. Georgia's been kidnapped."

Chapter 15

Carson raced into the ranch house to find Landry sitting with Rachel in the living room with a swarm of police officers. One of them was talking to the taxi driver.

Landry got up and rushed to him. "Carson."

He put his arms around her as she embraced him. "What happened?"

She told him what the driver had told police.

"Where's the note?" he asked.

An officer came over to him and showed him the note that had been placed into a plastic bag. There was an address and one message: *Come alone or your girlfriend is dead.*

"The taxi driver said Georgia called him Drake," the officer said.

Rage filled him as he looked at the officer. Then he started for the door. He didn't need cops. He only needed his bare hands. He was going to kill Drake.

Whit's palm on his chest stopped him. "Easy there, brother."

"Get out of my way."

"This isn't Myanmar."

Carson stared hard at him, fighting for rationality. Georgia in this kind of trouble brought him to his knees. He had to save her. She could not end up like Leif.

A police officer approached them. "I just received a call from the Hartman Hotel. Drake Foerster rented a room there."

"Get a crime scene team there," the other officer said.

"Already there. The lead investigator said there's evidence of bomb-making material there."

Carson flashed a look at Whit. Georgia's ex-boyfriend was responsible for the car bomb and the shootings. It had nothing to do with Reginald's murder. It had nothing to do with Stephen Chow and his botched mission, either. Carson had merely awakened Stephen to the fact that the data was missing. He'd added it up and went to search Leif's house. Only he hadn't known where to look and Leif's wife hadn't helped him.

"And some women's underwear. Did Georgia mension she was missing any?"

"No." But she may not have thought anything of it. Drake must have broken into his ranch. That filled him with rage. And disgust. The man was sicker than he'd imagined!

"We'll get her back," Whit said. "But we have to have a plan."

Carson calmed down. His brother was right. He had to think. "I need a minute."

He went upstairs and headed for his room. He'd

change into dark clothes and get himself good and armed. He agreed with Whit, but this was something he had to do alone. He was trained for this type of situation. No one else down in that living room was. And he'd be damned if he'd put any of his family in danger. The cops could follow him, but he had to be the first to arrive at the address Drake had left. He knew his kind. He'd lure him there and then try to kill them both. The psychotic, jaded ex-lover.

Passing Georgia's room, he stopped short when he saw all the items neatly placed on the foot of the bed. She'd left behind many of the things he'd bought her. That just made him mad all over again. Didn't she know by now that he loved her?

Loved her...?

Yes. He loved her. She completed him.

Hurrying to his room, he closed and locked the door. On his way to his walk-in closet, he saw the book on his bed. Going there, he picked it up. It was a copy of *The Tale of Peter Rabbit.* A folded piece of paper was sticking out from inside the cover:

> I know what you're thinking. That I'm wrong about you and your family, that I would fit in. You may see it that way but I don't. I can't be with someone who doesn't trust me or my word. I never said Noah was Jackson. How can I know that for certain? All I know is what I saw—a striking resemblance to Ruby's father, and to her. It's too much a resemblance to ignore. That's all I meant. But you'll ignore it to spare your family further scandal. I understand that.
>
> I've left the things I won't be taking back with

me to Florida. I couldn't resist a few of the other items, however. You had me figured out about that, Carson. I do love fashion. Please consider this book my token of appreciation for giving them to me, and for all the wonderful times I had with you. You're a special man who I will never forget. I wish you the best in your search for Jackson and also in your search for Reginald's killer. I do think the two are related.

In other words, she thought Emmaline might be responsible for his father's murder. His grip tightened on the page, but he kept reading.

If I discover anything definitive, I'll let you know. Unless you'd rather I didn't. Send me a text to let me know, but please don't try to contact me otherwise. It's best if we part ways now, and amicably if possible.
Yours in memory,
Georgia

He dropped the note onto the bed. Well, she sure sounded definite. She would also investigate Noah, which meant she had planned to stay in San Diego. Until Drake had intercepted her. And Carson hadn't been with her. He should have been with her. Moreover, he shouldn't have let her observation get to him the way he had. She'd shocked him, that's all. She'd shocked everyone.

Going to his closet, he changed into black jeans and a long-sleeved black shirt. He put on his black gun holster and combat boots, then went to his gun safe. He took out two automatic pistols and filled a duffel bag with ammunition and a few backup weapons.

Then he went to the window in his room, removing the screen and slipping through and into the night.

Drake leaned back on a recliner, laughing at a stupid sitcom playing on an old television. He'd brought her to a house he must have broken into. They were in the living room and he'd faced one of the wooden kitchen chairs toward him and made her sit there. She'd been working to loosen the rope.

"Whose house is this?" she asked.

His smile faded as he turned to her. "They're having a siesta."

What did that mean? Had he killed them?

"People who know them are going to start to miss them and come looking."

"Not tonight they won't. Shut up." His gaze went down her body and back up again. He'd looked at her like that several times since bringing her here and it terrified her. But she could not let him know how frightened she was.

"Do you remember that time in college when we studied for an English test together and left the library when it closed?" It was one of their best times together.

At first his expression didn't change. But then a small smile lifted one side of his mouth. "I remember a lot about us back then."

She feigned a laugh while she tried to loosen the knot in the rope tying her hands. "Your car wouldn't start so I rode you home on my bike." She felt a screw sticking out from the side of the chair and used that to saw the rope.

He chuckled. "I did that on purpose."

She stopped smiling. "You did?"

"Yeah. I wanted to be with you all night. That's the night you told me to go home because I had a girlfriend and you didn't want to make her jealous."

"You told me she was already jealous." The screw wasn't working.

He nodded. "And you said you couldn't be with me like that as long as I was with someone else."

She'd forgotten what she'd told him that night.

"I thought about breaking up with my girlfriend to be with you."

It had taken him a few months, but that's what he'd done. But by then Georgia had been dating someone else and then she graduated and they'd drifted apart until a few years later.

"Seems like the timing has never been right for us."

"No. So why not let me go, Drake? We can still be friends."

He grunted. "Why do people who are about to die always say things like that? As if I'm going to believe you."

"Killing me isn't going to solve anything."

"Killing both of you will."

"How?"

"It will give me great satisfaction knowing no one will have you and the one you did love is gone with you."

"I don't love him. I told you I'm leaving. Go check the taxi if you don't believe me. Ask the driver." She strained her wrists against the rope, frantic to be free of it.

"You love him. I saw you together many times. In

North Carolina. Here. He dotes on you." He growled the last few words.

Georgia suppressed a gasp. He'd followed her to North Carolina. He *was* crazy. Clinically. "Why do you hate me so much?"

"I didn't used to hate you. You used to be all mine."

"I was never yours. And you won't get away with this, not any of this!" The rope loosened and she slipped her wrist free. She felt scrapes and moisture that must be blood but she didn't care. She had to get away from Drake. But not yet. She'd wait. With all of his attention on her she didn't have a prayer. And his attention was focused on her, angry attention. She shouldn't have told him he was never his. Drake looked at her for a long time.

She wouldn't have the luxury of waiting for him to sleep or be distracted with the television.

Georgia gauged the distance to the stairs. So close.

He didn't miss her doing so, his mouth quirking in a slanted frown.

"Try it," he said.

The cold emptiness she felt and saw emanating from him kept her hands hidden behind her back. She said nothing.

"Go on." He stood up. "Try it!" he shouted, swiping his arm toward the door.

He didn't know her hands were free. Should she? Was now the time? What if he remained alert until Carson arrived? That made her mind up for her.

Jumping to her feet, she ran for the door. She made it halfway up the stairs before she felt him grab for her ankles. Rolling onto her backside, she kicked him in the face.

He yelped and fell backward but caught himself with the railing. Georgia scrambled the rest of the way upstairs. She ran through the kitchen and into a den area. There was nowhere to go but down a hall. At the end, she turned in to the master bedroom and stopped short. A middle-aged couple lay shot on their bed, blood soaking the sheets and blankets. The woman lay on her side and the man with his leg hanging over the bed, the covers off him. Georgia put her hand to her mouth and gagged in horror.

When she pivoted, Drake stood in the doorway, a gun hanging at his side.

Georgia backed away, looking for anything to use as a weapon. She picked up a lamp from a dresser and threw it at Drake. He batted that away, but as he did so she ran past him. He almost got ahold of her arm, but she slipped free and ran down the hall, through the den and the kitchen, toppling chairs over to hinder his progress.

She heard him curse as she made it to the living room, and then he tackled her. She landed hard on her stomach, her wrists stinging with sharp pain on impact.

Staying calm, she remembered what she'd learned in self-defense class.

Drake hauled her up with his arm around her neck. She'd have stomped on his ankles if it weren't for the gun to her head.

He would take her back downstairs and tie her up again, this time more securely. She wouldn't escape again. And when Carson arrived, he'd kill them both.

Through the back patio door, Carson saw Georgia nearly reach the front door. While Drake brought her down to the floor and began to force her to her feet, he threw a patio chair through the glass door.

As Drake turned toward the noise of shattering glass, Georgia stomped multiple times on his ankles, hard enough to make Drake wince and stagger. He clocked her with his elbow, sending her sprawling to the floor.

Carson fired his pistol, taking out Drake's shoulder. He dropped his gun and fell to the floor. But he pulled out a knife, and as Georgia sat up in a daze, he went behind her and put it to her throat, ignoring his shoulder wound.

Moving toward Drake, seeing his crazed eyes, Carson debated whether or not to put a bullet in his head. He could do it easily. He could have done it already.

"Don't make me kill you," he said.

"Drop the gun or she dies."

Carson moved so that he had a good angle and fired again, this time taking out Drake's elbow. Now he yelled in pain, dropping the knife as he fell to the floor. He still had one good arm and, unbelievably, tried to go for the knife.

Georgia swiped it away from his reaching grasp and scrambled a safe distance away.

Going to her, Carson knelt and touched her face where Drake had struck her. She'd have a fat bruised lip for a while.

"Are you okay?" he asked.

"I think so."

Carson helped Georgia to her feet. She was still a little unsteady from being hit. She leaned against him and looked at Drake.

He sat on the floor, holding his bleeding arm and staring at them with defeated menace. Had he even known Carson was ex–Special Forces? Carson was guessing not. He'd only seen through a jealous haze. No man was allowed to have Georgia, and if he couldn't have her no one could. A smarter man would have done more research.

As Carson met Drake's eyes, Drake's rage began to boil over, and he attempted to move.

Carson aimed his pistol, his other arm around Georgia. "I wouldn't if I were you. The next bullet will be in your head."

"Drake," Georgia said. "Don't. It's over. It's all over."

Looking from her to the barrel of Carson's gun, he returned his gaze to Georgia.

Pounding on the door preceded a loud "San Diego police!" And then the door was broken down and a swarm of officers entered.

Carson put his gun away and he and Georgia stepped back to allow police room to arrest Drake. Paramedics tended to his wounds and he was taken away on a stretcher. He'd be treated and taken to jail as soon as he was healed enough.

Another team went to work on the scene where the couple had been murdered. Drake wouldn't see the outside of a cell for the rest of his life.

Whit entered the house with a look of great relief when he saw Carson and Georgia.

"Sneaking out of the house?" Whit said to Carson. Georgia looked up from where she sat as a paramedic inspected her mouth.

Carson grinned. "Just like when we were kids."

"Not funny." He pointed his finger at his face. And then he phoned Landry to let her know Carson and Georgia were okay.

Now all he had to do was convince Georgia to come back to the ranch with him. Or maybe he'd come up with another surprise for her. But first he had a phone call to make.

Whit and Carson were still talking when Landry entered Reginald's old home office. Carson had just gotten off the phone with Aunt Kate for the second time. He'd spoken to her yesterday after dropping Georgia off at her hotel, where she'd insisted on going. Carson didn't have time to argue with her. He'd deal with her soon, though, and before she got on a plane.

"Was that Aunt Kate?" Landry asked, walking over to a bowl of jelly beans on the desk and taking a handful.

"Yes." Carson leaned against the desk next to where Landry stood, both of them at a slight angle to include Whit, who sat on the chair behind the desk.

"Did she find someone to help us find Jackson?"

"Yes." Carson glanced at Whit, who gave him a nod of encouragement. Carson looked at Landry again. "She's sending Derek Winchester. He's an FBI agent who specializes in missing persons cases."

"Okay. Good." She passed glances to both men. "Isn't it?"

"Yes." Carson cleared his throat. "But we need your help, Landry."

"Me?" She popped some of the candy into her mouth.

"We need you to pose as his live-in girlfriend," Carson said.

Landry stopped chewing her candy to stare at him. "What?"

"Emmaline comes to the ranch on occasion," Whit

said. "Just as she did for the reunion. We'd like to be ready for her next visit, one that perhaps we can coax her into making in the near future."

"That's right," Carson said. "She won't catch on to our suspicion while Derek carries out an investigation."

"But…I thought you dismissed the possibility that Noah could be Jackson."

"We have to be sure," Carson said.

Landry thought a moment and then nodded. "I think so, too. But to pose as a stranger's girlfriend?"

"He's an FBI agent. He'll be a perfect gentleman. You won't be expected to do anything you're not comfortable doing."

"Except be a convincing girlfriend?" Landry breathed a derisive laugh. "Right."

"Will you do it?" Carson asked.

She saw how serious he was and softened. "Of course. I want to find our half brother as much as you both do."

Carson was happy to see her gaining strength after struggling to accept what their mother had done and may have done.

"Great. I'll let Kate know." Carson started toward the door. "I'll see you two tomorrow. Whit, I won't be in the office until the day after tomorrow, maybe longer."

"Where are you going?" he asked.

"He's going to go get his woman," Landry said, eating more chocolate with a sly gleam to her eyes.

Yes, that's exactly what he was going to do. If he could convince Georgia. With Ruby's help, he had confidence he'd succeed.

Chapter 16

Georgia ached all over and her face was sore. Two days had passed since Drake was arrested. By the time they'd finished with the police, morning had come. It was late afternoon before she'd checked in to this hotel. Then she'd slept for fourteen hours. Carson had called her once, just before she'd fallen asleep, asking her not to leave California. *Not yet*, he'd said. Why not yet?

Her mother called and said she was down in the lobby, so Georgia had to let her into her room. She was sure she'd get more persuasion not to leave, but she'd made up her mind. She opened the hotel door to let her in.

"Tell me you're not really going back to Florida," Ruby said as she entered.

"I'm going back to Florida. We both don't need to be here." This was her first step toward putting herself first. Jackson was Ruby's son. She should be the one to stay until he was either found or the Adairs gave up searching. Ruby didn't need her to hold her hand anymore.

"Georgia," Ruby protested.

Ignoring her, Georgia resumed putting toiletries back into her suitcase.

"When do you fly back?"

"This afternoon." She'd go to the airport and wait for her flight.

"So you've made flight reservations."

"Yes. Just this morning."

Ruby came over to her and laid her hand on her arm, stopping her from putting her nightgown into the luggage. "Cancel them, Georgia. Come and stay with me at my new apartment."

"You have an apartment now?"

"Yes, Georgia. I feel like I belong here."

"Because of Hayden?"

"No. Hayden is a nice man and I enjoy his company, but I want to take things slow with him."

Georgia met her earnest look and had to harden herself from doing whatever Ruby requested. It was good she'd cooled it off with the rancher. It showed strength, and proved to Georgia once and for all that her mother wasn't after money in a man. Not that she needed it with the inheritance she'd received.

"You don't need me here anymore, Mom. You'll be very happy here. I can come out and visit you and you can come to Florida to see me."

Ruby shook her head. "Yes, I'll be fine. You don't have to take care of me. But stay. Just for a little while longer."

Long enough to allow Carson to seduce her into staying permanently?

A place in her heart swelled at the prospect.

"Don't you want to help Carson find Jackson?" Ruby asked. "Not for me, of course, but you've been helping him. Are you really going to drop that and go home?"

She was reaching now, but Georgia did want to look into Noah and see if she could prove he was Jackson. She wouldn't tell Ruby that, though. Although she would not be as protective as she had been before, there was a line to be drawn. She didn't want to hurt her stepmother, and hurt she'd be if Noah turned out not to be Jackson.

Georgia closed her suitcase. She was ready to go. Standing before her stepmother, she waited for her to relent and allow her to leave.

"I'll walk down with you," Ruby said.

They left the room and rode the elevator to the lobby. Georgia began to sense an ulterior motive in Ruby. Her stepmother kept glancing at her with a funny smile.

"What are you up to, Ruby?"

They went through the carousel doors and Ruby stopped on the curved brick walkway. That's when Georgia spotted the limousine.

"Mother…"

"Just give him a chance to explain, Georgia. You can be so stubborn sometimes."

The limo door opened, and Carson rose up from inside.

Ruby was about to walk toward a taxi when Georgia stopped her with a hand on her shoulder. "Why did you cool it off with Hayden?"

"I loved your father, Georgia. I'm not sure if I'll ever love anyone else again."

"It wasn't because you're afraid he'll be like Reginald?"

Ruby laughed, a breathy sound of incredulity. "Goodness, no. I stopped blaming Reginald a long time ago. He was only acting out of pain and misguidance from his parents. Had we not lost our son, he would have been a different man. I got the best part of Reginald. That's enough for me."

Georgia nodded with a soft smile. "I love you."

"Oh." Ruby moved forward and kissed her forehead, then put her hand on Georgia's cheek. "I love you, too, my daughter." She lowered her hand. "Now go and listen to what Carson has to say. And tomorrow, let me know how it went."

How what went? Ruby glanced back once with a sly smile before getting into the taxi.

After the taxi drove off, Georgia turned to Carson, dreading the sight of him because he always stole her breath and heart.

He invited her to the limo with his hand.

She rolled her suitcase to him. "Carson, what are you doing here?"

"Not letting you get on that plane." He nodded to the limo driver, who confiscated her luggage and hefted it into the back.

"There. Now you're trapped." Carson extended his hand again. "After you, madam."

With a harsh sigh, Georgia plopped down on the cushy seat and moved all the way over to the other side. "This better not be another one of your surprises."

"Oh, it is. The best one yet."

The limo started moving.

"Where are you taking me?"

"It's about twenty minutes from here. Enough time for me to talk to you about Noah."

She turned to look out the window. "You don't have to."

"Emmaline flew to Paris this morning, so I was unable to question her. But Whit and I did confirm that she had a son in Europe, a baby boy, who was born close to the time Jackson was."

Georgia turned to him.

"He died three weeks before Jackson was born."

Georgia inhaled sharply. "Then it's plausible—"

"It's plausible, yes, but we know that Emmaline was in Europe during the time Jackson was taken. How could she have kidnapped him if she was in another country? It's something Whit and I are going to investigate. My aunt Kate is going to send someone to help us. Someone who's experienced with these types of crimes." He told her all about their plan.

"Wow." Georgia faced forward. "So you do believe me."

"About that…" Carson took her hand in his. "Georgia, at the party when you saw Noah, I was too shocked to react rationally. I didn't mean to make you feel as though I was putting Whit and Landry ahead of you. I didn't mean to make you feel like an outcast. I was just shocked. I needed time to digest the idea of Noah being Jackson, the possibility of it. That's the only reason I let you go that night."

And neither of them had anticipated that Drake was as big a threat as he'd turned out to be.

"All of you were against me," she said.

"No. Not against you. Shocked. We all see the need to investigate Emmaline. Thanks to you, Georgia. You made us look there. You made us face it. I can speak for myself, Whit and Landry when I say for that we'll always be grateful."

If Noah turned out to be Jackson. What if he didn't?

"Stop thinking, Georgia. Even if Noah isn't Jackson, we all appreciate you. And I happen to love you."

That startled her so much that she didn't notice where the limo had pulled to a stop.

"I have a present for you." Carson got out of the limo and waited for her to scoot to the door and get out.

They were in front of a beautiful beachfront home, a big home. It had towering windows in front and intricate trimwork carved in stone. The front was bordered by a fence, and inside, curving flower gardens and trees lined a winding path to stone stairs leading to the porch and a double-glass front door.

"What is this?"

"It's our new home. Or yours if you don't want me here yet."

Her mouth fell open. "You…"

"Yes, I bought it. I actually bought it after we came back from North Carolina."

"I can't accept this."

"Come inside." He led her to the door and when he opened it, Georgia was lost in what she saw. Decorated cottage style, there was absolutely nothing that she'd change.

"I told the decorator what you liked. I think she got it right," he said.

Georgia turned in a circle. In the middle of the living room, rather than wide-open, there were several quaint rooms. An office. A den. The living room was spacious but filled with accents and furniture that created a cozy getaway. Through the dining and kitchen area, big windows offered an unobstructed view of the ocean. The deck back there had white wicker furniture adorned with pillows, and an old tin bucket held a bottle of champagne.

Slowly she faced him. "Carson, I…"

"It's yours, Georgia. Ours."

"Ours…" She shook her head. "I don't understand. Why did you do this? I don't deserve this. And I have no way of paying you back."

"Ah. That's another thing." He reached into his jacket and pulled out the Beatrix Potter book. "This is yours. Or ours, depending on how you answer a question I have for you."

"What question?" She started to smile because she had a pretty good idea what it was.

Carson walked over to her, reaching into another pocket of his jacket. Out came a ring box.

She covered her mouth with her hands, shivers of excitement tickling her skin.

He strode toward her, stopping when he stood right in front of her. "Open it."

Georgia lowered her hands and lifted the lid to reveal an impressive but humbly beautiful round diamond with an emerald halo.

"Will you marry me?" Carson asked.

She looked up at him, still a teensy bit uncertain.

"You fit in, Georgia. You fit me. No matter what happens or who crosses our path, you fit me and you matter more to me than anything or anyone. Do you believe me?"

Tears welled in her eyes and she nodded. "Oh, Carson." She threw her arms around him and began kissing him. She'd quit her job and start working here. She knew exactly which library she wanted to pursue. They could live here and Carson could work at AdAir. It would be lovely. A dream come true. "Carson." She kissed him more intimately. "I love you."

"Hold on, vixen." He took the ring from the box and, tossing that aside, lifted her hand and slipped it onto her ring finger.

"You knew the size."

"I've had enough practice."

She knew he was referring to all the times she'd bought her clothes. Laughing, Georgia took his hand. "I want to see the bedroom now."

* * * * *

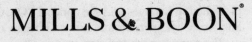

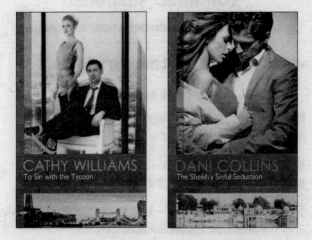

MILLS & BOON®
INTRIGUE
Romantic Suspense

A SEDUCTIVE COMBINATION OF DANGER AND DESIRE

0315/46